Martin's Working Nights Now

Katherine Dempster

This book is dedicated to everyone who has wallowed
away in jobs that felt like fluorescently lit coffins.

And especially for Lisa, who never became Martin, and
for Greg who desperately wants to be his best friend.

Contents

Chapter One

It's a living.

THE SIREN CALL OF another mundane day startled Martin awake.

Beep, beep, beep, beep, beep...

The angry mumbling of his wife to switch the damn thing off and get up overwhelmed his snooze button temptation. A pillow she launched landed in the doorway just as he passed through.

Tugging his robe closed against the slight paunch of his belly and the chill in the air, he shuffled downstairs to start the coffee. As the water brewed, he fixated on a stray thread that was on the verge of tearing a hole in the sleeve. Maybe Nadine would get him a new one for Christmas. It would be a pleasant change from the obligatory slippers she gave him every year.

The weather that week had been cool for the end of summer, closing out an uneventful season to make way for the next. Picking up his mug, he snorted at his bare feet before making his way to the front room. He had yet to wear a pair of those slippers. He hated how they felt. Too warm. What was wrong with socks when it was cold?

Another cloudy day.

The window in the front room framed the early morning sky, as if it were something to be admired. In the tightly packed houses on his street, lights flickered on as people went about starting their own days. He gulped the last of his hot coffee and ignored the crick in his back and the pinch in his hip as much as he ignored the dark cloud that lived above him during every waking hour. A floating hat of gloom that only he could see. Once more, it would seamlessly blend with the overcast sky.

"Daddy?" Harper, his four-year-old daughter and most important reason to carry on, padded her tiny feet down the hallway.

"Hey, Giggles. What are you doing up so early?"

"Mr. Jack won't stop whistling and I'm thirsty," she whispered, rubbing her eye with her tiny fist.

"He's at it again, is he?" Martin guided his daughter to the kitchen to pour her some juice.

Mr. Jack was the invisible friend who had become Harper's excuse for everything from being out of bed to spilled cereal. According to her, he had a tendency to whistle mindlessly. A detail that drove Harper up the wall. Martin smiled down at her when he lifted her onto the counter while he poured her juice. She was very much his daughter in the way she could always find something to be miffed about, although she delivered her complaints with smiles and giggles.

"I guess he couldn't sleep. He must be excited about me going for girls' weekend with Mom and Gramma tonight," she mused, sipping at the orange juice.

"Is he coming with you? Maybe he could learn to whistle new songs from the birds on the beach."

Harper giggled, "No, Daddy! Girls only! He can't anyway. Mr. Jack always stays here. You know that."

"That's right. My mistake. I thought he might want to join in on all the fun you're going to have."

"Martin, for god's sake, get her off of the counter. She could fall!" Nadine screeched as she shuffled into the dimly lit kitchen, flicking the switch and drowning the space with the bright pot lights above them.

He answered with his usual reply—a sigh and a glare — and set Harper on the floor beside him. She smiled up and ran off with her juice, most likely in search of Mr. Jack.

He set down her mug without a word and refilled his before setting the carafe on the counter for his wife.

"What time do you think you'll be hitting the road tonight?"

"Mr. Davidson says I should be able to do a half day today. Only two cars are being picked up so hopefully by mid-afternoon," Nadine yawned, filling her mug and holding the hot steam up to her nose. "Mom said we get the rental at three."

Martin hoped a break from work would brighten her up, even just a slice. Ever since she had started her position as a receptionist at Davidson Motors, grumpy was the best mood he could hope for. Not that she had been a ray of sunshine before that. The last few years had evolved her into a different woman, always nitpicking and rolling her eyes. The sunny days of their early courtship was left behind in college once the pressures of life slowly swallowed their light and pressed them through the dredges of daily adult life. His own abrasive responses certainly did not help, but he could only take so much when he dealt with the same unhappiness at work.

Beaumont's Discount Department Store was not the lap of luxury of Fifth Avenue shopping. In the era of online shopping, it held on by a thread, and the promise of low prices that continued to rise. His cramped office in the back of the store felt more like a crypt than a place to engage in business of any kind. Being the only employee in the Human Resources Department made it even lonelier. After fifteen years of employment, he had become too set in his routine to try something else, and the benefits program was not the worst. He preferred to think of himself as settled rather than stuck.

Monday to Friday, he would punch in and spend the next eight hours shuffling papers, dealing with complaints, along with the hires and fires of his fellow employees who never even bothered to learn his name. Chance Beaumont, the thirty-five-year-old frat boy who was the third-generation owner of Beaumont's, rarely stepped foot in the building, preferring to toss the meager profits from the company on poker tables when he wasn't golfing. Both of which he was sure he would go pro in any day now. The cocaine that he always found money for helped with those delusions while draining the company even deeper.

"I better get going," Martin sighed, leaning in to give Nadine a quick kiss on the cheek. "Have fun, but be safe, okay?"

He had only taken a step when she lightly wrapped her fingers around his wrist. "I'll miss you." Her voice was quiet, but her eyes were sincere.

"I'll miss you guys too." He took advantage of the rare tender moment to give her a proper kiss on the lips before he returned to his morning routine.

The bing-bong of the sliding doors at Beaumont's was the starting pistol that began his monotonous race to the end of his shift. A friendly nod of the head was the go-to greeting for the few others who he passed on the way to the back of the store and his cramped daily world. The blank eyes and tight smiles that were returned to him should be depressing, yet to him it made him feel a little less alone for a moment.

They had mounted the time clock for all employees just outside his door. The swiping of the thin plastic name tags that doubled as time cards was the only noise he would hear for the next eight hours. He slid his own through and clipped it back onto the pocket of his shirt.

Slipping his key into the paint-chipped door to his office, he tried not to compare the sound to the clanking of a cell door. He tossed the small cooler bag that held his lunch on the dented file cabinet in the corner and sat down on the worn cushion of his chair with a squeak. The inbox on his desk was empty. The inbox of his email was pure spam.

He sat back as far as the rock of the chair would allow and tapped his fingers on the desk. Not much to do until someone came to him with a complaint. There was no chance that there would be any new hires in the near future. Being a Friday, if there was to be anyone else let go, he would have been met by a file on his desk. After a quick look around to make sure he hadn't missed one, he was pleased that everyone made it through to another paycheck. As of late, there had been more staff quitting than being fired, leaving them with a skeleton crew to carry the weight.

One of the three fluorescent lights above him flickered and went dark. Standing with a groan, he steadied a foot on his chair and pushed himself up onto the desk. It wouldn't make much of a difference if it stayed off, but he needed to fill his morning somehow. A few taps on the bulb had it casting its yellowed glow over the room once again. He wiped his dusty fingers on his pants and looked around the room from above. They say perspective is everything, and he usually would agree. In this case, the different angle revealed nothing positive about the space except for the sight of more neglected areas that hadn't been cleaned.

Stepping one foot back onto the chair, his breath hitched when the chair's wheels slipped a foot away. Legs spread to near split, he raised his arms for balance as he struggled to pull it closer with quick jerks of his foot on the seat.

The crash of his body hitting the wall and the files that rained down on him bounced off of the close walls.

"Son-of-a-bitch!" Martin yowled, grabbing at the blot of pain that rocketed through his shoulder.

Grasping the side of the desk with his opposite arm, he rubbed at the site of the landing and circled his shoulder a few times for good measure. There didn't seem to be any serious injury, although his back was stiffer than ever. The pain was fleeting, which he was thankful for, but left a pull in his muscle and a tingle in his fingers. He stretched his arm, bending his elbow until the static in his fingertips disappeared. His hip cricked when he stood, making him not only feel foolish, but much older than the four decades he'd been alive.

"I'm fine! Thanks for asking!" he shouted to the empty air around him. It didn't surprise him that no one had heard the commotion all the way in the back of the building. The cashiers would be busy counting their tills to start the day and the only company he had was the custodian, Dan, who was no longer employed with full-time hours during the day thanks to cutbacks, or *cokebacks* as Martin liked to call them thanks to Chance's need for nose candy. The reasoning didn't hinder the resentment that he had filtered his injury and embarrassment into. He couldn't wait for the day to be over and he found himself on the couch with a beer in his hand. Still alone, yet so much better than the walls that were closing in on him. Full control of the remote, eating whatever he wanted, without pants if he so desired.

He dedicated the rest of his morning to cleaning up after the fallen files and filling out an accident report that he knew he would be the only one to read. He briefly inspected the spreadsheet that contained the names of the remaining employees and the checkmarks indicating completion of the HR packets he had placed in their lockers a few weeks ago. A laugh escaped him when he saw each name marked off. The store had become so barren of customers that the staff were willing to do the harassment training just to fill the time.

Opening his door, he slid his employee ID in the time clock to mark the start of his lunch break and set his lunch bag on his desk. He left the door open in case anyone else happened by and wanted to pass the time with a chat. He always left the door open during breaks for that purpose. No one ever stopped to chat. It was not as if there was a better situation happening in the break room. It was the most dilapidated part of the entire store; the spotting of the occasional rat did not leave a welcoming feeling, either. Most people took their breaks in their cars in poor weather or would stand outside on the loading docks to smoke or vape. People came and went so often, either from lay-offs or the inability to deal with the working conditions, that there wasn't much in the way of comradery.

The light above his head flickered again when he opened his lunch bag. He waited until it decided to stay on to set his food before him. A ham sandwich on white bread with mustard, an apple with a bruise that made it look as if it had spent a few rounds in the ring, and a thermos of milk.

A fitting feast for the day.

He picked at the decorative plastic that wrapped the thermos. It has once had a glossy print of red and blue plaid. Now it was mostly worn away to reveal the scratched aluminum underneath. It still kept his coffee hot or his milk cold, so it did the job. He poured a bit of the milk he had into the lid and took a sip, looking at his room-temperature sandwich. The same one he made himself every day unless he was in the mood for soup. Holding up one-half, he wondered why he always made it when he really never enjoyed it. He took another sip of his milk and tossed the sandwich in his trash bin.

He could make himself whatever he wanted, but he stuck with the same boring thing, just as he always did. Food that was as dull as the box he worked in, as disappointing as day-to-day life. Harper liked ham sandwiches. Maybe that was why. As if he could have a little slice of sunlight in the day. Regrettably, his office deprived him of sunlight and stole away the light of day. The light above flickered again.

Harper loved chocolate chip cookies as well. Any sweets, really, like most kids. Martin looked at the thermos of milk and decided to bring his own sunlight into the space. Locking his office, he turned the corner out into the storefront.

A radio station warbled from the speakers rather than the in-house, ad-free music that better-rated stores would have. Such as the store that was currently being advertised during the current commercial break. Martin shook his head, listening to the sing-song voice announce the amazing deals Beaumont's competitors were currently offering.

The snack aisle was practically empty, as were most of the others, when he stood in front of the cookie options. An off-brand chocolate chip pack would do just nicely. He picked up two packs and then set the second down. The splurge didn't need to be that big. It wouldn't be the best start to his solo weekend to be stuck on the toilet from that much sugar.

"Welcome to Beaumont's. Did you find what you needed?" the young man who rang up his order asked without looking up. His matching employee ID said his name was Ben.

"Yup. Just the cookies, thanks." Martin pulled out his debit card, watching how he could be served and completely ignored all at once.

"9.95."

"Yikes. So much for low prices, huh?" Martin joked to the side of the cashier's head and swiped his card. The employee discount had been dead and gone for over a decade.

"Thank you for shopping at Beaumont's, and we hope you visit us again," Ben said flatly.

"I guess I don't really have a choice, do I?" Martin laughed and finally caught his eye. "I mean, I work here, so…," Martin cut short when he saw the confused face that stared back at him and then pointed to his own ID clipped to his shirt. "Cuz I work here?" He tapped the badge.

"Oh, sorry. People come and go here a lot," Ben murmured and pulled his phone from his pocket.

"Yeah, well, I don't," Martin sneered. Ben had retreated to whatever was on his phone screen. "Are you kidding me?" Ben looked up with annoyance when Martin raised his voice. "I've worked here for forever!"

"Okay, geez. I'm sorry. I don't know everyone that works here, damn." He leaned back against the till with a roll of his eyes and went back to his phone.

"Are you shitting me right now?" Martin snatched up the cookies and his receipt. "I was the one that hired you last summer, Ben!" He emphasized the disinterested man's name and pointed to the name tag and then back and forth between his and Ben's, wild-eyed.

"Yeah, I don't think sugar's a great idea for you, my guy," Ben snorted and tossed the closed placard on the conveyor belt.

Martin watched him wander towards the back of the store, most likely to swipe out for his break, and ripped open the bag of cookies. One tumbled to the floor, and he stomped it into the worn linoleum floor, instantly feeling bad for the childish tantrum. He clumsily kicked the crumbs under the counter. Taking the long way around the store, he took the time to cool off and avoid seeing the obnoxious cashier again. He would close his door, eat his cookies, and try to reclaim the joy he had been sure they would bring him.

He slammed himself into his seat and tossed the cookies on his desk. The thermos sat open beside them.

Munching on the cookies, mindlessly dunking them into the milk, he stared at the wall in a dreamless daydream. They did not cheer him up as he had hoped. He frowned when he threw the empty package in the trash on top of the ham sandwich, then topped it all with the bruised apple that had sat at the bottom of his lunch bag all week. Clicking his computer awake, he went over a few files that had been unchanged for weeks.

The bulb above started to flicker again. A second joined in to cause his eye to twitch. Looking at the roster for the day, there was a highlight over an afternoon shift for the custodian, but no name was listed. Hoping to catch a break, he picked up his phone and dialed Dan's extension. A busy tone blared in his ear. He dialed again with the same results.

There was no way he would risk climbing back on his desk after almost breaking his desk. He needed help, or at the very least, a ladder. Stepping into the dim back hallway, he made his way to the custodian's room and gave a knock on the door. A scruffy face he did not recognize at first greeted him with a broad grin.

"Hey, man! What's up?" he asked, opening the door wider. He wreaked of the reason for his red-eyes and cheerful mood.

John? Jim? He knew his name. Martin was the one who hired him. He was one of the night crew that had survived the purge of employees.

Jake!

"Good, Jake. How've you been? What are you doing here so early?"

"Supe switched me to half shifts on days, for now, to cover for Dan." Jake tossed a cheese puff in his mouth and then wiped his fingers on his well-worn coveralls.

"I didn't know Dan was taking time off," Martin said aloud, but more to himself. Dan never took time off if he could help it. He also wasn't one for words, so it's not as if he would have told Martin anything about it.

"That's the thing. He didn't. They have no idea where he is. Just poof! Up and disappeared." Jake exclaimed, picking up a paper cup of coffee and settling in his desk chair. "He's been gone for a week, so they finally decided they needed someone until they figure out what they're going to do." He gestured for Martin to take a seat on the other side of the desk.

Martin tried to tame his jealousy when he looked at the space allotted for the janitor. Mind you, he shared the space with buckets, tools, and chemicals.

"What do you mean he's disappeared?" he asked, taking the offered seat. It was much more comfortable than the one in his office.

"That's all I know, man. He's just gone. Probably got sick of the job and moved to some beach town to retire. The guy was like, a hundred years old." Jake laughed.

Martin knew for a fact that Dan was only in his fifties, about a decade older than himself. He wondered how old the twenty-something Jake thought he was.

"That's so strange. I wonder why they didn't tell me it or about the change in staffing?" If Dan was no longer an employee, his file would have been set on his inbox to be processed.

"What is that you do here again…" Jake paused to look at his name tag. "Martin?"

Martin swallowed the irritated sigh that rose in his chest. "I'm Human Resources. I hired you, remember?"

"Oh, yeah, for sure. I totally remember that. I just didn't know what else, like, what other shit you're in charge of." Jake pushed a cheery smile across his face when Martin didn't respond. "So, like, are you in charge of giving raises?"

"No, that would be Mr. Beaumont." Not that Chance Beaumont would ever consider it for anyone other than himself. Martin looked at the phone off the cradle on Jake's desk.

"No ringy-dingy, no *worky*, right?" Jake let out a low machine gun of laughter. He stopped abruptly when he saw the nod and tight smile Martin returned to him. "Oh, shit. Are you in charge of firing, too?"

That earned him a genuine laugh from Martin. "I get to do the dirty work of it, but who it is would be out of my hands. Hiring is the only thing they trust my judgement on." He couldn't blame Jake for not giving his all there. He himself had just spent the better part of an hour staring at the wall. "Anyway, I was hoping you could give me a hand with the fluorescent bulbs in my office. One keeps flickering and driving me crazy." He stood and pointed to a ladder propped in a corner.

"Yeah, no problem. I got you. How many do you need?" Jake jumped up into service, hanging up the phone for good measure. He didn't seem to believe how powerless Martin actually was. That suited Martin's needs at the moment and went with it.

"There's three total, but only two are flickering. One worse than the other." Hoping for two brand-new bulbs was a lot for that place. Dan would wait days after the bulbs blew as if they were going to return from the lightbulb great beyond and begin to glow again.

Jake slid a long four-pack from a shelf and took one out. One was better than none. When he set the solo bulb back on the shelf and handed over the three, he pleasantly surprised Martin. He held them as if they were Fabergé Eggs while Jake grabbed the ladder and headed out down the hall.

They made quick work of the change with the assistance of the ladder and, within minutes, his office was awash in the bleak, steady light from above.

"Thanks for that. I tried to fix it by standing on my desk and tapping them, but it didn't help."

"No worries, man. You're lucky you didn't fall! That desk doesn't look too sturdy," Jake chuckled as he folded the ladder closed. Martin only rubbed at the dull ache that remained in his shoulder and pressed his lips tightly. "Anything else you need?"

"No, that's good. Thanks again." Martin stood in the doorway when Jake moved out into the hallway. He enjoyed having someone to talk to, and Jake seemed like a pretty nice guy.

"All right. Well, you know where to find me if you need me." He started back to his office with the ladder clanging under his arm, but stopped and turned as Martin was retreating back inside. "Hey, actually, a bunch of us are going out for drinks and wings tonight. After the afternoon shift up front is done. You should come."

Martin couldn't understand why he would invite him. He was never invited to anything. No matter the reason, he felt a rush of inclusive happiness creep over him. The staff up front that day were the same age or younger than Jake, so the idea didn't seem like much fun, but it was nice to be asked. He couldn't imagine what Nadine would think if he went out drinking with a bunch of twenty-somethings the very first night she was out of town.

"Tonight doesn't really work, but thanks for the invite. Have a cold one for me."

Jake shrugged and started off, calling over his shoulder, "Will do compadre. Let me know if you change your mind."

Martin sat and picked up his phone. Nadine had sent him a text, informing him she had picked up her mother, and they were on the way to the beach house, but he had missed it. Before setting his phone down, he sent a *drive safe and miss you* message and tossed it on the desk. He looked around the room, hoping for a make work project to kill the last few hours of his day to no avail.

He picked up his phone again.

Scrolling through all of his apps and a few levels of a puzzle game didn't even put a dent in the time.

He couldn't wait to be on his couch, remote in one hand, beer in the other. Tapping in the name of the pizza joint by his house, he perused the menu, deciding on what he would order.

A buzz and pop-up of a picture interrupted him. Nadine, Harper, and his mother-in-law, Jeanne smiled back at him with a backdrop of a rolling wave heading towards them under a bright blue sky. They had postponed the trip, which was a gift to Harper for her last birthday. Since she had requested a girls' trip to the beach, he had to ignore his pang of disappointment about not being included. He zoomed in on her beaming face. Perhaps they could plan a second trip there that he could tag along on. He certainly couldn't afford whatever palatial beach house Jeanne would have chosen. The woman had a lot of money, loved her granddaughter, and enjoyed spoiling her.

Thinking about their weekend put a bit of a damper on the solo weekend he had been planning. After spending all week sitting alone in his office, it didn't seem as exciting as the same thing on his couch. Even if it would be in his underwear with a beer.

Growing up, he had been in foster care for as long as he had memories and then more. A family was not something he ever felt for long and when he turned eighteen, aging out, he was on his own. It felt like he had always been on his own until Nadine and then Harper came into his life.

The light above him flickered again, and he loudly groaned. Pushing back from his desk, he leaned back to glare at the ceiling. A second flickered. The third joined in with a loud hum and then pop, darkening above him. His arms flailed when his chair made a crack, sending the back cushion and then himself onto the floor.

He lay staring at the fiendish fluorescents that seemed to have it out for him, defeat swallowing him whole.

"Screw it. I'm going out tonight."

Chapter Two

What could go wrong?

Nadine seemed surprised by Martin's text about joining the group for after-work drinks but said little else than telling him to have a good time and be safe. He wondered if she had the same hopes of a reset between them with the weekend break and saw him going out as a good sign. Either way, he was going to try to make the most of a crap day.

When he had popped his head into Jake's office to say he had changed his mind, he let him know they would all be gathering at The Dizzy Owl on downtown's main drag. Opening the door to the dank, windowless pub, it almost felt like a party in his small office for a quick second. Martin immediately regretted his spur-of-the-moment change of plans.

A loud local band blasted out from the far corner, competing with the rowdy raised voices and whoops that echoed around him. He looked down at his worn out golf shirt he had untucked from his khaki pants and compared it with the trendy plaid, jeans, leather, and intentionally ironic tees that adorned the much younger, cooler crowd. He kicked himself for not going home to change before he came, although he knew if he had, he would have realized his closet was filled with more of the same and would have chickened out and stayed home.

It was now or never. After all, it was just a beer; what could go wrong?

His hand was on the door in an attempt at a quick retreat when he heard Jake's voice call out over the ruckus.

"Martin! Hey, man! We're over here!"

Martin's shoulder's slumped when he let out a heavy breath and turned to find him at a long table in the middle of the melee of half drunk customers. He gave a wave and a forced smile and told himself one beer and then he would pick up a pizza and hit his couch. Just going at all was enough of an event for one night.

Ben, the cashier, sat in the middle of the group of Beaumont's employees and was so preoccupied with a pretty fellow cashier with rainbow colored hair that he didn't even notice Martin joining them.

"You made it! I wasn't sure if you'd really come or not," Jake added, pointing to an empty chair beside him, waving an unimpressed looking waitress over. "What's your poison?"

The waitress waited while Martin looked around the table. Beer seemed to be the drink of choice, which suited him. He asked what they had on tap. He couldn't make out a word as she mumbled an extensive list that bled into the rest of the noise.

"Yeah, that one. Sounds good," he said, stopping her mid spiel, when he realized he couldn't hear her above the crowd. He would drink whatever it was quickly and make tracks. It would be awkward to just get up and leave after being there for only a minute. He took in everyone circled into groups around the pub. No one else seemed as keen to leave as he was.

"How'd those lights hold up for you?" Jake asked, gulping half of his pint in one mouthful.

There was no point in telling him they were junk, just like everything else in Beaumont's. "Good. Thanks again for the help." He rubbed at the slight ache that remained in his shoulder at the mention and gave his arm a stretch.

"My pleasure, compadre!" He downed the rest of his beer and motioned for the guy next to him to pass him a pitcher they appeared to be sharing.

Martin recognized him as a floor stocker, but his name escaped him. He was a quiet guy who got his work done and then got the hell out of there the second his shift was over. Martin could relate.

"You're the HR guy, right?" he asked when he saw Martin looking at him.

"Yeah, Martin," he replied. He didn't know if he should hold out his hand for a shake or a fist bump. He stayed motionless and attempted a smile. Awkward was not a good look on anyone, but Martin was wearing the hell out of it at the moment.

The young man gave a nod and turned back to the conversation he was having without another word. Martin felt stupid for thinking it was a good idea. His knee began to bounce when he looked over to the bar to see how the waitress was coming along with his beer.

While one side of the table talked about what he assumed was a band coming to town, the other side was drowned out by the current one blasting away in the corner. They all seemed to be having a good time.

He stifled a sigh and mentally kicked himself for coming. No matter how dull his work and home life was, the excitement he craved would not be with a group of kids drinking themselves silly. It had been a long time since he found that to be a good time. Even before he had met Nadine.

The ache in his shoulder was starting to be matched with a growing thump in his head.

He noticed the server by the bar and thought of a way to leave early and more subtly than announcing it. Not that anyone they would care either way.

"Looks like a bit of a wait up there," he shouted to Jake. "I'm gonna grab my beer up there to save her the trip."

Jake gave a bob of his head and turned back to the group that held his attention.

Martin stood and wiped the sweat that had formed on his palms on his pants. Making his way to the bar took longer than it should with the jovial groups packed together around the tables. When he got to the long wooden sanctuary covered in sticky spilled drinks, he gave a wave of his hand to the waitress as she loaded her tray with drinks. She delivered his beer to him before heading back toward the shoulder to shoulder ruckus. It seemed to have become even more packed with revelers in the time it took him to cross the room. When he turned back to ask for his bill, the crowd had already swallowed her up and she disappeared into the bar.

"It's not like it was, huh, bud?"

Martin turned to find a man with scarce white hair combed over his ruddy pink head, raising a half empty pint glass to him. "Sorry?"

"This pub. Used to be the place to relax away from the missus and the screaming kids. Now it's all screaming kids as far as we can see." He laughed into his glass before giving a cough against the ale that went down the wrong pipe. Recovering, he watched another waitress step up to the end of the bar. "Although that's still better than lookin' at the missus, now isn't?" He let out a bark of a laugh that reeked of how many beers he had consumed before his current one that he slopped on the bar. "Still young and fresh. Been awhile since I've had a taste of that." The letch spat another laugh in his face, jostling his arm and almost making Martin spill his glass.

Martin could only grimace and attempt a grin as he took a gulp of his beer and pulled out his wallet. He slid out his credit card just as he read a worn sign behind the bar that declared *Cash only, ATM by the restrooms.* The only thing in his billfold was an expired coupon for a sub shop he had been meaning to try. He picked up his glass and moved as quickly as he could to grab the cash needed to leave. Another second with that drunkard would make him sick and he hadn't even had dinner yet to lose.

Begging his pardon and offering apologies, he worked his way through to the other side of the endless lineup to the ladies' room to find the machine and made quick work of his transaction. He finished his beer as he pushed through the crowd back to the bar. He was glad to see the drunken grandpa had made his way elsewhere when he returned. Hopefully, nowhere near a young lady.

Setting the glass down, he tried to get the bartender's attention to pay. It felt like hours before he finally locked eyes with him, only to have him point to his empty glass, give him a thumbs up, and then pull another pint. Martin let out a guttural groan. The damn place was feeling like it was attempting to hold him hostage. His couch had never felt so far away.

"Sorry, I just wanted to pay for this one and head out." Martin shouted as the band finished, making his voice carry to every wall in the room. A few annoyed eyes glared at him while he went red from the top of his head to his chest.

"Oh, no worries. Sorry about that, I thought you wanted another. Gimme a sec and I'll grab you're your bill from Jillian."

He slid the glass back away from Martin. To the bartender's credit, he was impressed that he could read the brewery off of the empty glass to serve up the same one Martin had begrudgingly ordered previously. You'd have to be pretty on the ball to deal with such a busy place. His silent box of an office seemed peaceful in comparison.

"Why let that drink go to waste when it's already poured?" A soft voice said, as if it was right in his ear. He turned to find a petite brunette leaning on the bar beside him. "You could always gift it to someone. Good karma and all, yeah?" She had an emerald lilt to her voice that matched her eyes.

The bartender stood with the pint in hand, waiting for Martin's response. "Sure, why not?" he conceded. "Put that one on my bill, as well." The bartender gave a surprised nod, and he set the glass in front of the woman. "I can always use the karma, right?" he added.

She looked to be in her early twenties, but there was something about her eyes that made her seem much older. She kept them squared on him and Martin kept his eyes on the bartender flagging down his waitress. There was an energy about her that put him on edge.

Were barflies still a thing? She seemed too put together and young to be what he remembered those ladies to be. No matter what, there was nothing but trouble he felt.

"Mighty kind of ya," she said, running a napkin along the condensation of the glass.

"Not a problem. Enjoy," he replied, mindlessly spinning his wedding ring with his thumb. He sighed as he looked about, trying to spot the waitress that held his escape.

"You seem like you're in quite the rush. Not the night you had hoped for?" She had a slur to her words, much like the last patron who had attempted to chat him up. At least she wasn't as repugnant as he had been.

"No, not my sort of night at all." He looked down to see her smiling up at him.

"Mine either. I was 'posed to have a nice dinner, but that didn't pan out," she confided with a smothered giggle. The glass sat untouched and full in front of her.

"Sorry to hear that." Martin was relieved when the bartender headed back to him with the bill in hand.

A glance down at the stranger held his gaze when she smiled again.

"Why don't you just stay for another drink and we can commiserate together?" she asked, her voice again sounding like it was so close to his ear that he should feel her breath even though she stood two feet away.

The pressure of the noise in the bar that had been ripping at his nerves eased and he felt the tension in his shoulder relax.

She seems like a nice enough gal. Perfectly harmless. She could obviously see that he was married by the ring on his finger and was only looking for someone to have a pleasant chat with. Two people making a dreadful night better with harmless friendship.

He blinked quickly, trying to look away. The more he stared, the more sure of himself he became and the reasoning in his mind became more clear, more reliable.

She stepped closer.

Just a nice young lady who shouldn't be left alone in a place like that, given her current state. What would be the harm? One more drink and then home. Easy peasy, nice and easy.

"Bud, are you ready to settle up?"

Martin jumped at the bartender's voice, "Yeah, sure, I…," he trailed off, still staring into her eyes, "I think we're going to get one more round."

The young lady smiled and looked at the now frustrated man behind the bar. As soon as she looked away, the explosion of music and gleeful shouts overcame him, unaware that the world had quieted when he was considering the young lady's suggestion. As the bartender walked away to fill the request, Martin felt an intense need to get out of the claustrophobic space.

"Actually, you know what? I better not. I'm driving and I'm really tired, anyway, so I should…"

Her hand reached out, and she caught his eye again. "One drink. I could use a friendly ear, and I think you could use a rant yourself." The desire to stay returned. "I'm not trying to get in your pants, if that's the worry, fella." His head felt foggy. "Look, that booth is free. Let's get you out of this noise and into a cozy seat."

It seemed like a good idea, and he followed her as she moved through the crowd. The waves of people seemed to push away from them like two like magnets rejecting each other. He thought of the alphabet magnets on his fridge at home. Harper was getting so good at making words with them. He should go home and make a little message for her to find when she returned from her girls' weekend. *When would that be?* He couldn't recall if it was Friday or Saturday.

Just a drink and rant and we'll all feel better.

The voice in his head was his own, but it didn't sound like his thoughts. In a blink, he was sitting in the booth with a fresh pint set in front of him. The stranger sat across with him, a full glass in front of her and the same tiny smile.

"Since you seem to have lost your manners, I'll introduce myself." She held out her hand. "Lyla. It's a pleasure to meet you…" she tilted her head, waiting for his reply.

"Oh, sorry. I'm uh, Martin." He wanted to leave.

"Grand to meet you, Uh-Martin." Lyla laughed at her own joke.

"No, just Martin."

"Just Martin, got it." She looked him over, watching him like a cat does a bird about to take flight.

The haze that slowed the world around him cleared enough to stop the spinning in his head and he settled into the stiff wooden bench of the booth. He couldn't remember why he was in such a rush to leave. Jake gave him a wave when he looked his way, and Lyla gave him one back.

"Friend of yours?" she asked.

"Co-worker." He took a sip of his beer and was surprised to find that it had become room temperature. He wiped his mouth and set it down. How long had he been sitting there? "Do you know him?"

He looked at his watch—it was already a quarter to eight. He pulled out his phone. No messages from Nadine. The pain in his shoulder felt like it was returning and travelling to his neck. He rubbed at the site, only making it feel worse.

"So, you were saying how much you hate your job."

"I was?" Martin didn't remember saying a thing about work.

Wait, did I? Yes, I did. We were just talking about Jake. Jake's here, right?

He looked over to the table where he had left Jake to find it occupied by an entirely new group of partiers. He hadn't noticed they had all left. Nice of them to say goodbye, he thought with a frown.

"I used to feel really stuck in my life, too. I get it." Lyla's voice rang out through the surrounding fog that made his head feel heavy.

Martin turned his attention back to her. Stuck. That was the perfect word for it. "It's just like everyday gets heavier, and deeper, like I'm slowly sinking into my grave."

He was taken aback that he said it out loud. That he had admitted he had let his mind get that bleak. He wondered if he really thought that way or if he was just being dramatic. Maybe he was drunk.

How many beers had he had? He thought it had just been just the one.

Lyla laughed, and it felt out of place for what he had just confessed. "You have no idea how much I relate to that."

The pain that traced from his shoulder to his neck throbbed and fatigue pulled at the gravity around him. He went to take a drink, only to find the glass empty.

"I think I better get going," he croaked, trying to slide himself from the booth. He would need to call a cab. There was no way he could drive home. His hand bumped into a glass, sloshing beer on the table. Wasn't it empty? Lyla laughed when he spilled, and he tried to focus on her. A tiny crimson puddle was on her top lip. "I think you have a bloody nose, lady."

She touched her nose and then her lip, looking embarrassed as she gave it a wipe with a napkin she had been putting tiny rips into and then shoved it in her pocket.

"I'm glad we met, Martin. You get it, you know? You understand how it feels to be powerless. I'm sick of all those bastards thinkin' they're so superior when they're nothin' but *dryshite*! I honestly thought I would be all powerful, but I wasn't. I'm not." Lyla leaned her head on her palm while she lamented to him, her voice even more weighted from drink. A full glass sat untouched in front of her. "But I am powerful, aren't I? We both are, no matter what anyone says. I'm a hell of a lot more impressive than these drunken cows, aren't I?"

He pulled out his phone to look up a number for a taxi service. The time that lit up was half past ten. It felt like he had only been there a few minutes.

The muscles in his entire shoulder felt as if they had been ripped and stretched from the bone. That embarrassing fall from his desk was worse than he thought and he needed to get home with some ice on it before it got worse.

"I gotta fix it…" he mumbled. "It's time to go. I need to fix it."

"You're right, Martin! We can fix *thissss*. Both of us, right? Why are we sitting here whining when we can just fix it all? I'll show them!" She threw up her arms in mock victory, her eyes as blurry as his. "We both will. I'm in charge of me, not them, and I know how to free you just like I'm gonna be! No one is the bosses of us, mate! You're not gonna regret this."

Martin peered at her through blurry eyes. "What the hell are you going on about?"

The light above the booth seemed to dim before the entire bar went black and Martin was no longer there.

Chapter Three

Death by snacks.

MARTIN BLINKED HIS EYES, unsure if they were open or not. The surrounding darkness was as thick as tar. The air hung heavy with a damp musty stink.

"Oh, shit," he muttered when he became aware of the pain that burned under every inch of his skin.

His stomach flipped between a rotting ache and a nausea that keep threatening to erupt and then back again. The ground he lay on was hard, cold, and a bit of a relief against the heat that boiled within him. He rolled to his side and rested his head on the rough concrete. The sound of a man whistling echoed from a distance.

"Hello?" he bellowed from his raw throat, nearly retching. No one answered.

He lay still, trying to get his bearings. Before he could figure out where he was, he needed to remember where he had been. The pint of beer he had not even wanted appeared in his thoughts. A bar. He had gone to the Dizzy Owl after work.

Could he have had that much to drink? His tolerance was mostly a beer or two a week, so it wouldn't have taken much. His stomach cramped, forcing his knees to curl up to his body. This was no hangover, that he was sure of.

Time was immeasurable. He had no idea how long he lay there until the pain subsided and he forced himself to sit up. The image of the woman he had met washed through his dizzy mind like a wave. Lily? Lola? He steady himself, holding his head against the spinning.

Lyla!

Her name had been Lyla.

What if she had drugged him? What for? There wasn't anything of consequence in his wallet. He patted his pants and found his pockets empty. Maybe she had.

Another clench of acidic burn tightened his stomach. He rubbed at his stomach, quickly smoothing his hand under his shirt, looking for injury. He felt relief when he found his skin intact.

Was it even a real thing to steal organs? It seemed as if it would only be movies. Waking up in pitch darkness with no memory of how you got there was equally horror-moviesque, so who knew what was possible? It did him no end of good to try to think of all the possibilities. At least he could tell he wasn't in a tub of ice.

The dank, cloudy mornings he despised began to look like sunshine and rainbows as the pain ripped through his body again. He contorted against the muscles that were folding on themselves before being pulled like an elastic band near to snapping. Whatever she had given them was certainly trying to kill him. Everything in his body wanted out.

"Lyla, you fucking psycho! Let me go!" he bellowed through clenched teeth.

Again, no one answered his cry. Other than the shouts of pain and groans of discomfort from Martin, everything else around him was silent. The darkness would press in and swallow him whole when the pain became too much for his mind to process and the momentary release from consciousness was the only thing he could pray for as time ticked on at a pace he couldn't gauge until another wave woke him into the cycle of nightmare that he found himself trapped in.

When he finally heard footsteps moving around quickly across the floor above him, he strained to hear what was being shouted through the icy cold vomit that tore up his throat and onto the floor below him. As the quick tip-taps moved closer, he tried to pull himself back from their direction in an attempt of protection against whoever was about to pounce on his location.

A door opened, sending blinding light into the space around him and causing him to howl with the pain it caused in his head. His eyes sealed shut against the un-natural brightness.

"Martin? Oh, my GOD! Martin, what's happened?"

He blinked his eyes, slowly adjusting to the assault of light. "Nadine?" *What was she doing there?* "You have to get out of here! I don't know what they're going to do to me."

Her hands felt like razors when she set them on his chest and then his face. "I've been calling and texting you all day! What the hell happened to you? Oh, Martin, you're burning up!"

When she helped him sit up, his bones felt as if they were dried twigs snapping under a heavy boot, and his shrieks filled the room. His head spun, trying to bring him back to the safety of unconsciousness. Nadine continued to speak her worry loudly and quickly, although he could only comprehend a word here or there.

When his eyes steadied, he could see that he was still in the clothes he remembered wearing to work the day before, but they were now filthy. Had it only been a day ago? He had no idea how long they had held him there. The streaks of blood and sick smeared on himself and the cement floor below told him it must have been longer.

"How did you find me? Where are we?" He could fight against the disorienting blur in his eyes to find enough clarity to answer the question just as Nadine replied.

"You're in the basement, Martin. The furnace room. I think you're sick, sweetheart. You're burning up."

The furnace room? Of his own house?

What the hell was going on?

"Why am I here?" Confusion and fright left him feeling like a child after a nightmare. He clung to Nadine's arm for comfort.

"Your guess is as good as mine," Nadine said gently, her voice now tinged with a hint of relief. "Let's get you upstairs and cleaned up. The nurse you called is waiting upstairs. She was pounding on the door when I pulled up. Nearly gave me a heart attack."

"Nurse?" He had no memory of calling a nurse.

Was it really just an illness, after all? It was possible that the night before had been nothing more than a hallucination. Could a flu bug torture his body so much? It couldn't be food poisoning. The last thing he remembered eating was milk and cookies. Death by snack would be a depressing way to go. Fitting, but depressing nonetheless.

Nadine helped him to his feet and struggled to get him out of the damp room and up the stairs. The light burned his eyes closed and doubled him over with the rage of agony that exploded in his head.

"I'm glad you had your wits about you enough to call her. I wish you called me, too. I had no idea what had happened to you." Nadine continued her rant of worry as they headed up the stairs gently, step by step.

The bathroom felt as if it had been miles away by the time Nadine had him seated on the toilet and stripped him of his soiled clothing.

"Harper," he murmured, exhausted. He had ruined her girl's weekend. Guilt swirled in to join the melting pot of emotions he found himself to exhausted to process.

"She's okay. She's in the car with my mom. Once we get you settled, I'll bring her in. She doesn't need to see you like this." Nadine pulled a clean t-shirt over his head. The soft cotton felt like red-hot blades. "Damn it, Martin. You had me so scared. I didn't know what had happened to you."

He was glad when she swallowed the rest of the admonishment that he knew she wanted to shout, but felt bad for worrying her. "I'm sorry. I don't know what happened."

"I just wish you had called me instead of a nurse. I wouldn't have waited all day to come home."

"What day is it?" he asked, flinching against the rough boxer shorts she pulled up his legs after she helped him weakly stand again.

"It's Saturday night." She started with him to the bedroom, twisting her wrist to see her watch. "It's nine already."

He couldn't believe he had been in the basement all day, not knowing where he was. The bed in front of him looked like heaven on earth until he lay down and found it feeling as harsh as the concrete he had been rescued from. Nadine turned off the overhead light and switched on the low light of the lamp perched on the nightstand when he started to wretch in response to the bright assault. It still felt too bright.

"I'm sorry. I'm so sorry I ruined your weekend. Is Harper…" Pain clipped his words, twisting him into a ball under the covers that he tried to kick away. "Is she mad at me?"

"Not at all. Turns out she thinks the ocean is the worst, so it actually worked out well coming home early." She rolled her eyes when she laughed. "The whole time she was whining about coming home to play with Mr. Jack, and how lonely Mr. Jack must be. He may be imaginary, but she wants nothing more than to hang out with him. You should thank him for getting us home early."

"I'm so sorry. I don't know what happened." Everything would have been fine if he just went home and sat on the couch with his pizza. His mundane life seemed like the enemy when it had been the thing keeping him safe all along. As if the universe agreed, another explosion of agony swelled in his stomach.

"Stop apologizing, Mart. You're sick. It's not your fault. I'm sorry you were alone when it got you." She tugged the blankets off that had twisted around his feet. The air felt damp and cold against his skin and the room spun again. "I was sure I was coming home to my man hungover and miserable from his night out, but there is no way this is a hangover." That was one thing they saw in common. She stood from where she had sat beside him. "I'm going to tell Mom that you're okay and send up the nurse, okay? Then we'll get you some rest."

The nurse. She had said that he had called for her. The gaps in his memory were not filling themselves in. "I don't remember calling anyone. Who is this nurse? I don't even know where my phone is."

"You must have called her before you went downstairs. Your phone and wallet are on the kitchen counter." He felt at the heat radiating from his forehead again. "I didn't even know the clinic did house calls, but she said you called earlier and she's been waiting at the door for a while. Good thing. There's no way I would have been able to get you to her when you."

"My wallet is here?" he said, almost as a breath.

He had been absolutely losing his mind with a fever. Now that he knew he was safe and had his family around him, he realized how ridiculous it was to think that someone had drugged him and stolen his wallet – or worse, his kidneys. It had felt like days that he had been held in a dungeon, with everything in his system coming out of any hole it could find, and he had been in the safety of his home the entire time.

Reaching out, he looked to Nadine's hand, who took his fingers intertwined into her own. "It's all okay now. Just rest." She let out a breath that she seemed to have been holding since she left the holiday rental.

Martin didn't like to worry her, but it was nice to see that she still cared enough for him to have concern. He didn't want to know what condition he would have devolved to if she hadn't rushed home to his rescue.

"I love you," he whispered against the stomach pain that still twisted his body.

"I love you too. Just promise you'll never worry us like that again." She disappeared into the dark hallway before he could give her that promise.

It felt good to have his family with him after going through such a fright, even though he would always feel bad for ruining their fun. When he was back on his feet, he would cash in a bank of holiday time and plan something for them all to do together. Chance Beaumont be damned if he declined the time off, as he always did. Whatever virus he picked up may have been karma for so stupidly thinking that it would be fun to hang out with kids that didn't give him the time of day; it was also a wake up call his people were already under his roof. Something out there was trying to tell him that his moping and complaining wasn't doing anything to improve his life. Believing that death had eyes on him made his meager life feel like it was worth fighting for.

A wave of icy agony slipped over the red-hot pain that had settled in as a constant cycle of torture and the fantasy of a happy future whipped away in a wretch. The edge of the bed slammed into his chest when he moved to make way for what threatened to forcefully leave his stomach. A few violent gags and coughs were all that his body could produce.

It was unimaginable that whatever he had caught was able to have a grip on anything within him when it felt like all he had left inside of him was blood and charred bones. No matter what, he was in bed, with his family, and safe. Sick or not, the worst had to be over.

His eyelids dragged heavy with fatigue and the insufferable lamp to his side. He wished he could close them without being rocketed into another nauseating spiral. Soon, creaks on the stairs and the banter of friendly voices distracted him.

"He's right in there. Last room on the right," Nadine said with her speaking to strangers sing-song voice.

Once the nurse gave him a once over, he would be on the road to recovery and they could all move forward with a new regard for each other. They had been sure the weekend apart would be a positive change for them, although the plague had not been a part of the hopeful assumption.

"Right. Thanks then. I've got it from here. Give us a few minutes to look him over, yeah? I'll let you know when we're done."

The too-cold temperature that burned him from the inside out began to shiver over his skin when he heard her. He knew that voice.

"How ya doin', Marty. I hear you're under the weather."

Fighting the pain that held him, Martin tried to pull himself back against the headboard when Lyla rounded the corner into his bedroom.

"What the hell are you doing here?" he screamed, when a broad-chested man with barrels for arms stepped in behind her and shut the door. He stared straight ahead, dead-eyed, in a tracksuit. The zipper on the hoodie was undone, revealing splatters of blood on his white t-shirt that dripped down from his shoulder to his waist.

"Oof. Can you stop with the dramatics? I feel like death warmed over," Lyla scolded, rubbing at a spot on her head. "If you calm down, I can explain. Let's just say I have bad news, and well, worse news, I 'spose."

Martin immediately found more in his stomach to pitch over the side of the bed. So much for the worst being over.

Chapter Four

Some bad news and some worse news.

LYLA TURNED HER HEAD in disgust at Martin's reaction to her arrival and he could not care less.

"What the hell are you doing here? I was sure I had imagined you." He tried to sound aggressive, only to come off as hoarse and exhausted instead.

"I get that. I'm quite the dream, right?" She laughed lightly as if catching up with an old friend, before rubbing her head again. "Christ. It's been forever since I've had a few pints. I remember now why I stick to the clean stuff."

"Why are you here?" In the shape that he found himself, Martin couldn't process the newest what-the-fuck moment. His attention snapped to another man who he had not noticed enter the room. This one, dressed in clothes that appeared to be several decades out of date and sporting a matching mullet, watched the interaction with amusement.

"Right. Straight to business and get us both back to resting. Smart." She moved to the other side of the bed with a look of disdain to the mess he had made beside him and took a seat on the bed's edge.

Eighties mullet and the bag of muscles who came with her remained motionless at the door. Martin was just as frozen when his eyes moved between the three.

"Ay, Marty, you look like shite!" she laughed again.

"What is going on here? Who are you, really?" The only thing he could be sure of was that she was not a nurse there to help him. Not with the meat-bag and the chuckle-fuck dressed in eighties-style plaid in tow. Being out-numbered was not a good feeling on a good day, let alone when you were as powerless as he found himself currently.

"It's going to be alright," Lyla purred, leaning forward, her eyes locked on his. She seemed to be trying to see right into his soul, a serene look softening her face. Martin twitched with a bolt of electric pain that bounced around in his stomach. "Hmm…maybe not. Godammit."

"What the hell does that mean?" Martin strained to not give into the tremors that built within him.

"Like I said. Bad news and worse news, I'm afraid. Looks like worse news than I had hoped. Not a lot left to work with." She crossed her arms and Martin growled when she and the eighties rocker snickered. "Okay. Alright. I'm the one who got flutered and fecked up last night. Time to pay the piper, yeah?"

Martin looked at her as if she had grown a second head. "What the hell are you going on about?"

Her flitty attitude did not match his of fright and complete confusion. The meat-bag at the door didn't seem to pay attention to anything that was happening, let alone care.

Lyla leaned away when Martin started for the edge of the bed again. He was thankful when he found his tank empty and leaned back against a pillow that felt like bricks, panting.

"Right, so if I'm being honest, I've been havin' a bit of a struggle lately and have been sort of acting the rebel. I know that has nothing to do with you, except you seemed to have stepped right out in front of my train wreck and so, here we are." She stopped and looked at Martin.

He assumed she wanted him to say something, or get even more angry. All he could do was stare and force himself to ignore the pain that took hold of him again. He couldn't even nod or glare.

"I guess you didn't so much step in front than get pushed," she shrugged and avoided his eyes. "I thought that my new life would be better. That I would be powerful and, therefore, happy, you know? Turns out I'm still serving the ones with power and I can't really say I'm thrilled. I saw the same thing in you and thought you were a good guy that had the same luck and lot in life as I had. Add the drink to that and I started making more bad decisions. It seems to be all I know how to do."

The pain built like boiling water pushing toward the edge of a pot. Her words fell into a constant buzz that he wanted to stop. Nothing she said made sense to why he had ended up doubled over in his crawl space.

The room returned to its spinning, first sideways and then head over heel, while Martin remained clenched in the bed. Lyla's face appeared almost nose to nose with him, pushing away the spiral of blurred ribbons the world had become.

"Open your mouth. Martin, I need you to open your mouth."

He hadn't realized how tight his jaw had become until his bottom lip popped away from the top when she pressed her finger into his mouth and lifted a black bottle to his face.

"There ya are. Give that a go," Lyla directed, sounding like she was miles away yet right in his ear as she had a way of doing.

The dry stone that his tongue had become watered, and he lapped about every inch of his mouth, searching for whatever elixir had just awoken inside of him.

Memories of his first taste of decadently cold ice cream, his first sensation of warm sun that somehow made his skin smell sweet, the vibration through his body the first time he experienced live music on a grand scale, and finally the exquisite release and euphoria he fell into the first time he had completely been with his high school girlfriend, Jackie. An exhaustion spread through his mind, down to his shoulders, before it glided through every muscle in his body, stretching his toes with sweet relief.

A sleepy smile stretched across his face that he did not notice. It had been years since he thought about Jackie. The seventeen-year-old Martin had been sure they were going to spend the rest of their lives together. Obviously they didn't. Such is the story of so many first loves. In front of him, he could see her bending down, her strawberry lip gloss coating his mouth. He lapped at the flavor.

When he rolled his shoulders he released a domino effect to the rest of his body. Stretching away the tension that had held a stranglehold on his body, he let his mind drift further into the memory. He wouldn't trade Nadine or Harper for anything, but the summer night's heat that had driven Jackie and him down into the cool relief of the basement after they had snuck his dad's beer from the fridge…

"Martin! *Jaysus* Christ, snap out of it!"

The familiar room of his youth dissipated and became the one where he laid his head down each night with his wife.

Lyla remained sat at his side, humor twitching on her face. "Pretty good, huh? I still remember my first taste. Nothing like it in the world."

Martin looked from her to his blanket covered body. The pain, the heavy head, the nausea: it was all gone. Lyla smiled with newly crimson lips when he looked back to her.

"Sorry," she wiped her mouth, leaving a pale pink behind. "I'm feckin' starving. I'm never going to drink spiked blood again."

When she smiled, he noticed her teeth. Impossibly long canines that she licked the last of the red stain from. He tried to sit back away from her. The relaxation that weighed his body down held him in place, his head lolling.

It felt wrong to be angry with the woman who had brought him such great relief, even when it was fair to assume the suffering had something to do with her to begin with. The punch drunk sensation eased and some control over his body returned. He slapped his cheek lazily in an attempt to sober himself further. He wondered if whatever she had given him was what he had stupidly ingested the night before. The cause and cure for whatever was wrong with him.

"What the hell is going on here? What did you give me last night?" He touched his mouth and his eyes grew larger than silver dollars when he saw the blood that now streaked his finger tips. "Is that blood?" Feeling around his face, he didn't feel anywhere it may have come from.

"Like I told ya. I've bad news and worse news depending on how you take it. I let you sit like this too long, it seems. I guess there's a reason we're not allowed to try this willy-nilly. If you had invited me in when you got home last night, you would have never found yourself in this position. Now I need to take care of it." Lyla frowned, looking him over.

It sounded like a threat, even though her voice was sweet. From what he could rationalize, he was the 'it' that would be in need of being taken care of. He'd watched enough mob movies to know what that meant.

One night out. One damn night out pretending his life could be different. This is what it got him. He needed them out of the house and away from his family. Calling out to them would only send them running into the very place they needed to stay clear of. If he had any strength at all, he would at least try to run. Moving his head seemed like too much of an effort. He was in a trap with no way out.

Martin looked at the two men who stood silently behind Lyla, one with an empty stare and the other with the same look of amusement dancing on his face.

"Having fun, are we?" he barked at the stranger, who only smothered his grin without a word.

Lyla gave a quick look at him and then handed the black bottle to the silent one. He took it robotically without acknowledging her. The way he stood motionless was becoming creepier than the woman who appeared to be drinking blood cocktails in his bedroom. The second man leaned back against the wall and started to quietly whistle. He recognized the tune but couldn't place where he had heard it.

"There's never an easy way to say this, Marty. You're a vampire now. Just like me. Well, not quite like me. You're in a sort of limbo between being a full-blooded vampire and, well, a corpse."

Martin's eyes blinked quickly, his face crumpling around an irritated sigh. The tension twisted within his body again, the relief of whatever she had given him floating away. Whatever game she was playing at, he was not interested in joining in. "I don't know what the point of all of this is, but I want you to get out of my house."

Lyla was obviously a psychopath who found glee playing with other people's minds. Lord only knew what drugs she had been slipping him since the night before. He pushed himself to sit straighter and pointed to the door. "Whatever this is, it's over. Go."

"I could do that, if you really want me to. If I do, you'll stay sick like this until you eventually die. I need you to understand that. Not the best way to spend your last days. If you have days left." She looked him over curiously.

He watched as the sharp fangs in her mouth flicked up and down into her gums in the way someone would twiddle their thumbs while in thought. There was no way that was just a trick of the eye.

There was no way that there were vampires, either.

Right?

The pain started again, burning and twisting his stomach; making his mind cloudy and his thoughts broken. The suffering that spread through every nerve in his body was real and it was returning. He knew that much. If she really was a vampire, if they really were real, he needed them as far away from his life as possible. How to make that happen while his body felt like it was dying from the inside out was the question.

"Listen, this is the problem we have. I'm not exactly allowed to turn anyone. Into a vamp, I mean. It's a really big no-no for someone of my age and rank to take it upon myself to become a mama," she said with a tight laugh. "I've gotten in trouble for playing with my food since I was a mortal little babe, and here I am again. This one won't get my pudding taken away, though. This one could have me turned to dust."

Martin tried to listen as he groaned, pulling his legs into his arms, willing the agony to pass.

Lyla put a hand on his back. "I can't leave you like this, Marty. This isn't right. I need to fix this." She spoke to herself, looking at him. The humor she had been hiding behind had slipped. "I can do this. I'm sorry, but it's the only thing that will fix this. It's all my fault. I admit that. I should have finished you last night. I had no right to start you off and then leave you. I'm always doing thing half-arsed and getting myself in trouble. Either way, you're going to find yourself with the same ending, right? I'll make it a lot more quick and painless than they will." She bobbed her head in agreement with herself.

He looked up at the sadness that now shadowed her face. "You're here to kill me?"

"I…well, I came here with that intent, yes." She pushed a short, sweaty lock of hair from his forehead. "Hearing you talk about your life last night, I dunno, if made me think you'd appreciate being one of us. The same way I thought I would, but my life is just as powerless now as it was forty years ago when I had a pulse. The whole lot is a mess. I don't want to, Marty, but we're both in it if I don't. I've dragged you far enough into my mistakes."

His stomach rolled with what felt like hot, wet flames up into his throat, choking him. If she wasn't going to kill him, whatever was wrong with him felt like it could do the trick for her. The worse he felt, the less fight he had against the idea. Pinpricks of light spiraled in his eyes as he heaved empty gags over the sheet, now soaked in his sweat.

Lyla stood away from him with whatever conflicting thoughts she was arguing about with herself. The battle tightening her petite, pale features.

"If anyone finds out I turned you, we'd both be as good as twenty-past sunrise." Her fangs flicked in and out as she thought. "You seem like a good lad, Marty. I know I fecked this one up pretty bad, but I have no idea how to fix it, otherwise." She moved impossibly fast to perch back on the bed. "Do you want me to take this all away? I can do it real quick and the pain will stop. Just tell me you're okay with it. Gag twice if you want me to." She attempted a pained smile.

It was clear even in the state he was that she meant to kill him. The sound of the Harper's giggle chimed in his ears and the way the sunlight hit Nadine's hair when she would putter in their small garden lit up before his eyes. Shaking his head, he pushed away from her and desperately held onto his stomach contents. He couldn't leave his family. He wouldn't. No matter how much he was suffering. "No. Please," was all he could sputter.

Lyla scrubbed her hands over her face and let out a frustrated snarl. "What is it about you, Marty? I couldn't eat ya. I can't kill ya. I really am a shite vamp, aren't I?

No wonder they don't let just anyone turn whoever they pick. It bloody drives me mad when the rules I hate prove to be right."

Martin dragged himself further away on the bed when she stood to pace along with her rant.

"I can't leave you to suffer like this. It's not my way to hurt people, I hope you know that. I mean, I eat them, but I don't try to hurt them. They certainly don't end up like you now." She grimaced when Martin let out a yelp of pain in response to a fresh wave of torturous heat rolling over him. "I need to do it, Martin." She started to him and stopped when he held up a shaking, pleading hand. "No, I'm sorry, but I have to fix this."

"Please. My family. Don't take me from them." His voice was raspy and exhausted.

Lyla snatched the black bottle from the stiff man and shook it upside down, finding it empty again. "Damn it. Way to feck it up again, Ly," she scolded herself. Martin watched her watching him, feeling like prey to an unsteady animal. He could tell that she wasn't murderous; she looked at him with pity, but was unpredictable enough to pounce at any moment.

His head lay heavy on the bed, knowing he didn't have any fight left. "Please. Just leave us. I won't tell anyone about you."

"Daddy?" Harper's voice called out from the hallway.

Martin tried to cry out when Lyla spat out a curse and moved with a flash to the door, twisting the lock and was back at his side faster than he could follow.

"Dammit! I'm gonna do it, Marty. I'm gonna try to finish the turn, okay? I just hope this doesn't kill us both." She grabbed the silent man and pulled him down to the bed as if he weighed less than one of Harper's dolls. His eyes stayed empty when her lips set upon his neck and then rolled back into his head with intoxication when she pulled her teeth from his flesh, leaving streams of blood rolling down to his crisp white shirt. Lyla pushed him towards Martin's horrified face. "Drink," she ordered. "Martin, for Christ's sake, open your mouth and drink!"

While intending to take a breath to scream, he felt his tongue rapidly being covered in a warm, coppery coating that sped up as Lyla pressed the man closer, forming a seal between their flesh and lips.

This time the pain increased, twisting within him, rather than the bliss the first last had brought him. He pushed away at the man, his energy rising, giving him the chance to fight when he felt his heartbeat thumping harder and harder in his chest. A pain started as a pinch deep within him bloomed into a ripping of agony that felt as if his heart was being blown up like an over-stretched balloon, each beat pushing it out larger and larger until his body seemed to burst out into the room as an explosion of light that burned his eyes closed.

His lungs tightened when the air they held trickled out from his mouth, that now hung agape. The heavy pounds within his chest silenced, and he felt himself laying flat on his stomach, the damp sheets warm against his cheek. The silent man and the effects of his blood were gone. He had never felt more alone in the now silent world that held him for what he was sure was eternity.

Was it death or limbo? There was no way to tell.

Lyla's face came into focus when she kneeled beside the bed. "Better?" She booped her finger on the tip of his nose with a quiet laugh. "I hope so, because I may have just made the worst decision in both of our lives. I hope I did it right, too. No promises. How's your brains, fella?

I didn't melt anything up there did I?" Her face twisted into a tight grimace as she waited for an answer.

Martin took stock of his body from tip to toes. The pain was gone, and the nausea had turned into growling ripples of hunger when a smell that hung in the air swirled about him. He inhaled the delicious aroma, causing his mouth to water and yelped when he wiped at his lips. His tongue ran over the spot of the pain, tasting a weak taste of blood that turned his stomach and then pricked onto a tiny dagger in his mouth. He froze, spread out like a starfish when his finger ran over a newly birthed fang and then a second on the other side. The smell shook him away from his new discovery when it danced in his nose again. He sat up quickly, faster than Harper on Christmas morning, and his eyes locked on the dead-eyed man who remained at Lyla's side. He rose to his feet, following his nose.

"Oh, whoopsie!" Lyla jumped up, pricking her fingertip on one of her fangs, and tapped her own blood onto the gently weeping wounds on the man's neck. The enticing scent quickly dissipated. "That's just a tease now, isn't it?"

Martin inhaled, trying to pick up the scent, finding nothing left. His body froze again when the air he had pulled into his lungs leaked out of his mouth without the will to replace the breath. He paused to feel the strange stillness within his chest before pulling in another breath for it to slip out again, like a tire going flat. He looked quickly to Lyla, bewildered by what he was now experiencing in place of the pain that had been eating him alive.

She put a hand on his shoulder, encouraging him to sit.

"Crazy, right?" she asked with a nervous grin tilting up the left side of her lips. "I'll never forget those first time feelings." She put two fingers to his neck and seemed pleased with what she found – or didn't find.

"What's happened? Am I going to be back to normal now?" He couldn't believe he was now a vampire. He couldn't even say vampire. The appearance of his deadly new teeth told him she wasn't a psychopath, she was a card carrying member of the undead, just as she had said. She could quite possibly be both, but he could not push himself to say vampire.

The thought alone should have willed his mind to panic, yet his body remained calm and motionless when he sat on the edge of his bed. His eyes squinted at the lamp that seemed to have brightened even worse on his night-stand. Holding a hand up, he shielded his eyes until Lyla switched it off. Immediately, everything came into focus around him, crystal clear and more illuminated than it should be within the shadows of the room.

"In a sense, yes," Lyla answered quietly. "Human Martin is gone now. You seem to have transitioned pretty well. I think a lot of it may have happened during the day. Probably. I think," she predicted, looking less than sure of herself. "Hopefully, now that you're one of us, vampire Martin won't get us both killed. I just have to find a way to hide you for a bit while I figure out what to do next."

"Daddy?" Harper's voice called out again while she jiggled the handle to his bedroom.

"Send her away, Martin. Trust me." The way she spoke so sternly worried him. There was too much to process without putting his daughter in any sort of danger.

"Daddy's okay. Please go downstairs and stay with Mommy, Giggles." He tilted his head and listened to the amplified sounds of her when he realized he could hear her all the way down the stairs and then speaking with her mother. They sounded as if they were in the room with him. He closed his eyes to marvel at his amazing ability, but they snapped open when he could not help himself from focusing on the steady beats of their hearts, his mouth watering with want. He slapped a hand over his mouth when he felt his lip twitch with hunger. One of the sharp new teeth pierced his tongue, causing another yelp to slip out. The canines felt too large for his mouth.

"Dod dammip," he muttered around his fangs, favoring the injury to his tongue. The blood stopped quickly yet left a taste in his mouth that made him spit into a tissue he plucked from the table beside him.

"Yeah, you'll find a nip of our blood will be pretty unpleasant compared to the living. It's pretty well like eating rotten fruit. Nothing but death left in us, Marty." She pushed the blood bag of a man forward again, and Martin grabbed him and tore into his neck as Lyla had done. The burst of flavor washed away the nasty taste of himself and he gripped the man tighter, greedily guzzling the blood that flowed freely into his mouth.

Lyla pulled him away, far too soon for his liking, tapping away his wounds with a dab of her blood like before. Martin looked at the now unnaturally pale man as he licked his lips in search of a stray drop.

"Let that settle in your tum-tum, Marty. It's best not to overdo it at first." She wiped the corner of Martin's mouth with her thumb and then gave her digit a lick. "That's more than enough to do you for a while."

"This has to be a fever dream. This isn't real." Martin knew everything felt real around him. The delicious, yet disgusting, drink he just imbibed certainly felt real. Everything but the possibility that he was now a member of the undead creatures of fictional horror. In real life, there was no way he would attack a man like a medium-rare steak.

"Sorry, fella. It's real." Lyla's back stiffened and she turned her head, listening to someone or something only heard by her. "I hate to turn and run, but for our own sake, it would be best if we kept our distance for a bit, so no one suspects us."

"Run? No, no, no, no. You have a lot of explaining to do. What the hell am I supposed to do now?" There was no way he could be left on his own to sort it all out. He hadn't even convinced himself it was all real yet. If he really had just made a meal of a man, how could Nadine and Harper be safe under the same roof as him? The vampires in the movies couldn't go in the sun, had to sleep in coffins, and could be taken out with garlic. He certainly didn't have a coffin on hand, nor did he know what to do if Nadine decided to make her famous meatballs! Lyla hadn't just given him some antibiotics and a date for a follow up appointment. She'd gifted him with his undead card. He needed a little more information before she left him to fend for himself.

She leveled herself eye to eye with him. "You have everything inside of you to survive for now. You've had enough to eat to keep your wife and kiddo safe until I can come back to see you. Just stay inside, say nothing about this to them, and wait for me. Tell them you're still sick. Stay in bed and keep those shades closed." Looking over the blackout blinds and curtains, she seemed happy with the shelter they could provide. "Give yourself a little break and I promise I'll be back as soon as I can. Just do not leave this house."

The thought of looking at Nadine and Harper like he had just looked at the man, the thought of doing to them what he had just done, was beyond anything he could imagine. "You can't leave me like this. What if I can't control myself?" He felt helpless for someone who now had the capacity to be murderous.

"You'll do fine. You'll be able to go for days without feeding." Reaching over to the sidelight, she switched it back on. Martin covered his eyes until she tossed one of Nadine's scarves over the shade, making it more tolerable. "Zip up, Tommy," she directed the motionless man who tugged up the zipper of the hoodie he wore, hiding the mess they had made of his t-shirt. She moved to the door, unlocking and then opening it before Martin could argue. "Hello? You can come up and see your daddy, now!" she called down to them as she turned back to find Martin trying to find his voice to tell them to stay away. "Oh, shite!" She pointed at his chest. "Lose the shirt! You made a mess."

Martin looked down at the dark red stains streaked all over himself and ripped it off over his head, giving his mouth a wipe, and hid it under the blanket just as Harper rounded the corner. He stiffened away from her when she bounded up to his side.

"Daddy, are you feeling better?" She leaned her head on his arm and he was relieved to find the desperate thirst he had felt just minutes before did not return. The sound in her chest was like a bass drum.

"He's looking much better, isn't he?" Nadine noted when she walked in to join them. She gave him a loving smile that he did not want to look away from. It had been a long time since he felt that tug of love in his belly from something his wife did. Nevertheless, he forced himself to look away, afraid she would notice something different in his eyes.

"We've done all we can for now. I'll check back in a few days from now." Lyla's jaw flexed with a stress she trying to keep in check.

"Wait! What until then? What do I do?" Martin's voice was desperate. As much as he had wanted that woman out of his room and his house, he didn't want to be left on his own to sort out what he now was.

"Just rest. Stay in bed, keep the blinds and curtains tight…," she cleared her throat and glanced at Nadine, "You know, to stop the migraines, and just rest."

"That can't be all I need to do." Martin tried and failed to not sound shrill. "Don't I need to sleep in.. uh.. a special bed?" The very fact he was still worrying if he needed to sleep in a coffin was as bizarre as it seemed important. He scowled when she smothered a snicker to his question. He couldn't believe all he needed to be safe was to lounge in bed and wait for Lyla to find her way back to him.

"What are you talking about?" Nadine questioned, concern dipping her brows. "A special bed for what?"

"It's just a touch of a fever still, ma'am. No need to worry." Lyla crossed the room and tugged at the pull-down blind and heavy curtains again. "No, this is all you need to worry about, Marty. It's going to be okay. Just stay here and I'll be back. You need to trust me." She leaned down to his ear and whispered, "For both our sakes."

She stood up quickly and snapped her fingers at the meal now known as Tommy. He faithfully followed her to the door.

"I'll show you out," Nadine offered, stepping out of the room in front them. Martin knew she was about to pepper Lyla with medical questions and hoped she could keep up with the front of being a nurse or a doctor or whatever her lie had been. It was enough for him to sort out if he was crazy or not. It was a whole other ball game if Nadine was sure he was.

Lyla took in a deep breath, as if she were trying to will herself the energy to deal with what she had done, and gave him a nod. Tommy started out on her heels like an obedient dog. The man in the dated clothing with the permanent smirk stay leaned against the wall, the quiet whistling again singing from his lips.

"Hey, Lyla! Aren't you forgetting someone?" Martin didn't know how he would explain the man's presence if she expected him to stay, or what sort of threat he posed.

Lyla poked her head back in the room to see where Martin pointed.

"Who? That guy?" She frowned at him.

"Yeah! That guy!" Martin agreed in a hushed shout.

"I dunno know who that is. I thought you knew him." She left down the hall without another word.

Martin pulled Harper to his side, suddenly more worried about the strange man in his house than the danger he might now bring to his daughter.

"I think you should leave," he advised, attempting to sound stronger than he felt.

"Daddy, you can't talk to him like that!" Harper pulled away from him and skipped across the room without worry. "That's my best friend! Come on Mr. Jack, I want to tell you about the beach. Did you know it's the worst?"

Mr. Jack?

Chapter Five

Ghosted.

MARTIN STARED BACK AT the man. Another addition to his *WTF* pile. The new guest stared back at him, showing no intention of leaving with Harper, who stared up adoringly at the man who they had been sure was imaginary.

Mr. Jack was real?

"Hey," the man dressed in ripped jeans and a sleeveless plaid shirt offered, before running a hand through his shoulder length golden mullet.

Martin went to stand before sitting down hard on the side of the bed. His movement was too quick and made him dizzy. "Who are you?" he asked, rubbing his eyes.

"I'm Dan. Dan Jack." He reached out a hand and then pulled it back, instead roughing up the blonde curls that hung down his neck. "Sorry, force of habit even after all these years." He let out a clipping laugh and a bob of his head. "Handshakes aren't what they used to be."

"Isn't he funny, Daddy?" Harper looked up at him, remaining at her friend's side.

"Hilarious, Harper. Can you leave Daddy and Mr. Jack to talk, please?" Martin wanted her as far away from him as possible until he understood who he was, or more importantly, what he was. Her own dad was enough of a problem now. An unknown man standing in his bedroom was icing on the crap cake.

"It's, uh, Dan. Jack is my last name," he corrected with his head bobbing along with nervous laughter.

"Yeah, that seems like the most important thing to get straight right now." Martin replied with dripping sarcasm. Anger was brewing in his core and he did his best to tamp it down before Harper noticed. "Giggles, why don't you go ask Mommy for a snack so I can talk to Mr. Jack?" He attempted to keep his lips stiff over his new dental work.

She beamed a grin at them both and obediently skipped down the hall to find her mother downstairs. He hoped Lyla had left without incident, even though he had never wanted the strange woman to be around more. The night was becoming beyond a fever dream. This was a night terror.

"It's Dan, man. My name is Dan." The guy gave a crooked grin.

He seemed harmless. Other than Martin had no idea of who or what he was.

Or how he had gotten into their house.

And why he was his four-year-old's best friend.

"Are you the guy that my daughter is always talking about? She calls you Mr. Jack."

"Yeah, that's me. She's a wicked smart lil' kid. She cracks me up."

"How did you get into our house? You're not a vampire, are you?" Martin realized that there was no sound of heartbeats from the stranger's chest.

When the chaos of the night was over, he was either going to wake up and for the first time in the history of man be grateful for a nightmare, or have a lot of learning to do with his new abilities. He sent out a wish for a nightmare with a pinch of his skin. He flinched when his skin split and a trickle of blood appeared. The tiny cut closed just as fast.

"Whoa, that's awesome! So I guess you're one of them now. That's fuckin' crazy. I didn't believe it when I first saw one outside through the window. I never thought I'd meet a real vamper. How's it feel?" Dan asked in awe.

Martin shook off his own growing wonder and forced himself back to the more important worry of the moment. "You didn't answer my question. Why are you in my house?"

"I guess that's a two-parter sort of answer, man. Like, for one, I have no freakin' idea. Honestly. I don't know why I'm here, but then on the other hand, this is sort of my house. I mean, it was my house." Dan looked around the room with memories dancing in his pale eyes. Stepping forward, the bedside light cast through him, making him more cloud than man.

"Holy shit!" Martin exclaimed. Mr. Jack was definitely not human. "What are you?"

"I'm a phantom, dude," he whispered dramatically, holding his fingers up like claws. "A spectral spectacle, a choice spirit, a bodacious ghoul!" His voice raised with every word. Martin stared blankly at him until he continued. "I'm a ghost, dude. This used to be my place before I died."

"A ghost," Martin repeated. "My daughter's best friend is a ghost. A grown man ghost, to boot." Looking down, he realized he was sitting in only a pair of boxer shorts while having introductions. He rose purposely slow in order to not shock his system again and stepped over to the dresser to pull on a fresh shirt.

"And her dad is a baby vampire! How cool is that? Harps is having a way more awesome childhood than I did. This shit is crazy, right?"

"That's one word for it." Martin frowned at the nickname the stranger had for his beloved daughter and ran his tongue over his newly born fangs, slowly learning not to stab his tongue. "So why can Harper see you and we can't," he paused to look at him, "I guess I can now. Why?" He returned to the edge of the bed.

"I have no idea. I don't even know how long I'd been here before, Harps. She was the first to see me. Cute little thing in her little crib. I was making faces at her and she started to laugh. Scared the shit out of me, to be honest."

"She's been able to see you since she was a baby?" Martin couldn't believe a man had been living in the background of their lives unseen for four years. He would think it was creepier if he still didn't have the taste of a random man's blood on his tongue. He ignored how his mouth watered when he thought of him and tilted his head to listen to his girls downstairs.

Harper was telling Nadine about Daddy meeting Mr. Jacks between crunchy bites of her snack. Nadine's responses sounded exhausted. He clicked the door closed, not wanting her to hear what must sound like a one-sided conversation with the air.

"She's such a cool little kid. I think I would have gone crazy if she hadn't seen me. Do you think that's how those scary ass polter-what's-its are made? That movie scared the shit outta me, but maybe they were just lonely, you know?"

"Honestly, Mr. Jack, I don't understand a damn thing anymore." His brain wanted to shut down with all of the shocks to his system and to his world in general.

"It's Dan, man. It's totally weird you calling me Mr. Jack." Dan gave a shiver of shrug.

"Oh, that's weird, is it? You have a very low grade for what is weird, considering." Martin rub at the spot on his head that would have started to thump with a headache under such stress. No pain grew. He assumed it must take pumping blood to cause a tension headache. Finally, a plus to being undead.

Undead. How was that possible?

He jumped when Dan spoke again.

"I guess being a baby vampire for a minute is a lot more to take in than being a ghost for so long. I've been roaming around here all by myself since eighty-eight. It's nice to have someone else to talk to."

"Is that why I can see you? Because I'm dead? Well, technically dead." *Or just entirely insane.*

"Maybe. I mean, it makes sense. I don't have a teacher like that hot little Irish piece that was here for you, so I've been trying to figure it out myself. Harps' been trying to teach me that computer of yours, but since I can't physically touch it and she's not the greatest speller yet, it's slow moving." He let out a rattle of laughter from deep within his transparent chest. "What's her deal, anyway?"

"Her deal? She's four. She's only had one year in school," Martin admonished, not liking the idea of his daughter's intelligence being questioned on top of everything else.

Dan laughed harder. "No, man. That Irish chick. What's her deal? She's smoking hot. For bloodsucking chick, I guess."

"Sorry, I don't know her *deal*. I barely know her." It had been just over twenty-four hours since his life crossed her path, ended, and started again as a vampire.

"So, is she like your mom now?"

"What?" Martin frowned at the question. "No, she's not my mom." He considered that she had just made him a baby vampire, as Dan had called him. "I don't think. I don't know anything about any of this." He held his spinning head in his hands.

"Imagine we hit it off, and I became like, your step-dad!" He busted out another laugh. "Harps would be like my grand kid and shit. That's wild, man."

Martin couldn't get a thought straight in his head with Dan rattling on. "Harper. Her name is Harper."

"Yeah, I know. She's always just been my little Harps, though, you know."

"No, I don't know! She's my daughter and I don't want you near her anymore! You're a grown ass man and a dead man to boot!"

Martin regretted his harsh attack as soon as he saw the hurt in the ghost's eyes. It couldn't have been easy only having a toddler as a friend for all those years. He didn't blame himself for lashing out, given the circumstances, but Dan was almost in the same boat as he was. A damned boat enroute to Hades, it would seem.

Before he could apologize, the ghostly rocker slipped away into the air in front of his eyes.

If they were both cursed with an eternal existence in that house, he hoped he would have a chance to make amends when his life wasn't imploding around him.

Sitting back on the bed, he sank into the fresh silence, his fingers tangled in his sweaty hair. He'd been dead less than an hour and he was already making enemies. For now, it was not something he needed to worry about. If Lyla didn't find her way back to him soon, he would be screwed.

She had said that if someone found out she had turned someone, both of them would be at risk of being killed off. He wondered if it was actually being killed if they already didn't have heartbeats.

By the time she showed up again - hopefully showed up again - he would have a list of questions a mile long.

Could that be how vampires are created? Turned and tossed? No wonder they weren't ruling the world if they were just clueless corpses roaming around looking for someone to slurp.

It seemed naïve to believe that she would come back for him when his very existence threatened hers, but there was a trust that he felt toward her that he couldn't quite put his cold, dead finger on.

Rising from the bed, he peeked out the window, half hoping he would see her, half hoping the sun would be high in the sky, unharming to him. The sky was dark, and the yard was empty. He pulled the curtains tight again over the blackout blinds.

Every vampire book, movie, and fable came to him all at once. There were so many contradictions, and so many terrifying possibilities before him. The mirror above their dresser caught his eye. When he stood before it, he could see himself just as before.

One question answered.

His face was pale and near gaunt, with unfamiliar shadows under his eyes and cheekbones. The stories with the heart-stoppingly gorgeous vampires were another myth, it seemed. That would have been a good selling point if he ever told Nadine what was happening.

Leaning forward, he opened his mouth wide to get a look at the fangs that now hung menacingly from either side of his mouth. Those would be hard to explain to Nadine. He gently pushed up, willing them to tuck up out of sight, as Lyla's had done. Nothing happened.

"Fangs, retract!" he ordered in a hushed voice, only to be embarrassed that he thought that would work.

He closed his eyes, stilling himself, and envisioned them popping back into his gums. As he sat there, he noticed how tense he had become. He ran his mind over each muscle that felt as if made from granite. To his delight, he soon felt a slick pop in his mouth. When he opened his eyes to his reflection, a normal, human looking smile greeted him.

For a brand new vampire, he was already finding superpowers. For moment he told himself there was a chance it might all work out. Once he figured out how to stay alive.

Or undead.

He wasn't sure what the correct term would be. Either way, he started to believe he could learn to survive.

Drinking human blood would have to be at the top of that list.

Just the day before, that thought alone would have made him nauseous. Now, it was how to get more of it that upset him. A little because he knew what it would entail. Moreso because he was already wanting more. The taste was still in his mouth like a constant tease, goading him to seek it out.

From what Lyla told him, he should be fine until she came back. There was a chance it would be too late, if possibly never. The soft thump-thump-thumps of Nadine and Harper's pulse called out to him from the floor below like a hypnotizing melody. It was beyond a worry that he could be a threat to the ones he loved the most.

The idea that he could hurt them in any way broke his heart. Just like the hearts that pumped just below his feet.

Thump-thump, thump-thump, thump-thump. His mouth watered with each beat. The warm blood that he needed to survive. The thick, crimson delicacy that was held buy not much more than thin, weak tissue paper.

Fangs popped back into his mouth, shaking him from the rabbit hole of thirst he had fallen into.

He covered his mouth, partially to hide the deadly teeth, partially out of the embarrassment of his horrific thoughts. His mind did not feel like his own. The hushed needs and cravings were a consistent hum, distracting him from his surroundings.

Growing louder, the beats were accompanied by the sound of the two as they ascended the stairs, each step drawing them nearer to him. The fangs refused to retract.

The more upset he became, the less he felt he had a chance to hide them away before his wife opened the door.

It wasn't so much that he wanted to drink from her anymore; it was that he didn't want to give her a heart attack.

He pressed his palms against the door, closing his eyes and hoping to find the strength to calm himself. Trying deep breaths did not help, as it only reminded him he didn't need to breathe any longer. The sensation made him uncomfortable.

"Dammit, Martin. Pull yourself together," he ordered, resting his head on the warm wood of the bedroom door.

Different images, from crashing waves to a warm breeze through trees, did nothing to center his mind enough as the sounds of his family came closer and closer.

The squeak of his office chair twitched in his head. It brought him into the dark, bland room, and staring at the blank computer screen across from him. He rocked in the broken seat, recalling each piece of office supply that littered his desk. The small framed drawing Harper had created drew his attention from the stapler that would only bend one side of the staple correctly. She had been so proud of it when she gave it to him for Father's Day, after making a trip to the store with her mom to find the perfect frame. Hot pink with a sparkle covered unicorn in the corner.

His mouth felt empty when the fangs slid back up into their gummy holsters.

He stepped back from the door. Was it the thought of his daughter or the numbness he found in his office that had calmed him? It had to be impossible that his cell of an office was his happy place.

The door swung open and stopped when it hit Martin in the head. Stumbling back, he was glad that his new vampire body saved him from the pain that would have caused.

"Martin! Are you alright? I'm so sorry," Nadine exclaimed, reaching out to touch his head. She frowned when he pulled away from her. He didn't know if she could tell that anything was deeply different within him and felt better with some distance between them. "What are you doing out of bed? The nurse said you need to rest more."

Quickly making his way back onto the bed and under the covers, he feigned a tired yawn. "I was just going to get a glass of water." Not that he was sure he could even drink it, but it seemed the easiest lie.

"I can get you that. Are you up for Harper to say good-night real quick?"

A moment of silence passed while he gave his body, and his cravings, a quick scan. Everything appeared to remain calm and in check. "Yeah, I'm good."

Harper ran through the door and crawled slowly up beside him, a grin from ear to ear. "Are you feeling better?" She waited for him to answer with a nod before she tucked in by his arm.

If his fangs made an appearance, all hell would break loose.

"I'm going to get your jammies ready, so a quick good-night and then meet me in the bathroom to brush your teeth, okay?" Nadine gave a stern nod and left them.

Martin pushed his lips tighter at the mention of teeth.

"I'm sorry you have an icky tummy, Daddy."

Martin nodded and gave her a squeeze.

"You're not going to be sick forever. Don't worry." She gave him a kiss on the cheek and hopped off the bed. "Night, Daddy. See you in the morning." Hopping off the bed to follow her mother's directions, she stopped in the door to blaze a smile back to him. "I'm glad you finally met Mr. Jack!" Her little feet skipped her away and down the hall.

The weight of the past two days weighed heavily on Martin. Little did anyone know he would indeed be sick forever. The escape he had craved had left him with a permanent wedge between himself and the ones he loved, with a lack of a beating heart to boot. The sweet well wishes of his daughter brought tears to his eyes that he wiped away when they slid down his cheeks.

Blood streaked his fingertips when he pulled them away. Panic rose again as he wiped at his face. Grabbing a tissue from the box on the nightstand, he scrubbed away any trace from his hands before going to the mirror to clean the rest. The last thing he needed was Nadine thinking he had a life-threatening illness like Ebola.

He smirked at his reflection. In a way, he did have something life-threatening, or at least he had. He was already dead. Ebola might be easier to explain. The tissues were tucked in the back of his underwear drawer, along with the bloodstained t-shirt, to be disposed of the next morning after Nadine awoke for the day. The t-shirt would be tricker to be rid of. Not like he could sneak it into the wash. Under the cover of the hallway's darkness, he should be able to slip in and out to flush the tissues, at least.

The dreary darkness of their house had been one thing he hated when they bought it. Nadine had insisted on the place, as it was all that they could afford near her mother. The only fresh light came from the bay window in the front room that he now saw as a death trap if he were to stand in front of it while the sun rose, as he had done so many times before.

It would be easy to explain away the need to stay in bed for a day or two, given that they all believed him to be down with the flu. After that, he would have to get creative as to why he wasn't eating or leaving the bedroom if Lyla didn't reappear.

He didn't even know if he could still eat or drink what he had just a day before. The movies told him there was a chance he would projectile vomit it across the room. Having a fake flu bug would be a great excuse to try it out. Probably best in private, though. Nadine had a very weak stomach.

The thought of never having another slice of hot, cheesy pizza was almost enough to send him into another fit of tears.

It would be enough to get through the night and into the sunrise of the next morning without worrying about what he could no longer have. If he was going to survive for his family, he was going to have to take one crisis at a time.

When Nadine slid into bed beside him after repeatedly asking if she could get him anything, he tried to ignore the steady pulse that tickled at her neck and listen to the stories of their disastrous beach day.

Harper didn't like the feel of the wet sand on her feet and hated wearing her water shoes. The ocean waves were too cold, and the sun was too warm. She had stated emphatically that she would not be sleeping in a strange bed for one more night and she could not stop worrying about Mr. Jack and her daddy being lonely. The mention of his newly discovered roommate had him scanning the room for any sign of him. It gave him the creeps to think of how many times he could have been watching them –

in the bedroom, in the bathroom, anywhere he pleased. Martin felt bad for thinking so poorly of him. He had only just met him and he seemed like a good enough guy. It hadn't been like the ghostly guest that had been rude, after all, and Harper liked him. For someone so young, she had an excellent judge of character, even if her only friend was a ghost.

"I'm not saying I'm glad you're sick, but it was nice to have an excuse to come home. The more she complained, the more Mom tried to spoil her, and that's just an awful mix," Nadine moaned, settling under the covers. "Anyway, I hope you feel better in the morning." She rolled over without another word and soon her breathing slowed and deepened.

It was beyond surreal to lie in the darkness beside his wife, tucked into the bed he had slept in for over a decade and tell himself he was now a vampire. Two nights before, he had been taking elbows to the ribs for his incessant snoring, dreading the sound of his alarm clock. Now he lay undead with the fear that he or the others under their roof would never be safe again. The thought alone should have him panicked, yet he felt calm, if not concerned. The changes in his emotions were as swift as the changes to his life. He tried to clear his mind of the questions that had mounted.

The steady thump beside him became deafening in the silence. There was no chance of sleep when he closed his eyes, making him wonder if he would ever sleep again. Another little tidbit Lyla had left out.

Reaching out past the sound of his wife, he tested how well his ability to hear had become. First, he heard the sounds of Harper's small snores and pushed on as soon as he centered in on her delicious pulse that had no right to be so tempting.

He found he could almost picture the expanse of sound as he pushed out further, hearing the hoot of an owl through the double-paned, closed window. The light rustle of wind through the tall oaks that were scattered throughout the neighborhood. He hadn't realized how lost he had become with the infatuation of his new skill, or that several hours had passed when he narrowed his ears on the couple that lived two doors down.

They preferred the stage of their yard for their constant arguments, whether it was the front or back, making their voices easily recognizable to everyone within three blocks. They were all well versed in the petty issues they were always at each other's throats for.

This time, however, their voices weren't shouting. What they spoke was definitely aggressive, but this time they spoke amidst moans and cries to the lord above.

Martin, realizing what he was eaves-dropping on, quickly shut his attention away from it and lay in the still in the dark. The sounds returned to him and he almost gave in to the temptation to listen more until he recognized that his body was enjoying what he heard more than he thought. The tent of blankets left him embarrassed enough to push the sounds of the makeup sex straight out of his head.

He had worried that Dan had been privy to the personal moments with his wife, a man who did not seem to able to leave the walls of their house, and here he was slinking around mentally in a near-strangers intimate moment.

The tent popped away faster than a crooked carny's circus leaving town. He lifted the blanket, surprised with the speed of the appearance and disappearance, and wondered if it was yet another vampire trait—vampire skill if you asked him.

Catching sight of Nadine's nightie pulled up on the side, he relished having the night vision he now had and took a moment to admire his wife's backside.

The front of his boxers again strained against his reaction. Tucking the blanket back down, he pictured his curious buddy settling down again, and sure enough, he was as flaccid as a popped balloon.

Apparently, his boners were much easier to control than his fangs.

That was a new little tidbit that he was quite a fan of. He hoped Nadine would be as well. The mood swings and wonky woodies felt more like puberty than becoming a member of the powerfully undead.

After trying out his new skill a few more times, he grew more tired than he had ever been in his life. A still blackness swallowed him whole, and the world slipped away into a dreamless slumber. He didn't move a muscle when Nadine slid out of bed shortly after to start her day, and he remained that way until the next sunset.

Chapter Six

Dinner Date

WHEN HIS EYES OPENED again, he wasn't sure if he had slept or if any time had passed. Nadine was no longer lying at his side; the blankets that had covered her were rumpled and unmade.

Listening to the house outside of his bedroom, he could hear his wife and daughter downstairs. The television was playing one of the cartoons that Harper loved to play on a loop. For a brief moment, everything felt normal, as if someone on high had granted the wish for it all to be a nightmare.

Reality crashed down around him when his stomach growled, and his newfound fangs slipped down and into the side of his tongue.

"Sonofabitch!" he cried out, covering his mouth. Footfalls started up the stairs and along the hallway. He didn't have a chance to retract them before Nadine opened the door, so he kept his mouth tight in a flat smile to conceal them, giving him a constipated expression.

"Hey, someone's finally awake," she said softly as she crossed the room to him. "Are you feeling any better?" He nodded his head a few times. "You've slept the day away. I was wondering if I should call the nurse to come back."

If only they had a way to reach her. Martin cursed her for still being AWAL.

"Mm good," he murmured through tight lips. "Jus' tired."

His wife watched him, looking him over to assess his sickly situation. With a sigh, she lifted a corner of her mouth into a complacent grin. "Okay, I'll leave you to rest more unless you need anything. We've already eaten, but I can make you something if you're ready to try food."

Spaghetti. Harper's favorite.

He could smell it on her breath from across the room. The smell was nothing like the tantalizing scent of warm, fresh blood that still danced in his nose, but it wasn't as repellant as he had worried it to be. Maybe garlic had to be raw to affect him. His nose twitched in distaste at the thought of eating even a mouthful of pasta. Nadine took his expression as a no and left him to rest in the darkened room.

As soon as he heard her turn on the tap in the kitchen, he bolted from the bed. Peeking out the window, he found the sky once again dark. When he moved to his dresser, the mirror above it told him he looked a little better than the night before except for the dark smudges that remained under his eyes and cheekbones.

He grabbed the bloodied tissues he had hidden and balled them into his fist. The hallway was thankfully dark when he shuffled along to the bathroom. His feet dragged, moving purposely slowly so as not to alarm his wife. Moving at the speed of light did not speak to being down and out with the flu.

After giving them a double flush, he headed back to his bedroom to work on hiding his toothy secret. The good news was unlike the night before, simply picturing them popping away out of sight was all it took. The bad news was the stomach rumbles continued, sliding them back down each time. There was no way he could make his way downstairs with such a risk, so he sat himself down on the bed. Even though he didn't need to breathe any longer, sighs were still his automatic reaction to his life, and they were becoming plentiful.

The one shining light in the evening was that he did not feel an unhinged craving to seek out his family for blood. He had been bracing himself for the crazed, uncontrollable frenzy that ravenous vampires suffered in the Hollywood portrayals.

Instead, he had a repetition of *gurgle, fangs, slide them away, gurgle, fangs, slide them away.*

Soon, Harper had come in to say good night. She gave a cheer that he was beginning to feel better, although a passing comment of how his skin felt cold to her sat nervously with him until she skipped away to bed.

Touching his arms and face, they didn't feel different to him, and he hoped Nadine wouldn't notice if Harper was right.

They exchanged very few words once she joined him in bed, mostly about how exhausted she was. In minutes, she was out, and he was left staring up at the ceiling. This routine could only last for so long before someone would question why he was stuck in one room or he found himself going mad with boredom.

Each time his stomach rumbled, Nadine would toss an arm with a slap, mumbling for him to stop snoring. The night was going to be insufferably long if he was forced to stay beside her, pretending to sleep. He had to escape the smother of those four walls.

Moving silently, he made his way out of bed and down to the main floor. As he turned on the television, he pleasantly discovered that he could have the volume on the lowest level and still hear it clear as day. It was so nice to watch the shows he wanted for a change that it took him a while to decide on what to pick. A few episodes in, the excitement wore thin, and loneliness set in.

In a hushed voice, he called out to Dan Jack, hoping that he could apologize, and he would have the chance for some company. He didn't appear or make a sound, not even his whistle. Martin attempted to stare at the television more until he grew restless. The rumbles in his stomach continued.

He paced from room to room, trying to ignore it. Standing in front of the large bay window, he watched the empty street. If he were to wait too long, he worried he would not be in control of himself once genuine hunger rattled him.

Digging through the basket of clothes in the laundry room, he dressed in jeans and a dark sweatshirt. Grabbing his wallet and phone from the counter, he shoved them in his pocket. There was probably no use for either being what he was, but the comfort of routine centered him.

It took him three attempts to work up the courage to open the door, not knowing what could be waiting for him. He pictured Lyla standing on the other side, smiling and eager to show him the ropes. He then pictured a cloaked figure laying in wait to cut his new undead life short for whatever reasons Lyla had wanted him to stay inside. The door creaked as it opened, forcing Martin to open it slower than he would have liked, stretching out the tension that grew within him.

The porch was barren, apart from the dying fern that lived neglected on a rickety metal stand to the side.

He looked at his watch. Not knowing where he was going, or what he would do when he got there, he had a few hours until sunrise to experience what the world around him was now.

Food would be nice. If only he knew how to get some. He tried to quiet his mind telling him what food now meant for him. A rumble in his stomach pushed him the rest of the way out the door.

He stood in front of his car. It felt foolish for a vampire to have the need for transportation. He knew he could move swiftly now, but he had had no actual practice at it. He didn't know how far he could go or for how long. Being his first time out, it seemed wise to have a quick way back to the darkness of his house if he lost track of time. Lyla had been clear that he had to keep the curtains closed tightly. The sunrise was not something he wanted to risk.

She had also told him to stay inside. His new life had him taking the risks of a rebel. He had a bit of a swagger at the thought until the hoot of an owl had him nearly jumping out of skin.

Turning the car off his street and onto the main road, he roamed without a destination. It took a few minutes for his eyes to adjust to the streetlights and glaring signs of fast-food restaurants and bars. If only it was easy enough to pull in and grab a bite.

He eventually parked in the Cluck Hut parking lot, looking up at the restaurant that he had spent many nights in when Nadine was pregnant.

A Cheesy Cluck with mustard, pickles, coleslaw on top, and a root beer, no ice. Every time.

It had been a disgusting order to him then. Now it was repugnant. The idea of eating the foods of his past turned his stomach now.

There were still a few people sitting inside, enjoying the greasy fare before it closed for the night. A couple flirted across the table. A group of college-aged kids drunkenly stuffed their faces. The staff stood blank-faced and bored behind the counter, waiting for closing time.

Looking from face to face, Martin wondered how he was supposed to pick someone if he were to choose to eat. Drink? He didn't even know what it was called, let alone how to do it.

It seemed unfaithful to pick a woman. Disrespectful to his wife. He supposed it was a little disrespectful for anyone that he was to use as a feed bag, regardless of who they were. It was a meal, not sex.

Frustration was building when his stomach rumbled again, inviting his fangs into his mouth. If he couldn't find a way to eat, there was a chance he would starve to death before anyone found out about his new situation. Agitation was turning to fear.

"This is fucking crazy!" he yelled out into the universe, slamming a hand down onto the steering wheel he still sat behind. Lifting his palm, he could see a bend in the spot where it had landed. At least if he had to overpower someone to eat, he would have the upper hand strength wise.

His emotions welled and dipped, anger-to-fear-to-depression and back. He blinked away the tears that reddened his vision, feeling foolish for having a breakdown in a Cluck Hut parking lot.

A heavy knock on his window startled him out of his burgeoning dead life crisis.

"What the hell are you doing here, Marty?" Lyla stood outside of the car.

Martin was so happy to see her, even though she looked positively pissed at him. Her voice was clear as a bell through the window, but he rolled it down out of habit.

"I think a better question is, where the hell have you been?" The anger of his words did not match his tone, which was filled with relief. Seeing her made it all too real, yet the frightening loneliness which had started to take root evaporated.

Before he could blink, the passenger door slammed when Lyla moved like heat lightning into the seat beside him.

"I told you to stay in your house! Are you trying to get us killed?" She did not match his happiness in the least.

For such a tiny woman, her energy was mammoth and intimidating. Martin quickly regretted his impromptu field trip.

"I didn't know if you were ever coming back. I can't stay inside for the rest of my life."

He did not want to take the time to think about how long that could be now. Either slayed on the spot by an unknown threat who had Lyla terrified, or all of eternity. Living in the moment had never seemed more important to his sanity.

"I said I would be back, Marty," she replied in a softer tone. "If I say I'll do something, know I'm giving you my word. I chose to turn you, and for whatever reason, chose to let you live. That means I am now one hundred percent responsible for you."

"So, you're not mad?" He was sure there was a catch. He couldn't get off that easily.

"Are you fecking kidding me? Of course I'm mad!" Her eyes flared with her impatient answer. "It's not like I don't have my own shite going on, Marty. I don't need to worry that you're out roaming the world willy-nilly when we haven't sorted out what to do with you yet."

He didn't like the sound of that.

"I was getting stir-crazy in there. You can't expect me to just lay there night after night listening to Nadine's heart pound like a drum beside me. I'm unconscious, like a coma during the day, and then forced to pretend to be asleep at night?" He frowned with a heavy sigh. "And what about when I get hungry? My stomach has been growling like crazy. What if I got too hungry and did something terrible to my family? What then, Lyla?"

Her face softened at his outburst. "Those rumbles aren't hunger and they won't last forever. It's just your body adjusting to its new state. Your stomach is going to shrink quite a bit. Your whole body is going to be making a lot more nasty sounds over the next few days, too. I wouldn't worry about it."

He didn't like the sound of that either. "Well, that would have been nice to know before you disappeared on me."

"I didn't disappear. I've been busy trying to sort out my damn mistake."

"Oh, that's a nice way to think of me." Martin stared straight ahead at the happy customers stuffing their faces.

Lyla snickered. "So, your plan was what? To head out on the town to grab a bite? Were you going to try eating that slop? It will make you crazy sick now, fella. That food is dead and gone for you."

Martin felt a flash of smugness at her guess, knowing he would not try that food. "I've sorted that out myself already." The thought of it making him sick was enough of a warning for him to not want to try to consume it.

"So, that plan was to grab a bite out of a human? How, exactly, were you going to pull that off on your own, huh?"

Martin's pride bruised when she laughed, even though he knew she was right and he was being a fool. "Which one were you gonna have a snack on, Marty?" She laughed harder when she pointed to the clueless people enjoying their night. "What's you flavor?"

His face tightened when he grit his teeth. "I don't know, alright? I don't know very much of anything anymore. All I know is this was stupid and I know that I have no idea what I'm doing, but I've just had the worst weekend ever that pretty much stole my entire life out from under me and left me floating about in limbo." It felt good to let out the rant that had been growing and poisoning him since he woke up in the cold room of his basement.

Lyla sat quietly for a moment. "You're right. I shouldn't tease you. You have to understand that I, in a way, became the mother and sole caregiver to a middle-aged man this weekend. It's a bit of a shock for me, too."

Martin looked at her to find her face drawn with the weight of her words. They were both in a tight spot together. It wouldn't help anyone to fight.

"I'm not middle-aged, Lyla." He smiled with a tilt of his head.

"You really are, though, fella." Her lip twitched up. "At least when you were human."

They rested in the change of mood, lost in their own troubles.

He hoped she wouldn't disappear as quickly as she had appeared this time. She was feeling less like a threatening stranger and more like the air that used to fill his lungs. There was no one else he knew who could give him answers; who could help him; who could keep him alive long enough to find his footing in the trenches between his old life and his impossible future.

It felt risking to break the peaceful silence, but he couldn't help himself. "How did you know I was here?"

Lyla's brows raised, excitement overtaking her in the dim light of the parking lot. "It was the weirdest thing. I've been having these little, I don't know, tickles I guess? Right at base of my skull. Little irritating vibrations that had been getting stronger." She wiggled her fingers at the back of her head. "Then they started putting thoughts, or I think, more like feelings, inside of me. It was yesterday that I realized it was you. It was feelings you were having. When you were frustrated or scared, I could sense it." She pointed at her head as if she had a third eye she had just discovered.

The intruding ability she had equally intrigued and violated Martin's sense of privacy. "That's bizarre. Are you sure that's what it was?"

"Oh, yeah. Especially when you were so randy last night. I was worried you were going to go full on with your wife. You're not ready to tackle that again yet, champ. You'll need to master a few things before you can enjoy that extra benefit safely."

Nadine had had nothing close to *full on* with him for quite some time. It had certainly been longer than the few days he had known Lyla. Embarrassment swallowed him whole when he realized she had sensed when he had overheard the crazy neighbors going at it. No matter how hard he wished, the car seat refused to swallow him whole and away from the humiliation.

"See, right there! You're embarrassed! It's all over your face, so it's pretty obvious as is, but I can feel it inside, too," she said with awe.

Martin groaned when he hid his face in his hands. It wouldn't help to correct her about what had caused his reaction.

"You don't have to feel embarrassed." She patted his arm as if he were a child. "It's all good, Marty. An important part of being connected is me being able to know how you are. Even where you are. It will help me keep you safe. Like, tonight. I could feel your tension building. It seemed like you were scared. I followed the feeling and found your silly arse parked in front of Cluck Hut like a shite-hawk."

Calling him an ass did not make him feel any more secure. It did feel good to know she hadn't completely left him on his own, even if it was only some sort of psychic connection. "What am I going to do, Lyla? I have no idea how to live like this."

"Of course you don't. You've barely stopped breathing. It's going to take some time and learning, but you'll do fine." The sound of one door slamming and the one beside him opening startled him. Lyla stood outside with her hand out to him. "Come on, let's go for a dander. You're not going to find yourself ordering any of those from the drive thru." She clucked her tongue and nodded toward the people within the restaurant.

Martin laughed when he stepped out of the car and locked the door. His humdrum life of just last week was dead and gone. He was now a vampire, chatting with a vampire, on the main street of the same town that had been smothering him his entire life. It felt wrong that everything looked the same, if not now too bright.

Lyla started for the sidewalk and down the street without another word. When he caught up with her, they walked along in silence until she stopped at a bench tucked under a low hang tree across from the town square park.

"We can't stay long, but I owe you some answers." She stepped up to sit on the back of the bench, motioning for Martin to join her. "Do you want to ask questions or just have me talk?"

He planted himself on the seat beside her feet. "I think my biggest question is why? Why did you do this to me?"

"That's fair. I guess the short answer was I got a little too scuttered on that bar blood and screwed up." She watched him watch her.

He stayed expectantly silent. There was no way that was going to be the only reason she gave for virtually killing him and he stared tight back until she continued.

"Right. The longer explanation would be that I've been spiraling pretty brutally lately. My own sire has been so busy lately that I've felt a little neglected. He is so important and I'm just his lowly youngest. I hate having no power in our world, you know. For Christ's sake, I'm a vampire. I should be living a life of jet-setting, and parties, and wealth, and power, but instead I spend most nights alone watching tv. Usually the same damn shows on loop. Not exactly the rockstar life, is it?"

"Why can't you live the life if you want to? You're immortal. You have super speed and you can hypnotize people. Sounds like you have everything you need to live that way." He could see why she needed a night to get blotto. The undead life had come with false advertising of glamor and power. An eternity of bland.

"You'd think, right? Except I'm not the only immortal zipping around the world. Not even in this boring ass town. Unfortunately, I have the least amount of power. I have elders calling all the shots. It doesn't matter that I have been a vampire for over forty years. I'm still a baby to them. Hell, you're practically still being born. Not really the ones to take on the world, are we?"

"Why do you let them control you?" Martin knew the answer before he even asked. That didn't change the fact he wished the answer would be different. The power structure held the rules, whether living or not.

"We're all controlled by something or someone, mate. You know that just as well as I do. That's how we ended up in this mess. I saw my misery in you and acted the big shot. Convinced myself that I was more important than I was. Thought that maybe if you were as miserable as I was, we could push each other to take on the world, or something. Listen, I don't know. I was hammered and angry. I guess I just wanted a friend. I don't have very many anymore." That was certainly a feeling he could relate to. She tugged at the coffee colored braid that was swung over her shoulder. "I was sure I was going to live this loud, exciting life when I met Owen and found out what he was. When he offered to turn me, I had myself convinced that the boring life I was stuck in was a thing of the past. What I didn't know was something you're starting to learn. We're even more powerless. It takes decades, hell, centuries to have the abilities vampires are famous for. Whatever the magic in our blood is, it's like wine. It needs to age to fill us with the gifts that we all want so badly. You say I can hypnotize people. I can only do it to feed. It's not like I can tell people to let me in their homes or have them hand over their money. Nothing like that. Not much more than you can do, really. I wish I had that sort of power, but I'm still waiting for things to develop, I guess."

"I really can't go into other people's houses anymore without being invited? That's not just folklore?"

"No, that's real. For whatever reason, we can't enter personal dwellings without permission. Just houses, though, so that's a blessing. Only houses owned by mortals, too. If a vamp owns it, it's just a regular building for us. Isn't that weird? Owen says it has to do with protecting their souls or something. A personal sacred space. Not so sacred to the ones that can hypnotize them, I'd say. Although, I don't understand most of what he says. He's over three centuries old, so very complicated things seem very basic to him. His answers lack a lot of details."

It seemed unreal to think what a conversation with someone who had seen so much would entail, considering the knowledge he would have compiled. "Is he the one that you're scared is going to kill us? Your sire, I think you called him."

"Owen? Oh god no. In human terms, I'm daddy's little princess. He wouldn't harm a hair on my head." She tossed her braid back and glowed with pride. "It's how I get away with things like nicking cash from my blood bags and hopefully for turning you. He makes sure I'm taken care of."

Martin's expression widened. That was the first hopeful thing he had heard in days. "And me? Does that stand for me? That makes me a sort of grandchild, doesn't it?"

Being under that umbrella of protection seemed promising. Maybe there would be a chance at freedom, after all.

"In a way, I guess. The line of connection isn't as deep once it's passed on. I'll gladly put in a good word for you, though." A single laugh shot out of her when she slapped a hand on his shoulder. "It's the other elders I worry about. Owen is going to chew my head off when he finds out about you. I'm honestly surprised he doesn't know already."

Martin did not like how she tried to hide the worry that clouded her eyes.

"You aren't allowed to make vampires? That's why you think we're in trouble."

"Hell no! I am so not allowed. Not someone so low in the ranks. It's kids having kids, you know. I barely know how to take care of myself, let alone you. That's why I suggested putting you down. It only seemed fair to not put you through all of this. It still might be a good idea to get out of town. I guess with you being unknown to everyone, you could do what I wanted to do and just get the hell out of here. Start a whole life somewhere awesome while you sort out who and what you are now."

"I have a whole life that I'm living, Lyla. I have a wife and a daughter that I have to look after."

She stomped her foot loudly beside him. "I know! I fecked up and I'm trying to make it right."

Martin wanted to get angry with her, but he couldn't. Thinking back to when Nadine told him she was pregnant came to mind. The wedding and HR job came shortly after, and it had all been for the best. Harper was the furthest thing from a mistake. She was what the universe brought to him as a gift. He knew that with all of his heart. His new life was already signed, sealed, and delivered. There was no room to rage about mistakes if he was going to make this life work.

"So let's sort this out the best we can. What do I need to know?" he queried, trying to stay positive and not drown in the negatives. Lyla smiled at his gesture of peace. "What do I need to be worried about? Other than those elders, of course. What about crosses and silver, and garlic?"

Just like everything else, he'd get things done that had to be done. No time to whine about what sucked in his life, when everything always seemed to suck. However, now he could literally suck life, so to speak. Score one for Martin.

"The garlic is kinda true, but that's just because our noses are so sensitive. It's not gonna kill ya, but it can be really unpleasant. I personally don't mind garlic. It's onions and dog farts for me. Those smells will blast me across a room. So nasty." Her nose crinkled, preemptively protecting herself from even the thought of the smells.

"Good to know."

That explained why Nadine's spaghetti didn't frighten him off.

"The silver is true. That's a big no no for us. It will rip right through you like a fang through skin. Gives a miserable burn, too. Takes forever to heal. Something about the makeup of the metal reacts to whatever is in our blood."

"Damn. Very good to know."

Martin was glad that he had gone with a gold wedding band. That would have been a nasty surprise.

"Fun fact: silver is the reason people think we don't have reflections. The only mirrors we don't show in are old ones with the silver backing. Thank god, they stopped making those. I'd hate to never know how my hair looked," she confessed with a giggle.

"I was wondering why I had a reflection. Seems a lot of what they say about vampires isn't true." It felt empowering to have some answers at hand.

"It's mostly based on truth, I'd say. Just wild interpretations mixed with folklore to scare folks. Take churches and religion and the mix. A cross isn't going to have us recoiling in fear because it's a cross. Vampires are way older than the first one of those that they threw around their neck. It's the imagery of the church that was scary."

Lyla frowned and looked up at the thin clouds that were gathering around the sliver of moon.

"Why would that be scary to you?"

"Not me, but our ancestors. The Christians found out about us and considered us demons or some bloody shite. They wanted to wipe us all out. Now picture a vast group of people who want to kill you and they wear the same charms and hang out in the same buildings. I think you'd avoid those things, yeah?"

Martin slowly nodded his head. That made a lot of sense to him; more than crossing two fingers could ward off a powerful immortal being that wanted to eat you. Even though he wasn't a very religious man himself, it was comforting to know he wasn't an abomination to whatever powers may lie beyond. He certainly needed the grace and help of any higher power that he could get now.

"Do you pray?"

Lyla slid down to the seat of the bench beside him, a look of confusion on her face. "Of course I do. How else would I eat? Eat well, at least."

"No, I mean prayer," he laughed.

"Oh, like the church stuff. To a God? I was never a churchy person to start with, even though most of my family was. I don't know. My heart doesn't beat anymore, but I like to think that I can still feel from it. It speaks to someone, I guess. That might be prayer. It might just be hope."

Martin looked over the quiet park where, just last week, he had sat in the sunshine. "That seems to me like the same thing."

"I like that. Maybe it is." Lyla joined his gaze over the shadows cast by the trees. "Speaking of prey, take a look over there." Across the park, a dark shape moved along the walkway. A man, staring at his glowing phone screen. "Ready to give it a go?"

It took a second for her meaning to set in. "Him? Now? I don't know, Lyla."

"You're not going to need to eat as often as you think, but you need to learn how to feed yourself. Come on," she insisted, moving in her flash like way towards the man.

The speed he tried was nowhere near her gale force movement, even though it was faster than he had ever managed as a human. He was proud enough of himself for not getting nauseous, as he had in his bedroom.

"Wait. Are you sure?" He spoke quickly and with a hush so as to not leave the man petrified of the two strangers stalking him in the night. As they approached him, he could see it was Ben, the cashier. "Lyla, stop! I know him."

"There's not very many people in this town anymore, Marty. You're gonna recognize a meal or two," Lyla teased flatly.

"No, I mean, I work with him. I can't have him knowing what I am." He was certain he didn't have it in him to take his life. "We need to pick someone else."

"Sure, Marty. Who? You tell me which of these humans you'd prefer." Her face lifted with knowing when Martin looked about hopelessly. "They're not your people any-more, fella. They're food. You just need to pick one."

"My family is not food, Lyla. It's not that easy." It was impossible to admit to himself that he was so different from them now.

"This dickhead isn't your family, now is he? Family is your people, mortal or not. Look at him!" She flashed toward him and back before Martin could react. Ben remained untouched. "He's scanning his own Insta, liking his own pictures. He'll taste like ego and ignorance. I like to think of that as the ice cream of blood bags. Come on. Let me show you how. He won't even know what happens. I promise."

She bounced on her toes with anticipation until Martin gave her a small nod. He had to learn how to survive and giving it a go on someone he wasn't a fan of seemed like the best option. "Okay, let's do it."

"Excuse me!" Lyla called out as she skipped toward her snack. "I'm so sorry to bother you, but I'm a wee lost." Ben looked up from his phone with a bothered snarl. Lyla closed the space between them until she was only a foot away. "Hiiiii…" She drew out the word with the hiss of a snake. Ben's face dropped, sleepy satisfaction clouding his eyes. "There you, go. Just like that!" She turned to Martin, who waved a hand in front of the now zombified man.

"Just like what? How did you do that?" Martin bent the few inches he had over Ben to look into his eyes, that stared right through him. "What did you do to him?"

"It's just like a spider, but we do it with our eyes instead of our fangs. Cool, yeah?" Lyla boasted as she slid her hand around Ben's waist. "That's step one. Step two is to listen to heartbeat." She waited while Martin steadied himself to focus on the consistent, calm *lub-dub* sound that rumbled Ben's chest.

His eyes went to the pulse he could see in his neck.

"Slow down, fella. That's step three. First, I need you to really listen to his heart. Get the rhythm in your head as if you were learning a new dance step. Bump, bump. Bump, bump. You hear that?"

Martin nodded, licking his lips. His thirst was overwhelming.

"You really need to pay attention here. If you don't want to kill him, and trust me, in the position I've put you in, you don't. You want to listen to the beat. When it starts to slow its tempo, you need to stop." She tapped her foot along to the thumps.

His mouth felt dry and hot. It was hard to pay attention to her direction.

"Marty, I need to know you understand this." She snapped her fingers in front of his face.

He blinked, pulling himself back into the lesson. If he was to survive and not harm his wife and daughter, he knew he needed to hold himself together. "Sorry, yeah, I hear it. Don't let it get slow. Got it."

"Part three you've already done, so I'll skip the explanation and just have myself a sip."

Her lips wrapped along his neck and Ben went limp, his eyes still staring off blankly. Lyla easily held him upright with one arm when she tasted him for only a few seconds before pulling away and wiping her mouth. A quick prick of her finger on her fang and dab of her blood on the puncture wounds had Ben as good as new; other than still being her mental puppet.

"He's okay, right?" Martin was surprised by how quick and almost clinical it was. Not the sensual slithering and moans of the vampire movies.

"He's fine. Just as yummy as I thought, too. It's all about the mood of the person. Bad mood, bad blood. Well, mostly. Virgin blood is my favorite. That's why I couldn't stop snacking on you."

The phrasing grossed him out, but the statement was just confusing. "I have a daughter, Lyla. I'm obviously not a virgin."

She almost dropped Ben when she shook with laughter. "Another misconception, my friend. We consider virgin blood to be someone who hasn't been tasted before. It's the purest blood. Whenever we have a sip of someone, a little bit of ourselves is left behind. It comes from our fangs. I think it evolved from marking our food."

"So, non-virgin blood is like taking a bite out of someone else's burger?"

"Precisely! Excellent simile." She helped Ben to stand on his own. "Now give my burger a taste!"

He moved slowly toward him, unsure how to approach. "Do I just...do it?" Trepidation held him in place.

"Time to give it a lash, Marty. No more stalling. I'm going to pass him over to you. I need you to look him in the eyes and relax your brain."

Martin followed the instructions, and a tightness came over his body as his mind slowed along with the world around him. Ben gave a slight acknowledgement of Martin's presence before slipping away to the dreamland where they had sent him. A strength rose inside of him knowing that he was in control. He took a moment to put the tempo of his heart to memory and went in for the meal.

The blood came easily in tiny pulses of waves that coated his tongue.

Bump-bump. Bump-bump.

He tried to balance the beat with the euphoria that washed over him.

Bump-bump. Bump…bump….bump.

He stood back with a rush when Lyla tapped on his shoulder with a strength that would have dislocated a normal human's.

"Slow down, Marty." He licked at his lips, cleaning away whenever hadn't made it into his mouth. "That was good. A little too excited, but he does taste good for such a bitter little man."

"It started to slow. His heart. Was I killing him?" That was something he was not mentally ready to deal with. Even if it was Ben.

"No, he was a ways away from dead, but it was a good time to start with how eager you are. The good news is you're never going to be unable to stop yourself from feeding on someone as long as you're in your right mind. You're not about to attack your wife unless you want to, if that's a worry. It's once you start that you can get carried away. Sort of like a diet, I guess. Hard to stop with smaller portions," she chuckled.

It didn't feel disgusting to taste the blood in his mouth, as he would have thought. It felt invigorating and powerful, just as it did when he had tried it for the first time during the haze and sickness of his turning. "I did it right? That was okay?"

"It was near perfect, my friend. Good work. How did he taste?" Lyla wagged her eyebrows.

"It was…," Martin stopped when shrieking came from beside them. The rush of excitement drained away.

Horror twisted Ben's face as his hands dragged along his neck, which still trickled blood.

"Oh, feck!" Lyla shouted, and jumped to regain Ben's attention. She whispered words of soothing and content-ment returned to Ben's face. Repeating the finger poke and dab, the blood clotted instantly and the puncture wounds disappeared. A scarf from her purse was used to clean the rest of the dinner mess they had made and Ben was soon back to staring at his Insta and continuing on his way.

"There's an excellent lesson. Always clean up after a meal before sitting back for a chat," Lyla muttered with irritation. "I told you I wasn't ready to be a sire. Dammit, that was close." She stomped her foot, watching Ben meander out of the park.

When the shock of Ben's screams passed, Martin gave Lyla a light punch to her arm. "Come on, Mom. You're doing the best you can." A twitching smile on his lips preceded a relieved laugh.

"Oh, no. You will not be calling me that." Lyla swung her bag over her shoulder and looked at her watch. "Not to sound like a mother, but to paraphrase what mine used to say, the street lights will be off soon. Time to head home, Marty. I hope tonight helped you some."

The attempted jovial moment was gone. Martin looked to the sky, wondering if he would ever see the light of day again. Even if he didn't, he could say that he didn't feel as trapped as he had just hours before. "I'll get the hang of it."

Lyla leaned forward for a quick and awkward hug. "I'll be around, don't worry. Just try to lie low."

The weight of having to return to his prison weighed heavily on his shoulders. "Do I really need to stay in my house all the time? I can't live like this forever. People are going to start asking questions."

Putting a hand to her forehead, Lyla frowned. "That's a good point." She closed her eyes in thought, stretching her neck back and forth. "Okay. Feck it. If you can find a way to live your life under the radar, you should be fine." She opened her mouth to say more and then clamped it shut to stare back at him before she started again. "I'll take care of it."

"Well, my life is nothing if not under the radar," Martin sighed. "I just have to find a way to do it all at night now."

She turned to leave before turning back. "We're gonna sort this out, Marty. I swear to you, we'll be back to the boring lives we hated soon enough." She gave a sympathetic grin and shrugged. "Now get home before you get cooked."

He didn't share her amusement when she said the words. "The sun really will turn us to dust?"

"Not right away. It hurts like nothing I've ever felt before, though, trust me. It's a burn that takes forever to heal, too. Real nasty situation. Not as bad as some of those UV lights they've made, though. Those are beasts!" She gave a shiver and started out into the night.

"Bye!" Martin shouted sarcastically. He was not yet used to her appearance and disappearances. She merely waved a hand in the air and kept walking.

Making his way back to the Cluck Hut parking lot, he marveled at the lights that danced in reflections in the puddles along the road. The air smelled of evergreens and flowers as strong as the perfumes Nadine always sampled during Christmas shopping, but never bought for herself.

She never bought anything for herself, really. Martin had started the morning of his new life complaining to himself about a ragged robe and the slippers she bought him, never giving a thought to how she lived the same life as he did.

A job she hated, a house that wasn't preferred. She went to bed every night exhausted after a long day of misery at work and then taking care of their energetic daughter and grumpy husband. Never once getting a simple bottle of perfume that he knew made her happy. All they saw was the cost, not the joy of it. Not that cost wasn't a tremendous obstacle in their lives.

Nadine had been brought up in more than comfort, but she had always wanted to carve her own path. Her mother was given a few graces with her only granddaughter, to spoil her more than they'd like. Beyond that, Nadine insisted on standing on her own two feet. Growing up as he did, everything in one bag as he was shuffled from house to house made her staunch need to make her own way something that he always respected.

The realizations blasted through him like a breath of cold air in mid-winter. The blood that now mingled with his own made his mind more focused and more expanded all at once. If a douche like Ben could bring such enlightenment, he wondered what an actually intelligent person would do. It didn't seem to bother him he was now thinking of people as different sorts of meals. Not with the high of a fresh nosh blooming inside of him.

The lights inside of the Cluck Hut were off and his car was the only one in the lot when he returned. Sitting behind the wheel, he tried to decide his next move.

Lyla had said he could leave his house now.

His office was the perfect place to hide from the sun. Getting to and from it didn't seem like a possibility unless he could dig a tunnel from his basement to Beaumont's.

After pulling onto the road, he kept scanning between the sky, the clock, and the road until he pulled into his driveway. The house was still dark.

Opening the door as quietly as he could, he slipped inside and replaced his wallet, keys and cellphone where they had been and sat on the couch with a groan. He really wished he had someone other than Lyla to talk to about his new life.

"Mr. Jack?" he whispered. "Sorry, I mean Dan. Are you here?"

No one answered. He considered the possibility that he had just been a hallucination from the mess he had been through while turning. Dan Jack felt like a genuine memory. The hurt in his eyes when he had snapped at him sure felt real.

He considered pouring out an apology to the silent air, hoping he would hear it, but the rush of the blood was wearing off and all he could think of was going to bed.

There was no way he was going to make it into work. That much he knew.

Fatigue wearing him down, he shuffled over to his phone, tapped the number for Beaumont's and left a message that he wouldn't be in. From the weight of his tongue, he must have sounded drunk or beyond ill when he spoke. Not that it mattered. He wouldn't be missed for a day or two.

Each step on the staircase felt miles high. His body willed him to lie down as the world around him spun. Fighting his eyes to stay open, he stumbled down the hall and into his bedroom.

Nadine lay in bed just as he had left her.

The mattress enveloped him when he lay in the sheets that had never felt so soft. The soft breeze that blew across him began to lull him to sleep.

The fresh, cool breeze from…

The window!

Nadine had opened the window after he had left, leaving the blind hap-hazardly tugged up and the curtains splayed open like a pervert's trench-coat.

With every ounce of strength he could will, he dragged himself to the death trap and tugged it all shut. One night as an out-in-the-world-vampire and bedtime almost killed him.

Crawling in beside Nadine, the sound of her heart beating was more soothing than enticing this time.

"Love you," he murmured before the world shut off and he was gone again.

Chapter Seven

Big lies and tiny bubbles

WHEN THE WORLD SWITCHED on again, Martin sat alone on the bed. It was a struggle to remember the last dream he had before his daily comas became his new normal.

Had it been about pizza?

No, that was the last food he had wanted to eat. There would be no more dreams, no more delicious meals shared with his family, no more light of day. Every sunrise, the sudden blackness that came and went, in what felt like a second or two, would take time to get used to.

A feeling of helplessness washed over him. Anything could happen when he was in such a state. There was a chance Nadine would realize he was ice cold and without a heartbeat; nothing but a corpse laying beside her. Every time he closed his eyes for the day, he risked waking up in the morgue. It was hours of powerless darkness which seemed impossible to wake from.

He scrubbed his hands over his face, pushing away the foul mood he had awoken to.

Was it because he was hungry? He listened for a rumble or growl from his stomach. It sat as still and silent as the rest of him. Lyla hadn't told him how often he would need to eat. Not often wasn't really something he could plan out on his calendar.

His cellphone flashed a few past messages from Nadine. He had lied and said he had a doctor's appointment set up for that afternoon and she had offered to get an extended lunch hour to accompany him. He insisted it was not a big deal and that he would be quick and then go straight back home to bed.

Listening to the noises in the house, he could sense that she and Harper were both downstairs watching TV. He tapped out an apologetic text saying that he had fallen asleep as soon as he got home and that he was now awake.

There were already lies building between them that did nothing to make Martin comfortable with the choices he had planned out for himself. Being a newly born monster didn't seem like something that would come with honest and open dialogue, though.

Getting out of that room—that house—was the beginning of his new life and the only source of tamping down the deep depression that was constantly building under his uncontrollable mood shifts.

The first step was a call to Beaumont's. By the time he awoke that day, there was only a small crew of staff left on for the short stretch until closing. There was no point in bothering with a call to Chance Beaumont, who would probably have no idea who he was, either from his lack of knowledge of the business he ran or from the party powder he snarfed up as fast as his nostril could swallow it.

Flipping through the contacts on his phone, he decided to call Ted, the store's manager. Equally uninterested in his job as everyone else, Martin knew he would at least pick up for the power trip.

When he did, it was a quick conversation, which he was glad for. He came up with a sympathetic lie of childcare problems, his inability to work from home, and they quickly agreed that he could work just as effectively at night as during the day. He knew the lazy man wouldn't want to pick of the slack of Martin's job (not that there and was much slack to pick up) and was proud of the razzle dazzle he managed when Ted repeated his plan as his own, wanting off the line more than caring what Martin did with himself.

A day shift in the smothering office already felt as if could be a night shift with the lack of light and fresh air. One piece of his pre-dead life was back to as it was. It may be the part that he hated the most, but it could be the foundation for what he could see being a functioning future.

Lyla's suggestion of just leaving town and starting a new life wouldn't quiet down.

He allowed a moment to daydream of telling Nadine about what had become of him. The revelation would intrigue and excite her, making her want to join him in his immortal adventure. Her face would light up when he told her he could give her a youthful forever and they would fall in love in the way they had once been before the weight of life pulled them into the undercurrent of adulthood. They would pack up Harper and make their way to every corner of the globe, living freely and making the world their own. Penniless and homeless.

It was easy to see how Lyla could slip into a deluded view of the afterlife after a few drinks. The unending unknown was a lot to swallow if you looked too far ahead.

Barely born. That's how she had described him. He couldn't look after himself in the world as he was, let alone keep his family safe on the road. He didn't even have a passport. Would a vampire need a passport? Not if he had the super-mind control that he had assumed he would have. Becoming a vampire was really a disease more than the incredible, all-powerful beings of folklore. It wasn't flying through the night seductively, living life like a murderous rockstar. It was a tummy trouble that never ended.

"Someone is looking better." Nadine walked into the room. With her hair tangled up on top of her head and wearing pink flannel pajama pants, she set a teetering basket of laundry on the end of the bed.

Martin snapped out of the imagined world and back into the current one. "I am. Sorry I didn't see your texts."

She pulled hangers from the closet to set away the laundry. "It's alright. I assumed you were out to the world again. Whatever this bug is, it's been knocking you out."

"Yeah, it's been a doozy," Martin agreed. She didn't know the half of it.

"You made it to the appointment, though?" Her eyes stayed on the task at hand, hooking shirts and hanging them up.

"I did, yeah." His tongue slid over the nestled fangs and prayed they wouldn't make an appearance.

He had hoped to have some time to search online for a harmless ailment he could feign for the time being. Options for his newest lie came in bursts of suggestions that all seemed too ridiculous or too serious. He stalled too long, and the silence hung heavy between them. The lack of a further reply stopped Nadine in place.

"And?" she inquired with a nervous laugh. "What did they say?"

"Allergies," Martin blurted and snapped his mouth shut at his ridiculous fib.

Stupid, stupid, stupid. There was no way she'd buy that.

"What? Allergies wouldn't have you that sick, would they?" She hung up a sweater and turned back to look him over. "You were barfing your brains out, not covered in a rash or anything."

He was glad that she didn't totally dismiss his faux ailment. A minor victory. His mind spun a new yarn, just as he had with Ted. "Yeah, I, uh…it was a bad virus that leads to allergies. Apparently, it's been going around. Nasty, nasty bug." It was not something he would ever believe. If he still had the need for air, he would have held his breath until she spoke.

"Oh, man. That's awful." She stepped back from the bed. "Is it contagious? Still, I mean. Should Harp and I keep a distance for a bit? Last thing we need is her out of school right now. I'm out of personal days." Her lips twisted down with worry.

"No, it's…uh, something I ate, they think." That and something that was eaten from him, he lamented silently. "Probably something bad in the water or something.

Probably at Beaumont's." There was no part of him that felt bad about dragging that place through the mud, even if it wasn't true. "It, uh…attacks your stomach lining and the fever and all that. Just like what I had. The doctor's sure that's all it was."

"That's so awful. Do they know how long you'll be down with it?" She pushed the basket to the side, sitting on the bed beside him. "You're looking a lot better already."

A look of interest replaced the worry when she looked him up and down. The twinkle in her eye wasn't one which was seeing him looking better. It was the same look she would give him when they first got together, especially after a healthy sized glass of red wine. He felt a cold blush wash his cheeks when she put a hand on his thigh.

The interesting moment was gone just as fast when she moved her hand up to his cheek and then forehead. "You're still freezing! You should get under the blankets. That's so weird. I think you're going to need a couple of more days."

He did as she instructed, not wanting her to look further into the changes he was going through. Not that believing he was a vampire would be at the top of any rational person's list of illnesses. The tent in his boxers was something else he wanted to conceal. Any other time she gave him that look, he would have been more than happy to see where things went.

Lyla's voice telling him he wasn't ready to go *full-on* yet nestled him down in a flash.

Who knew what could happen with his new body and appetite? It wasn't worth the risk, even with how long it had been since she looked at him that way and not knowing if she ever would again. Having her that close would also make it impossible to hide his still heart and icy body. Suspicion was not want he needed on day one of his plan.

"I'm well on the mend. The doctor said the worst is over," he lied and felt hope with another lie that popped up to explain the previous one. "The bad part is the allergies. It affects the skin and stuff. The sun. I can't go out in the sun right now. It's gonna give me really bad rashes for a while." He nodded along as he spoke, as if to force her to believe him. "The meds that he gave me make it worse but will make it better eventually."

If only he could zombify her like he had done to Ben. It wasn't worth the risk of failing and terrifying her. Lies were his only defense and weapon for the time being. Lyla had said it only worked on someone you were attempting to nosh on, so it would be pointless to try. He wasn't about to snack on his wife.

"The sun? Is it bad? Did it happen today?" She walked to his side and took his hand to look over his arm.

"No, it wasn't too bad. It can be, though, so he said it's not worth the risk."

"Where's the medicine they gave you?" She looked around the nightstand and then at the dresser.

"It, uh, was a shot. That's all I needed. Modern medicine, right? Pretty amazing stuff," he lied. It would be amazing if there was a shot to return him to the living, breathing man he had been the week before.

"That's good, at least. How long do they think the side effects will last?" She started back on the mound of laundry.

"Probably just a few weeks or so, and then it should go back to normal." He tucked himself down under the blanket, pulling it up to his neck, hoping to warm his skin to the touch if she were to inspect further.

"A few weeks? Do you have that much sick time left?" She didn't say it, but he knew she was thinking about the loss of income. Plans to cover the difference were already scanning in her eyes.

"Well, that's some of the good news there. I spoke with Ted." He swallowed a laugh when she dramatically rolled her eyes with a crooked grin.

Ted held no place in Nadine's heart after the few encounters they had. Especially after he had convinced Chance Beaumont to make him full manager from assistant when the last guy left after having had enough, and then do away with the assistant manager position all together. The move gave him a raise, more power, and took away Martin's chance to get out of his cupboard life and into the front office.

"What did that sleaze have to say?" She folded the laundry with a force he could tell was meant for Ted. The light-hearted exchange had him standing at attention for her again. He bent his knee up to hide his admiration. This was the longest conversation without a fight they had had in months. Step two in his back to normal routine would have to be asking Lyla how and when he could attempt being back to normal with his wife. As if she knew what he was thinking, she gave him a sly look, folding a towel against her chest. He knew he needed to speak with Lyla again ASAP before these moments drifted away. It wasn't clear if it was concern over his illness or if there was something that had changed inside of him in the process that was attracting her to him again. He allowed himself to be lost in his thoughts for too long again, and he saw her flirtatious look turn into returning concern. "What did he say?"

"I'm going to be working nights now. Just for a little while." Martin forced himself to keep eye contact with her when her face dropped.

"Nights? How's that going to work?" She tossed the folded towel onto the bed and crossed her arms across her chest.

He had her on the hook of his lie. Now to reel her in. His plan may just buy him the time he needed until Lyla sorted out whatever it was that she needed to get the threat of death lifted from their heads. She didn't seem as concerned the night before, so he figured it came down more to the politics of their world than actual death. Regardless, he would stay under the radar and make like everything was normal. He sat up against the headboard with a hopeful sparkle in his eyes. "Not much different than now. I'll be home in time to help get Harper ready for school, and then I'll sleep during the day." That just left dinner to avoid. "Just until the doctor clears me to be good in the sun again."

Sooo…never. He swallowed his sigh and smiled tightly at her.

One day at a time, Martin. One day at a time.

"And Ted's okay with this?" Her eyes narrowed at the idea of Ted being okay with anything that benefited anyone else.

"I don't think he cares one way or another. As long as my work gets done, there's really no change."

Not that there's ever any work to be done. He pressed his cheerful expression deeper onto his face, willing her to be pleased with his plan.

"Do you think you'll be good with that?" The financial strain in her eyes gradually lifted. "I mean, will it work for you?" He knew she was suppressing a grin at the thought of a few nights without him snoring beside her.

Even though she hadn't noticed the lack of sleeping he had been experiencing for the past few nights. He wasn't about to complain about that and face the questions he couldn't answer. Keeping her happy and on board was all that mattered.

"I'll make it work." That was going to become his mantra in the coming days. Hell, in the coming years, possibly. Having the private space of his windowless office, he hoped he could have Lyla stop by and help him adjust more to what she had created. The world seemed less daunting and almost manageable for the first time in days.

Nadine chewed the inside of her cheek while she mulled over what she had been told. "This is just until you're cleared to go back on days, though, right?"

"Yep, not for long, I'd think."

He knew it would be, but they'd cross that bridge when they had to. Getting back to a routine outside of the cell of his bedroom, learning to live as a vampire, and staying under the radar of the elders that had Lyla so worried was all he could fit on his metaphorical plate.

"Okay. If you wanna give it a try, let's do it." She hung the last of the laundry and set the basket on her hip. "When did you want to try it out?"

Sooner rather than later seemed prudent. "Tomorrow night. I should be back on my feet and ready. I already feel much better."

She gave him a long stare, as she was weighing his words with how he looked. Whatever she saw, she decided to agree and gave him a shrug. "Okay. If you say so. Just don't push yourself, okay?"

"It'll be fine. We'll probably barely notice a difference." Martin fussed with the pillow behind his head.

She hadn't noticed that she had been sleeping beside a creature of the night all weekend, so being alone wouldn't be so bad. It certainly seemed safer.

"Did you want to rest some more, or did you want to come down and watch TV with us?"

Getting out of the room was exactly what he wanted. "I'll be down in a minute. I just want to have a shower real quick."

"Smart, you're going to start to stink like a corpse," she laughed.

Martin froze at the phrasing she had chosen, giving himself a quick sniff. Strangely, there was nothing to be smelled. Not rotting, not sweating. He managed a nervous laugh.

Starting out the door, she stopped with a hand on the door frame. "Did you want me to fix you something to eat?"

"Oh, no, thanks. I had a sandwich after the doc's. I'm still not very hungry." At least only half of that was a lie.

Nadine still lingered in the doorway. "And you're sure you're good to get back to work so soon?"

"All good. I'm sure."

He followed her out into the hall, and they parted ways without another word at the top of the stairs. It had been a couple of days since he had had a proper shower. A few quick washes in the sink were all he had managed between pretending to sleep, being virtually dead, and fleeing into the night the evening before.

Looking at his face in the mirror, he could see he did look better. Healthier than he had been in years. Whether it was the night before's meal or an effect of being turned, he looked rested and, he had to admit, a little radiant. His jaw sported the same light five o'clock shadow as it did when he met Lyla. Would his hair still grow? He looked at his nibbled fingernails. It would be a blessing to break that habit.

He would be nibbling people now instead of his own fingers. The thought made him queasy and a little snacky all at once.

Stepping into the steaming shower, the hot water felt good on his skin. He gave himself another sniff, wondering why there was nothing to be found. Good, bad, or otherwise, he was odorless. As he slathered on some of Nadine's body wash, the sweet smell lingered on him. He breathed in the floral and vanilla of the bubbles and smiled. Each layer of scent exploded in his nose. That shower always had a bottle of that exact wash in it, and he had never experienced how lovely it was. He realized the same scent had drifted off of Nadine when she sat beside him. Her warm hand on his thigh.

Scrubbing himself down, his new best friend popped up to show his admiration for the cozy smell, as well as the memory of her touch.

Listening to see where everyone was, he looked around mischievously before taking a handful of bubbles south.

An electric current of pleasure exploded within him, nearly knocking him off of his feet. One tiny touch was enough to feel better than any orgasm he had ever heard of, let alone experienced. Shocked, he saw he was no where near finished with that graze of his fingers. Giving it another testing touch left him starry-eyed and out of breath in half of a second. He covered the guttural moan with a soapy palm.

If that was how sex started for vampires, he was sure he would never survive completion. He sat on the edge of the tub, catching his breath and staring at his seemingly harmless boner in awe.

He dried off gingerly and dressed in loose sweats. No wonder Lyla told him he wasn't ready to go full-on. It may just kill him.

But what a way to go.

"Daddy!" Harper called out cheerfully, changing Martin's mindset in an instant when she ran into the bathroom and wrapped her arms around his leg. "Mommy said you're feeling better!"

"I am, Giggles. Don't you worry about me."

He swung her up into his arms and playfully over his shoulder, as if she weighed no more than a feather. The trill of her laugh trailed along with him when he carried her down to join Nadine on the couch.

It was the first day of the rest of his life and for the first time in a long time, he felt hope. Who knew dying was all he needed to do?

Chapter Eight

Blunder buffet.

HARPER ONLY MADE A bit of fuss when she heard the news of Martin's new schedule. The fit that she threw when it was time for him to leave was a bit more of an event. After promising to be home before she woke, with what felt like three hundred hugs, and more than a puddle full of tears, she relented and let him out the door with her arms wrapped around Nadine's neck.

The change was hard on her, but at least Martin was still on the right side of the soil. She was a resilient little girl and he knew soon enough she would adjust.

The store was silent when he slid his key into the back door and made his way through the loading dock to his office. It felt as if he had been gone for weeks, not just a few days. He set the lunch cooler, which he had tossed some meaningless food in, on top of the dusty file cabinet, and took his usual seat in front of the ancient computer screen. It all looked the same as he'd left it, including the empty inbox on his desk. Switching on his computer, the inbox of his email only held spam.

He rocked back and forth in his chair, listening to the rhythmic squeak, his eyes closed against the same boring view he had come to loathe. There were worse jobs, he was well aware, and there were worse outcomes for what had happened to him. That didn't change the creeping self-pity that easily returned in that office.

A steady beat joined in to the song on the broken chair, causing him to freeze in place. He wasn't alone.

Rising from his seat and poking his head out the door, the heartbeat was loud and clear. The custodian's office. Before he could head toward it, Jake slid a bucket out the door with a mop, screeching along to the music that was blasting from the enormous headphones he wore. Martin's face twisted in response to the noise, and he almost covered his ears against the bombarding beats. The extra sensitive hearing was another gift of his afterlife that he was having trouble adjusting to.

"Oh, hey, guy. How's it going?" Jake asked, sliding the black cans from his ears.

"You scared me. I thought I was here alone," Martin said, relieved that it was only the bumbling janitor.

"You scared of me? That's a laugh, compadre," he exclaimed, laughing at him.

Martin didn't get the joke. He also didn't understand why Jake wasn't surprised to see him at the store so late. "I see you're back on nights now, huh? I've just started, myself." He didn't know if he should provide more of a reason so as to not raise suspicion, but Jake didn't seem the type of guy to put a second thought into what he was told."Yeah, they have me on split shifts now. Fuckin' sucks, but you know how they love to save a buck."

"That they do." Martin stood in the doorway watching Jake watch him. "So, I guess I'll get back to it."

"For sure, yeah. You do you," Jake nodded, pushing the bucket back and forth between them. "And, hey, no hard feelings, right? Hustlers gotta hustle and all that shit."

Martin rarely understood what that fool said, but this was next level. Did he mean the negative reception his arrival at the pub had received? Not something to be sorry for, so why would he…

Hustlers gotta hustle?

The anger met his eyes before a word could be said. He didn't want to believe it. He had no other choice when Jake held up the mop in front of him like a stoned member of the knights of the round table.

"Oh, shit, man. I thought she would have told you! I didn't mean for this to happen. I swear! I just bring them to her, she does what she does, and then they go on their way without knowing a goddamn thing. I swear I didn't know this was going to happen!" He stepped back toward his door, holding the mop out further.

"You asked me there to be a fucking snack for Lyla?" Martin closed the space between them so quickly, Jake stumbled over the bucket, slipping down onto the bubbling spill he created. The fast action left Martin nauseous. Luckily, he was too enraged to let it slow him down. "You set me up?"

Why hadn't Lyla said anything to him about that? He was just starting to trust her. The sting of the lies pressed into his stilled heart.

"It's not like that," Jake objected with terror, holding him in place on the wet floor. Martin stepped forward with a snarl, and his fangs joined the argument. The increase in his heart rate nearly made him drool. "Okay, okay, it's kind of like that, but she's never done anything like this before. I swear to you, I thought it was harmless. I'm begging you, man! Please don't kill me!"

Martin stepped away when tears started down the panicked janitor's face, grasping the mop to his chest like a life preserver tossed in a storm. He had never made anyone have such a guttural reaction before, let alone have been the cause of it. Taking a once over of himself, he felt the metallic pooling in his mouth that he had felt before both times he had fed. Every muscle in his body was tensed and ready to pounce. He was more animal than man in that moment and he was suddenly more than Jake. His fangs slipped back up when he put even more space between them.

No matter how angry he was, he wasn't about to take someone's life, was he? No, he couldn't. Could he? His anger at Lyla was not strong enough to wish she was there with him; being a buffer between what he was and what she had made him. He would certainly have words with her when he saw her next. Whenever that was.

"I'm not going to kill you, Jake. I just can't believe you would do that to me." His rage dwindled into an ember. If vampires used people for food, why should he be surprised that some of those people had found a way to claim a piece of the pie for themselves? "How much did she pay you?"

The mop lowered from in front of his face. "Fifty bucks." He raised it again when he saw Martin's eyes bulge.

"Fifty bucks? You ruined my fucking life for fifty-fuck-ing-bucks?" Martin roared. He paced back and forth, willing himself to calm down.

"I know, my guy. I know. I'm so sorry. I didn't know she would ever do anything like this. She's never done any harm or anything, you know? It was like feeding the birds and the birds, like, slip you cash after."

He looked down at him and could see him as nothing more than pathetic; cowering in dirty bucket water, petrified of Beaumont's HR rep. It was enough to make Martin laugh.

The humorous shake of his shoulders confused Jake, and Martin gave him a half-smile.

"This entire world is fucked up, isn't it? Dead or alive, it doesn't matter. Everyone is eating everyone else in one way or the other, aren't they?" Martin's laughter deepened into lunacy until he could speak anymore.

Everyone was just trying to get by under the strain of everyone who had crawled above them or the ones who were born into a situation that made them hold the heavier end of power. Jake was no different. He was doing what he had to in order to keep himself moving along the unbalanced line of life. Martin now literally drained the life from people now. He'd be a hypocrite to be angry.

When he settled himself down, he walked to him and stuck out his hand.

Jake looked nervously up at him, not moving a muscle.

"It's okay. I'm not mad. Well, I'm not at you. Come on, get up." Martin held his hand closer to him until he finally took it. He launched him up quicker and higher than he had planned, thanks to his new strength. "Sorry about that. You good?"

The coveralls he wore were drenched, and his headphones had slid across the floor from him, but he nodded. "I'm good, yeah." The color returned to his cheeks. "Are we…you know, really good?" He bobbed his head nervously, as if he could convince Martin that they were.

"Yeah, we're good." Martin wiped the bubbles from his hand on his pants. "At least now I have a snack for my lunch break hanging around."

Jake paled again and started backing into his office. "Come on, dude…"

Martin laughed, lighter this time. "I'm just screwing with you, Jake. I'm not going to eat you."

Relief dropped his shoulders and he nervously let out a rapid fire chuckle. "I never know with you guys. Lyla always says that too, but then—boom—there's a weird empty void, you know? Like, in my memories. I'm pretty sure that chick is snacking on me." Jake laughed again, which made Martin feel queasy. It was bizarre to hear someone speak so lightly of a vampire sneaking sips from his veins. He looked at his neck. The pulse beat steadily, albeit still a little quickly.

His stomach rolled again and then rumbled. There was a chance it was just the strange noises Lyla said would happen. It could just be the munchies from listening to increased heart rate while talking about blood snacks. He didn't want to risk the chance that it was because he was hungry.

"I better get back to work, then," Martin advised, knowing there was no work to be done.

"It's so crazy that you're still working here. If I was a vamper I would be living in a huge fuckin' mansion somewhere, right on a beach, with supermodels for my meals, right? You guys are wasting your lives!" He fell into a fit of his machinegun paced chuckles.

"You'd think we would, huh?" Martin lamented. "It is what it is."

"Lyla says it's not that easy, though." Jake lifted a shoulder and pushed the mop around in the puddle he had created with his stumble. "From how she tells it, I wouldn't want to be a vampire."

"You don't say?" Martin blurted, his tone dripping with sarcasm. "Must be nice to have been given the choice."

Jake stopped and looked at him. "Yeah, I mean, sorry about what happened. I've been doing this for years and she's never done anything like that. I swear." Fear that the argument wasn't over had him stepping back again.

There was no way Martin would take his word for anything anymore. Lyla's reaction to their current situation spoke to her being shocked by her behavior, though. That he could believe.

"If you want, I could cut you a deal on me," he raised his eyebrows, as if he had come up with an idea worthy of a genius. "Yeah, like, you could pay me and then when we're here and you need to eat, you don't have to go out and find someone."

Martin liked the idea of having someone on hand if needed. On the other hand, there was a good chance he would taste like skunk weed and flaming cheese puffs. He had said it was probable that Lyla had tasted him on more than one occasion, and he had enjoyed what she had guided him to so far. He felt disgusted by the memory of using humans as food, while his stomach stirred and gurgled for more.

"How much are you thinking?"

"I dunno. Maybe a hundo a week?" Jake's eyes widened at the thought.

"A hundred bucks? You know where I work. Where would I get an extra hundred dollars a week? Are you crazy?"

Even if he could afford it, there was no way it would be worth it. His stomach objected to him shutting down the idea. Lyla had paid Jake for the procurement of victims, yet had just taken what she wanted in the park with him.

Was it laziness or was there a certain gift Jake had for finding the good stuff? It didn't seem like that was the case when Martin himself had himself been on the menu. Maybe it was like fast food. The ease of getting a quick bite without any of the preparation. If that was the arrangement, death as in life would repeat itself. There wasn't any money for restaurants and take-away; be it burgers or humans? His stomach was getting louder. Not only that – he only charged her fifty dollars for fresh virgin blood. This clown was now thinking he was worth double that?

Disappointed drooped Jake's face. "How much would work for you? I know you'll be happy with what I've got."

The sad pandering of his blood as product was off-putting to the point Martin almost walked away. It was almost impossible to believe that he had been working down the hall from a man that not only knew about vampires, he had been using them for financial gain. He had even used him for financial gain. The hunger inside of him pushed his anger to the surface, agreeing with him that Jake had wronged him.

He had no right to put him in that situation and then charge him for his survival. He owed him.

The few feet between them closed before Jake could even drop the mop. The same tightening of every muscle in his body that he had felt in the park with Ben returned when he locked eyes with Jake. He didn't fall completely under his spell in the same way. His mouth lulled opened, muttering unintelligible words that Martin ignored.

With Ben, Lyla had captivated him first. He wondered if he wasn't strong enough yet to do it all on his own. Regret shook him from within. If he wasn't able to go through with it, there was a chance that Jake would know what he had attempted to do. There was no way to know how much he knew about his precarious situation with Lyla. What if he had connections with the elders that she feared? What if he wanted to take revenge?

Here he was, an immortal being with the power to treat humans as he pleased, and he was being owned by that moron. His fangs slid down with such force that an ache throbbed in his gums.

Enough was enough. He locked his eyes on Jake's and pushed his will onto him. It was time to take control over something, and Jake was it.

The sleepy, dazed look glazed over him in seconds, his body going limp. Martin grabbed him just as he fell.

"You got this. You got this. Just like before," Martin pushed himself, leaning in and out from his neck like a child attempting to skip double-dutch. He focused on his heartbeat, which had calmed under his spell. The tempo became a drum in his head, just as Lyla had instructed.

Flavor erupted across his tongue when he finally worked up the nerve to sink his teeth into the paper thin skin on his neck. It didn't taste foul as he expected, although it didn't compare to the other two he had sampled.

He was glad to not find himself as lost in the experience as he did in the past and could easily swallow the warm meal at the same time as keeping his attention on the beat.

Thump-thump…so delicious…thump-thump…so warm and somehow sweet…thump-thump.

Pride blossomed inside as he successfully fed solo for the first time. Now, all he had to do was finish, like Lyla had. Close the wounds, keep him calm, and then send him on his way. If he could manage that, he could have a bite whenever he was hungry and Jake was on shift.

Thump-thump…thump-thump…

His throat filled with blood, making him sputter and spit a mouthful on the floor beside him.

"Oh, god." He stepped back when the weight of the meal hit his stomach. Having done everything that Lyla had instructed, he never stopped to think about portions. He had gorged himself well before Jake's heart had given a sign of distress.

The contents of his stomach pushed to be released against the desperate swallows of air Martin pushed down to keep it all in place.

You can lead a horse to water, but you never think it will drink until it pukes.

Martin snapped out of his distress when he felt Jake rousing in his arms. He ignored the protest in his tummy and made quick work of dabbing a fingertip of his blood on the tiny holes he had created, staring into Jake's eyes until he could see the world returning to his mind.

"Whoa, you okay, compadre? You look like you're gonna pitch." He looked him over and then looked ill himself when he saw the blood that Martin had spat on the puddle of bubbles on the floor. "What the…" A look of suspicion and then unease shadowed his face. "You good?"

Martin wiped at his mouth, glad to find his palms clean of blood and then down at his shirt and tie. Not a drop of blood to be seen. He may have a problem with portion control, but he was at least finding himself to be quite the tidy diner.

"Yeah, I'm just exhausted. From the turning and all that." Martin stepped back, putting a few safe feet between them. "Makes me feel sick."

Jake wiped the mop over the blood, clearing it into the rest of the wet spill. "Sure. That makes sense." He dunked the mop in the bucket. "Why don't you take the rest of the night off, my man? I can cover for you. Just leave your badge and I'll swipe you out when I leave."

Going home, undoing his pants, and laying on the couch sounded like heaven. A burp would be glorious. The blood filled him like an overfilled balloon. "Are you sure?"

"Yeah, no worries. I'll leave it on your desk. Go on home and get some rest and shit, okay?" He sounded nervous even with the friendly grin he pushed up onto his face.

"I think I will. Thanks, Jake. I owe you one." Martin unclipped the ID badge from his pocket and tossed it to him.

Martin walked to his office door, realized he had nothing to gather, and started for the door.

"See you tomorrow, compadre," Jake called out.

"Yeah. Thanks again."

"No worries. First one's free," he added. Martin stopped in place, turning to face him. Jake held up the badge. "Swiping you out. First one's free, but the next one will cost you." He bobbed his head up and down before going back to mopping without another word.

There was no time to worry if that was what he really meant or not. He needed to hit the couch and digest his buffet of blood. A cloud was settling over his mind and his body felt heavy. The stress and anger he had been feeling drifted away as he left.

After pulling over several times to wretch, he made it home without actually losing any of his stomach contents. He had not felt so full since Tricky's Tacos tried out an all-you-can-eat taco Tuesday when he was sixteen. Not a smart move being across the road from the high school. They went out of business soon after.

Just thinking of the smell of those tacos made him gag as turned the key in his front door. Then pizza came to mind. Then a taco made out of pizza. Each time he thought of another food concoction his stomach rolled.

Kicking off his shoes, he moved as quickly as his stomach would allow and lay face down on the couch. He managed to drop the zipper of his pants before collapsing. If he didn't have to eat often, as Lyla had said, he was sure he would never eat again. He cursed her for not warning him about overeating, as if a grown man couldn't know that already, and wondered if vampires could drink the fizzy tablets that Nadine would plunk into water whenever anyone had a tummy ache.

"You look like hell."

Martin's head shot up in the direction of the man's voice to find Dan Jack sitting in the recliner beside the couch. "Dammit, you scared me!" Martin exclaimed in a hushed whisper.

"Sorry." Dan shifted on the chair that he appeared to be seated in, yet hovered just above.

Pushing himself up, Martin waited to make sure his stomach will still before he spoke. "Where have you been?"

"Here." He gestured to the surrounding house. "I'm always here."

"I wanted to apologize for how I spoke to you the other day. I was kind of freaking out."

"Waking up as a vampire would do that to anyone," he jested. "I was a mess for the first decade after waking up a ghost." Dan smiled when Martin didn't know how to reply to that. "How's it been going?"

"As good as it can, I guess. I don't really have anything to base it on." Martin ran his tongue over the canines that now dropped half an inch when he was hungry. Or mad. Or horny. A sigh sank and rose in his chest.

"I didn't even know you guys were a real thing." Dan shook his head. "Honestly, that's more of why I wasn't coming around. It kind of freaked me out. When I saw one munching on a lady outside that time I was sure I was seeing things. That or I'd somehow been sent down south, if you know what I mean."

"If it makes you feel any better, I didn't think they were real either. Same with ghosts, too," Martin admitted with an uneasy laugh. "But here we are."

Dan shrugged in agreement.

They sat in silence, Dan lost in thought, Martin glad his stomach was finally seeming to empty. He wondered where it was going and realized he hadn't used the toilet since he had met Lyla. Presumably, being a vampire would free up a lot of time for him if he never needed to go again.

"Hi, Daddy." Harper walked into the room, her balled fist rubbing at her eye, a rolled piece of drawing paper in her other hand. "I missed you."

"What are you doing up, Giggles?" Martin shifted over to make room for her on the couch. It was far too early for her to be up and not expect tantrums by lunch time, but he had missed her too much to worry about whoever would be dealing with that at her pre-school.

"I couldn't sleep. Mr. Jack read me books, but I missed you being here." She crawled up beside him and rested her head on his arm. "I drawed you this." She held up the paper.

Unrolling it, he found a family portrait drawn out in crayon. Unlike the drawings of the past, this one included Mr. Jack. He held it up to show him before he noticed with horror that Harper had drawn her father with fangs.

"What...uh, what's this here, Giggles?" He tried to keep his voice even and calm.

"It's your bat teeth, like *Veromika* Vampire." A long yawn stretched her jaw.

Veronica Vampire was one of her favorite cartoons. He looked to Dan and found him watching the interaction with what looked like childlike guilt, a tiny smile dancing on his face.

"Why does Daddy have bat teeth?" he asked coolly. There was no way she could know.

"Mr. Jack said you're like her now. That's why you have to work nights."

Martin's worry turned to rage. Dan's amusement held firm.

"Why would Mr. Jack say that?" he questioned Harper with his eyes on Dan.

"Come on, dude. You know how she gets when she's asking questions. I read her every book she had and she wouldn't sleep because you weren't here. You should thank me for explaining it all to her." Dan smiled at Harper and rocked on the recliner. "You were totally cool with it, weren't you, little chick?"

Harper grinned up at her dad and nodded. "It's okay, Daddy. You're different like Mr. Jack now, but you're still my daddy."

The innocence of children would never cease to amaze him. She was acting as if he had nothing more than a new food allergy. In a way, he supposed he did.

"She was fine with it. She's wicked smart," Dan advised with pride.

"I'm well aware that she's smart, Dan. I just think it was something that you had no right to tell her."

He stewed in the glare he gave him, knowing it was coming from a place of jealousy due to Harper's ghosty friend having more time with her than he had. It didn't feel good to feel replaced.

"Were you going to?" Dan stopped rocking in the chair and leaned forward. Martin pressed his lips closed, unsure of how to answer. "Exactly. Now she knows, she knows not to tell Nadine, and you have one less thing to worry about."

Martin's fangs snapped down in response to Dan's curt tone and he hid them behind his hand. Harper looked up at him like he had done a magic trick, trying to pull his hand away to see.

Dan's transparent chest shook with laughter. "What are you gonna do with those, dude? Suck my ecto-plasm?"

The question hung in the air before its ridiculousness lightened the air. Harper giggled along, clearly not knowing what the men found so funny. The world was officially and unendingly bizarre for Martin.

"Fair enough, Dan Jack." Martin managed through his laughter. When they pulled themselves together, he picked up Harper and stood her on her feet. "That's enough fun for tonight. I want you back in bed, Giggles. You can't be tired for school today."

Another yawn escaped her when her shoulders slumped. "Alright," she moaned.

"And remember what I said, Harps. This is our secret," Dan added, pointing to the three of them. "Mommy can't know yet, right?"

"Right, Mr. Jack." She dragged her feet toward the stairs. "Night. Night, Daddy. Love you."

"Night, Giggles. I love you too. I'll see you tonight." He smiled at the slight wave she gave over her shoulder when she started upstairs.

Martin stared at the space on the seat she had just sat. "Is it weird that she's not scared about all of this?" It didn't seem right that she was taking it all with a grain of salt. Kids were supposed to be scared of monsters.

"I don't think it's weird," Dan replied. "She was cool with me from the start."

"You said she was a baby when she first saw you." Martin pushed away how strange it was that a grown man had been hanging out in his daughter's nursery.

"Like I said: she's wicked smart. She just understands things. She knows you're not going to hurt her. You're just her dad, dude. She loves you. Kids are way more kind than what we all turn out to be."

"I just worry that it's too much for her. I didn't even know her best friend was a grown ass man, who is also a ghost for god's sake, and now all of this. It's pretty fucked up." It was out of his hands what had happened to him. He wouldn't let it hurt his daughter.

"Are you pissed?" Dan asked when her footsteps stopped in her room. "That I told her?"

"I mean, I'm not happy, but I'm not happy about a lot lately." Not that he was happy about much when he had a pulse.

"Understandable." Dan conceded. "You're being real chill about all of this, if you ask me."

"You think?" Martin wasn't one to give himself the slightest compliment, so it meant a lot to hear, whether or not it was true.

"For sure! That hot chick who came around was stressed as hell about all of this and you've just been putting one foot in front of the other like you always do and you're getting shit done. Gotta respect that, dude."

Dan held out a fist before frowning, remembering he was translucent. Martin reached out a fist anyway, bumping the air. He could feel a cloud of chilled air around his hand.

It was strange to think how much Dan knew about them. He had been an unknown roommate for as long as they had lived in that house. The loneliness was on a level that Martin couldn't fathom. His clothes were definitely from the 1980s. He had said he died in eight-eight. That's a long time to be alone as a being you didn't understand. He hadn't made it a week yet and was overwhelmed, no matter how chill Dan thought he was.

He wondered if there was a next level once you died or if Dan was just stuck within the walls of that house for all eternity. Even as a vampire, he had a few options to end it all. Unless then he would end up like Dan was now.

Longing for the days of not knowing there were other things than being a regular, boring human, he was glad to have Dan to talk to, at least. "How long do you think you'll be here?"

"No idea." He shook his head and ran his spectral fingers through the curls of his mullet. "Honestly, I don't know. I'm starting to forget the time I've already been here. My memory is gone to shit," Dan lamented, stilling in the chair.

"You had said you died in eighty-eighty. Do you remember how?" Martin wondered to him, settling back onto the couch.

"Not anymore." His head tilted just slightly to the side as he considered what he did remember. "I know it was eighty-eight, though, because that was the first year Crüe didn't tour. Shit, I was so pissed because I was sure I would see the next year. Instead, the universe kick-*stopped* my heart." His laugh over his song title's word play didn't reach his crystal eyes. "All good, in the end. Harps has been great at helping me find videos on that computer. Crazy that the whole world can live in that box."

Martin agreed with bob of his head and made a mental note to see if there were any CDs at Beaumont's to bring home to him. They would probably be horrible bootlegs knowing the quality of their products. It would probably be better to go online and buy them like everyone else now did. Like Dan said, life was in that little box now.

"So, that's about all you remember of your life?"

"I kind of remember the people who were here before you. A group of guys. I think they were just before you. Sometimes I think that's when I was alive. I think I lived here with a bunch of friends." His expression darkened as he dug through the moments that still hung in his mind. "Maybe not," he blustered and seemed to want to blow off the question. "I guess I'll have you as a roommate longer than the others, now." His eyes darkened and he frowned even as he made the joke.

Martin didn't want to push him. From the looks of their current lives, he was right. They would have a long time to get to know each other. He gave only a nod and clicked on the TV that filled the void for a while until sleepy comfort sank him into the couch. His eyes weighed as much as his body.

"Whoa, dude!" Dan's shout shook him awake. He stood beside Martin, pointing behind him, where he had his hands grasped comfortably behind his head.

When he sat up to see what had caught Dan by surprise, he saw his hand was wildly smoking. A slim ray of sunlight shone on the back of the couch where his hands had just rested.

"Shit!" He shook his arm as if to put out a flame and ran to shut the curtain tighter. The beam still shone through.

"Looks like it's time to hit the coffin," Dan teased.

Martin growled at the black streak across the back of his hand that was haltingly disappearing. The sunlight glowed from the kitchen, creating the beginning of a barrier to the stairs.

Helping out with Harper in the morning would not happen if he wasn't able to keep the light out. He wondered what would be easier to explain: boarding up the windows or smoking like burnt toast.

With a frustrated look to Dan, he zipped upstairs and into bed beside a still sleeping Nadine.

He was dead asleep before he could mouth a thank you to his new friend, Dan, for saving him from becoming overcooked bacon.

Chapter Nine

Husbandly duties.

THE NEW SCHEDULE SOON became the new routine and within a week, they had settled into the clockwork boredom that had created the bones of their lives in the past few years, except for the undercurrent of worry that had built within Martin.

Lyla hadn't shown hide or hair of herself, which left him with something to stew about and no one except Dan to talk to about it. The return of Moping Martin had even affected him. The fun-loving ghost had made himself scarce as of late. Martin couldn't blame him. That poor soul couldn't even escape the house. He didn't need Martin's whinging as well.

At least when he was at Beaumont's, his family wasn't in as much danger of whatever Lyla was worried about. He hoped.

Jake had been around most nights, and to Martin's chagrin, had not spoken to Lyla either. Every evening when he punched in, he considered asking Jake to punch out for him like he did the first night and use the dark cover of night in an attempt to find the disappearing vampire and to find out if she was alright. Knowing he had the skills of a paper pusher, not an elite detective, he chose to stick with his routine as she had asked by the time he reached his dented office door.

He had found a way to make Jake's presence worthwhile by using him to practice feeding. At least that's what he told himself he was doing to lessen the guilt of making his co-worker his personal juice box. As far as he could tell, he had mastered wiping the already burnt-out mind Jake was working with and was proud of the control he had over his thirst. Each night he had his little snack and was on his way, letting Jake get back to dragging his dirty mop around the empty store.

The comfort of his office improved when he turned off the flickering light for good, not needing it to see about the tiny space anymore. At first, the computer took a little adjusting, as it felt like he was looking directly at a solar eclipse. Once he could manage to keep his eye on the screen, he took to searching any site he could find for vampire lore, hoping to decipher the truth from tales.

Lyla had already busted a few myths, and a few seemed too far-fetched to believe, such as shapeshifting and starting fires with his mind. It would be a dangerous power to have when he was in a mood. Turning into a bat and flying high above the town, seeking out anyone who had wronged him and turning them into human flares. He knew Lyla would tell him he was wasting food.

He laughed wistfully, missing her.

Not only was it nice to have another vampire around to show him the ropes, but he had also grown fond of his new friend-by-circumstance. His mind tried to call out to her, wishing she could sense him like she had when he was in the Cluck Hit parking lot. No response ever came.

Several blogs warned that killing a sire would result in the same fate for those who shared a bloodline. That gave him hope Lyla was still alive, or at least undead, and was just off being Lyla. Ignoring the hard possibility that he would be notified of her death by receiving his own was difficult.

Until he heard it from Lyla, it wasn't true.

Unless he never heard from her again.

His knee bobbed quickly as he read articles, posts, and blogs that all had their own idea of what this unknown world was. This was not something he could research blindly on his own.

Both of his knees started to bob. He launched from the chair and out the door once the walls felt as if they were closing in on him. It seemed impossible to have an anxiety attack without the need for air or a heartbeat, but he was sure that's what was happening.

Pacing up and down the poorly stocked shelves of the store eventually slowed the tornado of thoughts that had tried to swallow him whole. Even though it was already a fairly empty store during opening hours, the silence of the overhead speakers and the dimmed lights gave it a cavernous sensation which creeped him out. It felt foolish to be put on ends by the banal box store he had spent so many hours in.

Perusing the food aisles, he reminisced about all the foods he would never have again. No more pizza rolls, peanut butter sandwiches, or ice cream for him. Just Juicebox Jake. It didn't help that every time he fed from him he got an intense case of the munchies. Beggars couldn't be choosers, he supposed.

The rows of off brand food would have to be off limits if he were to keep himself from spiraling into a pit of depression. Instead, he wandered over to the small clothing department and flicked through the racks of cheaply made clothes that were almost all marked as clearance, despite the regular prices on the tags. He started to try on a hat for a laugh until his lifelong fear of lice had him setting back on the hook. When there was an outbreak at Harper's daycare, he used up every day off he had to stay home with her and keep away her from the itchy little blood suckers.

That phobia, and what he was now was, was not lost on him. Not knowing if lice would latch on to vampires was much more of a worry.

He looked at the ties; the fabric was thin enough to be sold in a Halloween store as costumes. The ones he received for Father's Day were a much better quality.

Each tie brought a memory of Harper smiling with hope and pride as he opened it, pretending he had no idea what could be held within the gift that Nadine had wrapped with her.

He missed Harper. He missed his life.

The next day would be the first of the weekend. When he mentioned his desire to maintain his sleeping schedule, Nadine had mixed feelings. It made sense to get used to the flip-flop of hours while being mindful of his so-called sun allergy. She voiced her concern that it left little time for the three of them to spend time together, but said she understood. The lie was enough to get through the two days off from Beaumont's, but it did nothing to allow him to spend time with his daughter. So far, there were no benefits to having a vampire dad that he could see.

If he was being honest, there wasn't a benefit to being a vampire at all that he could see.

He moved over to the electronics department. The television brands were ones he had never heard of, or seen in any other stores. It was incredible to him they could sell knock-offs like Singsong and Bosy. It was even more baffling where they found such junk.

Lost in thought, searching through obviously repackaged DVDs, Jake suddenly appeared and startled him.

"I get all my vids here," he announced. "Well, except the ones I watch on my phone, if you know what I mean?" He gave a cartoonish wink and his quick patter laugh.

Martin didn't know if a vampire could turn green, but the thought of Jake watching porn grossed him out.

"Sure. Yeah," was all he could manage. He knew it had to be the weird stuff, being that it was Jake.

"Any word from Ly yet?"

"Not a word. You?" Martin asked with mentally crossed fingers.

"Nothin', I'm sure she's just busy." Jake's head bobbed along with agreement to himself. "I hope she turns up soon, though. I could use the business." His voice trailed off as if he just remembered who he was talking to. "How you holding up, compadre?" He ran his hand through his frizzy blonde curls that he wore in a messy halo around his face.

"I'm good. Be better if she were to show up again. Does she tend to disappear a lot?" Martin kept his eyes on the

DVDs, attempting to keep his tone casual to hide his unease.

"I mean, yeah, I guess she does. She a vamp, man. She does what she wants." His laughter ricocheted around them.

If only being a vampire meant the freedom to come and go as you wanted. Martin's experience was a wee bit different so far.

"Can I ask you a question?" Martin looked up to see Jake lift his shoulder with indifference, "Why does she pay you for getting her," he faltered, trying to find the right word, "uh, people."

"I think you should ask her that." He wouldn't meet Martin's eyes.

"Why? It just seems strange that she pays for what she can get on her own."

"I don't know what I can say, you know? She looks after me, I guess."

Martin couldn't understand why she would look after a random stoner when she complained that she never had the money to get out of town. Jake's frown told him he wasn't going to share anything else, whether it was because he couldn't or he really didn't know why.

"Hey, would you mind swiping me out again? I need to take care of some stuff for her," he lied. He just wanted out of there. He needed to feel fresh air on his face and to be under his own roof. Another night of playing hooky wouldn't hurt anyone.

"Sure, man! No worries. Get outta here," Jake answered with a little too much excitement. Martin didn't care enough to think further into whatever the reason was that made him so glad to have him leaving. He just gave a nod and headed straight for the parking lot.

Soon he was pulling into his driveway to find his house was still as dark as it had been every early pre-dawn morning. He arrived earlier than he had been the rest of the week, so he wasn't surprised. Nadine would be working her Saturday short shift at the dealership that she did once a month. He knew she would still be in bed. It seemed best to use the time to be next to her rather than wake up Harper and have her wake the house with her early morning exuberance.

Cracking the bedroom door open slowly, Nadine rolled over to watch him slip into the room.

"What are you doing up? It's your sleep in day," Martin whispered, stripping off to his boxers and sliding in the still made bed side beside her.

She slid a little closer to him, revealing a worn face with dark circles shading her hazel eyes. "I haven't been sleeping very well this week. It's strange to be alone."

"Maybe your mind just wants to stay awake to enjoy the silence without my snoring," he jested, knowing that wasn't the case. He would have been the same way when she was away at the beach if he hadn't been in the middle of turning into a walking, talking, undead mosquito of a man.

Nadine allowed herself a soft laugh. Martin had forgotten how much her sing-song giggle was so much like Harper's.

"Working nights seems to suit you," she declared with a twitch of her lip. "Or maybe it's because you've been staying out of the sun. Either way, you have this," she tilted her head with regard, "glow now." She reached over to run a finger down his cheek. "It's certainly keeping you cool."

Martin tried to hold on to the moment building between them and force away the tension that gripped him at the mention of his body temperature. The way Nadine was looking back at him captivated him. To his delight, she had become more and more flirtation over the last few days. Whether it was a change in his behavior, or some magical vampire allure, he didn't care. As long as she kept looking at him with those thirsty eyes, he would be perfectly happy.

Her hand traced up and down along his arm when she wiggled her head across her pillow to meet him nose to nose. Martin's faithful soldier reacted immediately, as it had been doing ever since he had been turned. Nerves rattled him when he thought about how explosive their encounter could be after he almost passed out in the shower from giving himself just the start of a *handshake-how-do-you-do*. Sex with his wife, especially after so long, could break it off. He was sure of it.

Nadine was whispering to him, her breath on his lips. All Martin wanted to do was be in the moment, Unfortunately, all he could think of was if she kissed him, would his fangs pop out? He wanted to be with her more than anything, but the risks grew more briskly than his boner.

"Was that Giggles?" He sat up in bed, looking toward the door, knowing their daughter was fast asleep.

"I don't think so," she replied with a frustrated edge to her tone. Her hand returned to his arm, startling him. He moved faster than he would have liked to and knocked the glass of water she had thoughtfully left him on his nightstand. The clatter onto the hardwood was enough to distract Nadine from the speed with which he had flinched.

She sat up with a sigh that turned into a groan that was seeped in frustration. "Well, if she wasn't up, that would do it."

Martin used his shirt to mop up the spilled water as Nadine moved to the door and pulled her housecoat from the hook. "Sorry!" Martin blustered. Even though he didn't know how to handle his new vampire-powered sex complications, it didn't mean he wanted the moment to end.

"I may as well get up. My mom's taking Harper for the day so you can sleep. You might want to set an alarm, though. She's bringing her back after they go out for dinner. They should be home around eight and we don't need you dead to the world when they get here." Martin stood straight when she described him as such and his soldier was immediately at ease. "Mom's been getting snippy about having her so much." She twisted at the tie on her robe. "I guess it's a lot more work when you don't just sweep in to spoil her and then off to her real life and boyfriends," Nadine snickered before staring at Martin frozen in place, a forced grin pressing his lips tight. "You okay?"

"Yeah, all good. Sorry about the water." He continued to push the shirt around in the puddle with his foot.

"Alright." She looked him over with suspicion. "It would be good for you to spend time with her tonight. She's starting to think of you as a creature of the night, I think," she gave another quick laugh. "I found the drawing she made of us, and I swear she made you a vampire in it."

The drawing! He had forgotten to hide it from his pocket. She must have found it when she was doing the laundry. Panic rushed his thoughts. Playing dumb would just lead to more conversation on the matter. He decided to lean into it.

"I saw that," he admitted with a guffaw that was a little too forced and much too loud. "Probably because of that Veronica Vampire cartoon." He tossed the soaked shirt into the hamper in the corner of their bedroom and searched in vain for something else to busy himself with.

"Anyway, I'm going to have to stay late tonight. Mr. Davidson, in his moronic wisdom, is going through with the blood drive tomorrow to bring in more business on a Sunday." Her eyes rolled. "In what world do we need more business on Sundays? The prick just wants to seem like a savior for it and won't be lifting a finger. Just like that damn toy drive he had me working overtime for last Christmas." Martin still had blood drive ringing in his ears. "Do you know he didn't even donate to it? Not even a buck, let alone a toy. He probably won't show up tomorrow until the press, who he probably bribed for a photo op, show up."

Blood drive. Martin nodded along, as if he had continued listening.

"Any chance you could get up early and come by? I could use your support." He kept his head bobbing. "Really? You think you can make it? The hopeful ring in her voice made Martin quickly catch up with everything that had been said. "It's inside so if you can make in between the car and the buildings you should be okay. You don't even have to donate."

"Oh, sorry. I mean, no." He hated how quickly her face dropped. "I want to, I swear, but, you know, the doctor, what the doctor said about being out in the sun." Her anger lessened, although the annoyance stayed staunch on her face and in her posture. "I know this won't be for long," he lied. "I'm really sorry."

"I get it. It's alright." She stopped her stomp into the hallway when she reached the door. "Do you think you could cover yourself up and use a bunch of sunscreen when you get up so you could mow the lawn? Once it's dusk. It's a mess front and back and I haven't had a chance to get to it with all the house chores on top of work."

"I'll try, but I don't know if I can." He stopped when her eyes narrowed with a frown.

"Well, whatever you can do this weekend would be a big help, Martin," she snapped, her arms crossed tightly against her chest. "I understand that the doctor says you need to stay out of the sunshine, but the workload is getting a little one sided and it's frustrating not knowing how long this is going to go on."

'Preaching to the choir,' he thought to himself. "I get it. I know you've been picking up the slack, and that your mom has really been stepping up." It was hard to hide his irritation, even though there was no way for her to know the real reason. At some point, he was going to have to find a way to tell her. With the little information he had, even if she did believe him, he wouldn't be able to explain the mountains of questions he knew she would have. That or she would think he was nuts and either leave him or have him committed.

"Whatever. It's fine. I'll try to get around to it," she replied coolly and was out the door.

Martin knew it would only fuel the rumbling fight if he went downstairs, so he opted for a quick shower and to hide in the bedroom. He needed to find as many alarms as he could, anyway. If he was to be up before sunset, if it was even possible, he would need to have enough of a noise explosion to shake the dead. He would sacrifice the few minutes he could have with Harper that morning for more quality time when she returned home.

As long as he could wake himself up and not have his mother-in-law find him cold and pulseless in bed.

After a quick search on his cell, he found that sunset should be at eight-eighteen. The two old analog clocks tucked away on the shelf of his closet were plugged in beside his cellphone, and he set them to go off at seven-thirty. If he could rouse from the dark sleep, he would have time to get dressed, sort out the shape of himself before they arrived, and then he vowed he would be cutting the grass by eight-nineteen if could settle Harper in front of the TV.

Laying down after he heard Nadine advise Harper to leave him be so he could sleep, he readied himself for the sunrise to steal him away for the day. As his eyes grew heavier than the weight that sunk his body into the mattress, he thought of Dan Jack.

"Hey, Dan, buddy. If you can hear me, I could really use your help," he mumbled out into the surrounding ether. "I really need to be awake before Harper gets home. I don't know if you can, but can…can you…" His voice grew weaker, "Can you try to wake me up before eight?"

The last words were barely audible and the last thought Martin had was that he hoped he had spoken them, not left the most important detail in his thoughts. The black emptiness of the day swallowed him whole.

AAAAAAHHHHHHHHH!

The room spun back into a blurred view around him; the noise of the alarms pulling him back. His scream of confusion and fear twisted itself into the cacophony of beeps, music, and news radio that vibrated every surface of his bedroom. Blinking away the cobwebs of sleep that tried to pull his eyes closed again, he could see he wasn't the only one shrieking and doubled down gutturally when Dan's transparent face came into focus just inches from his own. His mouth was wide with the effort he gave, screaming *wake up* over and over.

Martin struggled against the sleepy weight that tried to hold him when he reached for each alarm to switch them off. "Jesus, Dan! You're gonna give me a heart attack."

He hovered in a sitting position just above the side of the bed. "Yeah, I don't think that's gonna happen, Daddy Dracula." He smiled broadly when Martin leveled unimpressed eyes at him. "I guess it worked! There's still a bit of sun out there and look at you awake like normal. How do you feel?"

His body fought him with every movement until he got his feet on the floor, scrubbing the sleep from his face with his palms. At most, he felt hungover. "I think I'm good," he managed through a yawn. After attempting a few steps and more than one full body stretch, his mind slowly cleared. Knowing that he wasn't entirely controlled by the sun gave him a feeling of control over his new body. His stomach rolled and his eyes burned.

"Why don't you grab a shower and I'll go keep an eye out for Harps?" Dan offered, and Martin took him up on it with thanks.

A cold shower with a few slaps across his face had him good to go as much as he was going to get. Timidly peering around the corner from the bottom of the stairs, he found the main floor dim from the dusk. Not wanting to tempt fate anymore, he chose to head out to the garage to get the lawn mower ready. Worst case, he could call Harper and her grandmother in to meet him in the s garage's shield from the light.

"You should have seen your face, man," Dan chuckled as he appeared through the garage's cement wall. His face lit up with pride when he saw Martin's jaw drop at his mystical appearance. "Pretty wicked, right?" He waved a hand back through toward the house. "Harps thinks that's my best trick."

"Just when I think I'm getting used to what I am now, something else pops out and shocks me," he returned with a shake of his head.

"Literally pops out when it comes to me," Dan grinned at his own joke. "So, what's going on out here? You gonna be the new ghoulish gardener?" He wore his pride of his banter on his face.

"Technically, aren't you the ghoul?" Martin teased, earning a laugh and misty offer of a fist bump. When he reach his hand out to meet his, the mist floated around his arm with a chill. "I've been dropping the ball with things thanks to my new *allergy*," he air-quoted and gave a tug to the mower's pull cord. He nearly ripped it clean off, luckily starting it on the first try. His newfound strength seemed to be increasing. The mower sputtered and coughed at his feet. He kneeled down to find the cause of the block.

"Damn, man! You're a beast." Dan watched with admiration and gave him a ghostly high five.

"It used to take me half an hour to get this…oh shit!" he exclaimed and jumped back when a splinter of wood shot like a bullet from the mower, grazing his arm that he had lifted to Dan's high-five. The dagger slipped through

Dan, leaving a trail of his chest's fog to the point in the drywall it lodged.

"Oh, shit! That mower is a vamp hunter! Tried to stake Daddy Drac," Dan marveled, staring at the broken branch that was now a part of the garage's wall. "I guess yard work is a tough gig for anyone," he added with a look of empathy, softening his sarcasm.

Martin didn't have time to process that a poorly main-tained lawnmower could be enough to end his undead life when the phone rang. The shock of what had almost happened had him moving at an inhuman speed to the kitchen counter where he had tossed his phone.

"Hello?" he asked quickly.

"Martin? Is that Martin? Are you alright?" Nadine's mother Jeanne's voice asked on the other end. "You sound out of breath."

More than you know.

"No. I'm not…I just…" He took a blink to compose himself. "I just ran to grab the phone. What's up?" He pressed a sense of calm into his words. "Are you on the way with Harper?" His hand ran up and down his side, searching for broken skin, and found none.

"Actually, no. I'm on my way to get Nadine."

"Why? Is she okay? What's happened?" The panic bubbled again.

"No, no, nothing's wrong. I'm just stealing your girls for another weekend. I hope you don't mind." The line was silent when Martin didn't know how to reply. "We're going to have a sleepover, just us girls, at my house tonight. Then tomorrow while Nadine is doing her little charity thing at work, I'm having a grandma-grand girl day. My gentleman friend, Daveen, has a beach house that's for sale and invited me to have a look, since I'm in the market. It seems that maybe you could use some," she paused to clear her already clear throat, "some time for yourself to heal more from your ailment."

"They're going with you all weekend?" he finally managed. "They don't even have clothes or anything. Harper needs her bear-bear." He started for the stairs to gather her things. The thought of her being without her creature-comforts made him feel sick.

"No, we're all set there. Nadine came home on her lunch break to get what they need. I'm picking her up from work so we can get a jump on our girly time."

They were just going to leave without a word? Nadine must have been more angry with him than he thought. He was angry with himself that he wasn't quick enough to make it up to her. The damn lawnmower almost killed him for his attempt.

"When will you all be back?"

"Oh, I don't know. Tomorrow afternoon, maybe after supper. Anyhoo, we have to go now. Say bye-bye to daddy, Harper."

He could hear his daughter call out goodbye and that she loved him before Jeanne made kissy sounds into the phone and hung up.

"They're not coming home tonight," he sputtered to Dan, who held his hand over Martin's back as an attempt at ghostly comfort.

"I know, man. I saw them come home and Harps told me. I didn't want to say anything in case Nadine changed her mind. That chick can dig her heels in when she's mad, huh?"

Martin ignored that last part and tossed his phone back on the counter. "Harper doesn't even like the beach."

"I know, man."

"I was sure that I was going to find a way to make this weekend normal. Like how it used to be," Martin lamented.

"I know, man," Dan repeated. "Why don't watch TV and pretend we can still drink beer?"

The two walked glumly to the couch and plopped down in unison, with Dan landing just above the surface as he did.

Martin clicked on the TV and scanned the options. "I wish I could still drink beer."

"I know, man." Dan threw his arm along the back of the couch behind Martin. "Me too."

They stared at the TV until Dan nudged Martin to let him know it was almost sunrise. When he woke the next night, they had still not returned. Nadine replied to texts checking in on her with curt answers of "I'm fine," "it's fine," and "we're fine."

It did not feel fine to Martin.

Sunday evening, he awoke to a welcome noise in the house below him and was glad to see their faces, even though Nadine was still answering any question with quick snips. It was better than the silent treatment he was used to. Harper filled the awkward silence by griping about how awful the beach still was until it was time for her to go to bed and Nadine shuffled her to her room.

It felt unfair how his wife was treating him. It's as if he could help the fact that he couldn't go outside during the day now, anymore than he could fix the plethora of fresh problems that Lyla had gifted him.

When Nadine didn't return from upstairs, he planted himself on the couch to stew in his annoyance. Dan didn't join him that night and he didn't blame him. He wasn't much company in that mood.

The sun was a ways from rising when he felt childish for keeping up the unspoken argument and made his way up to bed. It would be a couple of hours until Nadine would be up for the day and he was down for the count. To his surprise, Nadine curled up against him when he settled under the covers and they stayed that way until her alarm stole her away for the day.

When he awoke, the tension remained, but he could tell that Nadine wasn't as angry about their squabble. Martin wondered if she would have carried it all on as long if she knew *Van Helsing's* lawnmower had almost taken him out. That was a can of worms he would keep sealed.

A big hug from Harper and a chaste kiss from Nadine marked the end of the weekend, and he headed in for his first night shift of the week.

That was not the weekend he had hoped for.

Chapter Ten

Fighter Jets and fireworks.

BEAUMONT'S WAS EMPTY WHEN he made his way through the back hallway to his office. The familiar creak of his chair was the only noise in the building as he rocked back and forth, his hands clasped behind his head and his eyes to the dark ceiling. It was going to be a long night if he didn't even have Juice Box Jake around; not only for his nightly snack treat, but it was nice to have someone he could talk to about what was actually going on in his life. Even though Jake's mind was usually elsewhere, it felt good saying the insane new bits of his life out loud.

As he swung himself forward to push off from the chair and head out for a stroll in the store, his inbox caught his eye.

There were a few file folders thrown on top with a yellow sticky note on top.

Martin—I hope you're gonna be back on days soon. Chance has asked me to replace the employees that have left and we just had another bunch stop showing up. I guess he found the money for them somewhere. Ha ha.

Ted

The files contained the exit processing for the employees that quit without a word. Something that had become pretty commonplace, if not more frequent than in the past. He couldn't blame them for walking away, picturing the feeling something like movie heroes walking in slow motion away from the explosions. He would give his left arm to be able to do that. Definitely his left fang, at least.

It wasn't a surprise that Ted would be pissed about having to do all the hires and paperwork. He would drag his feet to reload a stapler. As a manager, all he had ever managed to do was irritate everyone around him. When he actually showed up, that is.

There were four employees to process, which took up very little of his time. Once he finished the paperwork, he duplicated it on the computer, and then stuffed them in his file cabinet to rot. It was the most work he had done in months. Under the files, he found a stack of applications that had been filled out by fools who didn't know what they would be getting into. He knew Ted had placed them there because he couldn't be bothered with sorting candidates, so he went through them, attaching a sticky note to ones that had virtually any experience. He almost felt bad about being a part of bringing them into the moldy fold of Beaumont's. Telling himself it was a job that could mean a roof over their head and food on their table made it a scratch easier. Knowing how much they would be paid for their effort made it a very small roof and very little food, but it was something.

His phone buzzed, and he tossed the papers to his desk, curious who would text him in the middle of the night.

Hey. I'm sorry about this weekend. I've just been overwhelmed with work and you being sick and then the change in schedule. No one even donated to the blood drive.

Martin was glad to see his wife reaching out and ignored the way his mouth watered at the mention of her charitable effort.

It was childish of me to run off like that. I really am sorry. I know you've been having a hard time, too. I can't sleep without you here, and it's making my head foggy during the day. I haven't slept at all tonight because I didn't apologize before you left.

He started typing out a reply and back spacing it all and then doing the same again. He couldn't think of the right thing to say. It would be freeing to pour out his heart and tell her everything that was really happening. Lyla, and the elders, and Jake, and how their family will never be the same ever again because of him. He wanted to tell her how they were the first thing he thought of when he thought he was going to die, and that living as a blood-sucking monster for all of eternity is worth it to have them in his life. That he knew he had been just as much of a problem in the marriage as any other factor that they fought against and he wanted to spend the rest of his unending life making her happy.

But he didn't.

Telling someone they were a vampire wasn't really a text. Instead, he apologized for the grass, said he missed her too, and that he was sorry his new 'allergy' was taking a toll on everyone.

> It wasn't just the grass that made me so mad.

Martin waited as the dots showing her typing again appeared and disappeared.

> I thought we were going to have a moment. A moment – moment. Like we used to.

Martin's brows dipped to his confused eyes before he realized what she meant. He thought of how to reply when the dots returned.

> I know it's been a while. We've both been so busy and tired. I know I haven't been the most flirtatious. I'm just always so frustrated and drained lately.

He didn't move a muscle, watching the dots.

> I thought we were finally going to have some time, just you and me, and I real-

ized that was exactly what I needed to ease some of that frustration.

Martin strained against his khakis and a fang framed grin shone across his face.

I was mad because you pulled away and I thought you didn't want me any-more.

The smile slipped from his lips. He had thought she was only mad about the grass and that he was working nights. He had no idea that she wanted him as much as he wanted her at that moment. His hands flexed, open and closed, over his phone while he decided how to reply. It's not like he could tell her the reason that he couldn't be with her that night.

Sorry, babe. Just getting used to my new magical dong and fangs. Gotta worry about that blood lust now that I'm a vampire lol.

If he waited any longer, he knew it would just hurt her feelings that he couldn't reply.

Without another thought, he texted he was on his way home. He switched off his computer, swiped out, and was in his car before the message even made it to her.

Pulling into the driveway, he could see Nadine on the porch, her robe tied tightly around her. He tried to keep his body under control. Running at her with lightning speed, or popping a fang as a greeting, was sure to kill the mood.

"Hey," she said bashfully.

Martin could tell she felt exposed by the honesty in her texts.

"Hey," he returned with the same nervous energy.

A little nibble of her own lip was all it took for Martin to get the courage to make it happen. Fangs be damned.

They locked around each other and clumsily made their way inside and up the stairs before he could psych himself out with any more what ifs.

Nadine pulled away long enough to giggle and shush him as they passed Harper's door before Martin kicked their bedroom door closed behind them and they tangled onto the bed.

The room detonated around them. A mix of blinding light and Nadine's euphoric face swirled before his eyes. Every muscle, every nerve in his body hummed with a rapturous bliss that left him delirious and floating outside of his body. The pleasure he was surprised to find with drinking blood couldn't compare to what he could experience with his wife. If someone had told him fighter jets were crisscrossing the ceiling above them in an explosion of fireworks, he would have believed them. He felt as if they were hovering in the air, held together by an electrified web of frenzy as they pulled each other closer.

His attempts to remind himself to keep his fangs in, to go slow, to keep his newfound strength in check were eventually drowned out by the sounds of ecstatic moans that poured from the two, leading to Nadine finally collapsing beside him. The intense, orgasmic gratification stopped as quickly as it began. The room appeared around them again and a panic of losing control replaced the fervent frenzy that had just consumed them.

Nadine lay panting, her hand on her sweat soaked hair, and a grin that would split her face if she could possibly be anymore happy.

Martin looked her over as he did a mental check of himself. His fangs were still tucked safety in his gums, he couldn't taste blood—his or hers—and he was pretty fucking satisfied!

"Are you okay?" he asked, worried that he may have hurt her.

"Okay? Damn, Martin. Where did that come from?" She pulled him down to her and pressed a heavy kiss on his lips before she stared into his eyes, trying in vain to catch her breath. "Crap! We didn't wake up Harper, did we?"

Martin grabbed the blanket to wrap around his waist and tip-toed to the door, listening for any sign of her. He could hear her soft snores easily, but that would be hard to explain to Nadine and would unquestionably lessen the afterglow.

Cracking the door open, he gave a quick glance toward her room and found it quiet as he knew it would be. His head snapped in the other direction, to the staircase, when he heard a snicker of a laugh with a whistle.

"Way to go, dude," Dan, who was hovering his head around the corner from the stairs, cheered in a hushed voice.

"What the hell? Get outta here, perv," Martin scolded with just an inkling of pride in the smile he smothered.

"Oh calm down, lover boy. It's not like was watching. I could hear you from downstairs!" Dan nodded his approval of what he had overheard.

Shooing him with his free hand, Martin swallowed another self-pleased smirk and closed the door behind him, as if that could keep the spectral spy from entering.

Nadine held the sheet to her chest, a glow still in her eyes and her reddened cheeks. "Who are you talking to?"

Looking down, he shrugged and pointed to his blanket covered crotch. "This guy. He's out of hand tonight," he half-lied.

"You might want to reconsider trying to scare him away, if I were you. I'm a big fan of that perv," she teased. "I'm finally ready to get some sleep, but I'm gonna need an encore of that in the future." She held out her hand to gesture for him to join her in bed. "Oh, I didn't have a chance to tell you. My mom is buying that beach house. She says it's a gift for Harper," she said with a half-hearted scowl. "She wanted to put her on the deed. A four-year-old, for God's sake." She shook her head at her mother overreaching once again. "We compromised by putting my name on the deed and she's going to add it to the stack of things going to her in her will," she laughed. "So maybe when your allergies clear up, we could drop Harper off and make a weekend of it." A seductive invitation slid across her face. "Although, with what I want to do, we won't have to worry about being outside."

Curling up behind her, he couldn't remember a time in his life he had been happier.

"We'd have to be outside if we want to recreate that one Spring Break," he suggested, even though he knew they'd never be able to do anything in the sun again. The moonlight would be a worthy equal.

"I don't think my body is as limber as it was then. We may need to pick a lower tree," Nadine tittered.

For the life—or unlife—of him, Martin could not pinpoint where exactly they had let the fun fade away.

His body still hummed with pleasure after Nadine's breathing slowed and she drifted away to sleep, her lips still tilted up with happiness.

The thump of her heart matched the thump of Harper's down the hall, making a relaxing metronome-like tempo fill the air around him as he held her in his arms. Time passed too quickly before her alarm was announcing their evening together was over. Before she rose for the day, she spent a few extra minutes smothering Martin with kisses until Harper's calls for breakfast pulled her from the bed and out into the day.

The sunrise pulled him away soon after and when his day death released him, his smiling lips soon found Nadine's before he had to leave for work. Harper took joy in teasing her parents for being *smoochy faces* around bites of her spaghetti. Again, time moved too quickly before he had to give them each a kiss and head out into the night.

That one night made up for the weekend, without a doubt.

Hell, Martin would admit it was worth being turned!

Even though he drove to work, he still felt like he was floating on air. It surprised him when he found himself whistling a tune as he crossed the parking lot and into Beaumont's. He would have thought he would have to breathe to be able to do it, although he sure knew he could still sigh, so it marked it down as just another vampire quirk in a long list of discoveries. The one he used last night had been his favorite, hands down.

Nadine's warm skin was still on his fingertips, and the melt of satisfaction on her face filled his mind when he entered his office to find more folders set on his inbox.

Ted had managed to hire two more staff and lose another three. The pool of willing applicants was going to dry up quickly at that rate. There were only so many people in that small town, and even less that would last at Beaumont's.

Finishing the paperwork as quickly as he could, he filed away the last folder and wandered out to the store when he heart a familiar heartbeat. After that tumble with Nadine, he had worked up an appetite for a little Juice Box Jake.

He stopped in an aisle of stale bread and cereal when he heard Jake's laughter and a light return of a woman's.

"You started to make me worry, chick. For real, though," Jake guffawed. "Martin's gonna lose his shit when he sees you're back."

Lyla's voice had Martin moving at a clip to where they chatted, Jake leaning on a gum display beside Lyla, who had perched on the conveyer belt beside a register.

"Lyla, my god! Where have you been?" Martin demanded. Her calm, pleasant smile infuriated him. "You can't just disappear like that! I didn't know what had happened to you. I didn't know if me or my family was in danger."

"Whoa, whoa, whoa, Marty. Slow down," she insisted, jumping down and closing the space between them. "I'm glad you missed me, mate." She slapped a hand on his shoulder that Martin shook away.

"You can't just disappear, Lyla." The anger was dissipating seeing she was in one piece. "Last time I see you, you say I'm a barely born vampire and then you just leave me on my own?"

"Aww, did someone miss their mommy?" Jake teased.

Martin spat, "Don't call her that," at the same time Lyla did the same.

"Geez, sorry. It was just a joke," Jake apologized with surprised eyes above his frown.

Lyla ignored him and kept her attention on Martin. "I get it. You're pissed at me. Take it down a notch. I wasn't out having a grand time, yeah? I have a lot of things of my own to deal with." She picked up a gossip magazine and flipped through a few pages before setting back and grabbing another.

"You couldn't have touched base with me? Didn't you worry about me?" His voice was weak when he asked the second question, embarrassed that he had asked. Especially in front of Jake.

Lyla was kind enough to pay no notice of his uncomfortable bashfulness. "I knew you were fine. I told you, I'll know when something's wrong. You've been doing great! It's been crazy for me, if I'm being honest. I've been sorting out the trouble I got us into and making amends with the ones that could give us grief. Owen has been helping me and, in turn, you, Marty. I've been kissing the ring while you've been getting it off with the Missus. I'd say you're having a better go of it than I have." She raised a knowing brow and gave him a sly grin.

Martin's embarrassment doubled down. "How do you…," he sighed deeply and covered his face with his hand. "You can't feel that or anything, can you? You can't see us, like in your head, can you?" He kept his fingers over his eyes, not wanting the answer, which only caused Lyla to crack up more. Just when he finds the one benefit of being a vampire, it could be ruined by the thought of some sort of psychic threesome that he didn't know about. It would be hard to explain to Nadine why they'd never be able to recreate that moment with her again. It would be even more hard to resist it.

Jake joined Lyla's laughter, the confusion as to what they were laughing about tight on his face.

"No, Marty. I'm not creeping on you when you're havin' a ride. I told you, it's your emotions that I can feel. There is no way I'm slipping in your head and watching. Jaysus, that would be weird as feck!" She marched herself around to the till and started pushing at random buttons.

Relief loosened Martin's shoulders when he could see the very idea of it made Lyla uncomfortable. He shook his head at Jake, who had raised a high five to him when he figured out what they were talking about. He shrugged and took a pack of gum from the rack he had draped himself on and pulled out a piece.

"Hey! You can't just steal that," Martin blurted. "This place is broke as it is, and you get away from that register," he demanded of them.

Lyla looked around the counter and pouted, shrugging when she saw the irked look that Martin gave her. It looked like stealing from the people she fed on and her ancient sugar daddy weren't the only way she kept money in her pocket.

Jake pulled a second piece from the pack and stuffed them both in his mouth, chewing widely. "What are you gonna do, compadre? Tell Ted on me? I think my secret about you is a little bigger." He winked and his chest shook with his chuckle.

Lyla moved in a flash and smacked his arm. "Don't you even think of trying to threaten us, little man," she warned him, looking coolly up at him.

"Easy, it's just a joke, chick. Chill." Jake tried to keep his voice light even as he nearly knocked over the rack when he stumbled a few steps away from her. "I know where my bread is buttered."

Lyla gave him a flat stare before turning back to Martin. "I swear, if you eat too much of this one, you'll eventually lose a lot of brain cells."

Jake gave another perturbed look that he turned back and forth between the two. "That can't happen, can it?" he asked her, scratching his head.

"There's a reason I only had you once and won't come back for seconds," she demurred, making her way back to banging at the register and pushing the buttons.

"Oh, whatever, you're just giving me guff. I'm awesome and you know it," he insisted with a broad grin that brought the sparkle back to his eye. He laughed harder when Lyla rolled her eyes at him. "You know you want this."

"No, thanks. I may have had a sip once or twice, but when it comes to what I want, it's not that." Lyla gave his shoulder a consoling squeeze. "You know I'm not into sausage."

Jake acquiesced he would not win that battle with a bob of his head. "Anyway, I'll see what I can do for you," he advised Lyla, and stood from the gum rack. "Come see me tomorrow." He gave Martin an exaggerated grin and started for the back of the store.

"What's that about?" Martin asked, a little disappointed that her appearance now seemed more to see Jake than him.

"Just business, nothing to worry about. So, how was it? The first time as a vamp?" she deflected.

Martin crossed his arms across his chest and swallowed the grin that pulled at his lips. "I don't want to talk to you about that. It's private, Lyla."

"I get it. I won't bring it up again." She watched him until he couldn't hold in his happiness anymore and his smile escaped. "It's pretty awesome, though, isn't it?"

"Holy shit, it is," he admitted and then waved away the continuance of the details. "Why are you here? Just to tease me?"

"No, that's just a plus." She climbed over the counter, stuffing the magazines she knocked over back with the others. "I know I haven't been around much and I still owe you a lot, especially answers. I guess you could say I was getting the answers to give you." Martin looked at her expectantly until she went on. "Yeah, that's the thing. I don't have a lot yet."

Martin groaned. "So, I have to keep hiding out? How long do you think I can hide this from my family?"

"Marty, you're going to have to find a way to make it work if you want to stay with your family. I can tell you that the elders I was worried about are off our backs now. That's the good news. Owen really came through for us.

But you're a vampire now. That's never going to change. Just like me. We all have problems, fella."

Martin slumped when the gravity of it hit him. It had all happened so fast, and he had kept so much of his life the same. It had felt like it was something he had been waiting to pass. Whatever trouble Lyla had gotten them into would fade away and he could go about his life.

But his life ended when his heartbeat stopped. There was no changing that, and he knew he had been hiding that truth from himself.

"My family is safe now, though, right?" he questioned quietly.

"I promise you they are, Marty. Safer than ever now that they have us looking after them." He looked up quizzically, and she expanded her thought. "Us meaning the vampires. I may be low on the chain of anyone with influence, but I'm friendly with quite a few who matter." Her smile faltered and she looked to the front sliding doors.

Martin slightly nodded when she didn't continue. "Okay." It was strange that he didn't hold Lyla to blame for the spot he found himself in. He didn't know if it was another vampire blood mystery or if he was admitting to himself what his life was now and that there was nothing he could do to change it.

"I'm really sorry, Marty. You have to know that I know this has all been a fecking disaster for you. I had no right to pull you into my pity party and do something beyond stupid, but now that the dust has mostly settled, I can honestly say that I'm glad you're in my life now. You're a great guy and I promise that I'll help you through this. We'll find a way to make it work. I'm getting my shite together. For both of us."

"Get your ancient vampires to give me a few million bucks so my family and I could run away to a private island and we'll call it even," Martin jested, his mood a little lighter with her declaration.

"If I could do that, I'd already be on that island, wouldn't I?" she returned, relief in her eyes with Martin's joke. "Seriously, though. I've never known anyone who was turned and then stayed with their family. It's unheard of, but Owen said that if that's your wish, it's the least we can do after what I did." Her face darkened with what Martin perceived as shame.

"What else could I do? I can't leave them. They're my family. I love them."

"I think you're loving Nadine a little more now, too, aren't ya?" She clamped her lips when Martin shot her a look. "Sorry, I couldn't help it."

Martin considered what she had said. "What do you mean, it's the least you could do?"

"I promise all honesty to you from here on, so you should know that there was a big argument about what to do with you once I can clean to Owen. We're lucky that everyone holds him in such regard, because I'm sure everyone else would be voting either to give you the final death or to make you join a hive somewhere far away." The lighthearted smile she gave him was forced.

"Join a *what?* What does that even mean?"

"Hive? It's what we call a group of vampires that live together. A sort of flop house for vamps who have nowhere else to go." She looked pained when Martin's face widened with frustrated shock. "It's better than meeting the sun!"

"Final death, Lyla? There really were people who wanted to kill us?" He had been coming and going to work, thinking she was exaggerating the danger they were in. If someone was on death row, you don't tell them to go to work as usual and just lay low. He felt sick thinking that something could have happened to his family.

"I know! It was bad, Marty. I told you I wasn't off having fun. I was terrified! The same could have happened to me, which is only fair because I am the one that fecked everything up." She held her hands up in defeat and gave an exaggerated shrug of her shoulders, shaking off the emotional outburst in seconds. "We're good now, though. We just have to figure out the details, I guess. I'm taking on my issues one by one. I promise."

He had been going about his life not knowing how close the end he really was. "How are you so calm about almost dying? They were seriously going to kill us over this?"

"We're already dead, mate. The threat of final death is always lurking around the corner. Especially if you're going to try to live among the living. Trust me, you'll go mad in an instant if you think about it."

It was hard to see it as clearly as she did, but it did make sense. Even when he had a pulse, if he were to think about dying everyday he wouldn't be able to function. There were just as many threats when he was a human between accidents, disease, and ailments. The difference now was it was rule-wielding elders lurking in the shadows and stake-throwing lawnmowers at home.

"So now that you've taken care of them, am I going to see you more? Am I going to have help to sort this all out?" Martin wondered, hoping he would. One evening with her taught him how to eat. Now he needed to learn how to thrive. He ignored the fact that his only hope was a hot-mess who had already almost gotten them killed. She was all that he had and he was going to take what he could get.

"I promise I will be around a lot more. I know it's been hard," she admitted, her eyes looking anywhere but to Martin before she zipped across the small space between them and pulled him down for a quick hug. "We'll figure this out." She moved to the door and clicked the lock open before he could return the embrace. "I'm off to continue my apology tour now. Lock this behind me," she instructed with a finger pointed at him. "Oh! Before I forget, I have a phone now." She pulled a small flip phone from her pocket. "Silly little thing, isn't it? I've never wanted one before but, a, uh, friend said it would be responsible to get one."

She zipped back to the register and grabbed a pen to scribble her number on a scrap piece of paper. After she left it on the conveyer belt, she gave him a thumbs up and was out the door.

There was no sign of her in the parking lot by the time Martin made it to the door.

The past twenty-four hours had been a lot to take in, even with what the past couple of weeks had dropped on him. For the first time in a long time, he had things to do at work, and something to be excited about at home. He considered that he may have actually even made some friends. Fatigue frayed the edges of his nerves and his stomach rumbled. Before he could even process a minute of it, he needed to eat and wandered off to find Juice Box Jake, before it was time to punch out for the night and begin another day.

The mundane case of the Mondays that he lived with were as dead and gone as his pulse. Lord only knew what waited for him next.

But first—a snack.

Chapter Eleven

Blood thirsty and bankrupt

THE NEXT FEW DAYS were the same as his *new* new normal. He didn't want to jinx himself by admitting that it was shaping up to be a life which he enjoyed. If there was one thing Martin knew, a sunny sky was just one waiting to rain.

Testing the phone number Lyla provided had become a nightly routine, and a small glimmer of peace settled over him each time she answered, the bother ringing clear in her voice. Whatever the apology tour she said she was on was taking a toll on her. The breakdown she was in the midst of when she turned Martin must have been quite the spiral; not she was one to open up about anything.

The early mornings with Nadine had been just as explosive as the first time, and they were thoroughly enjoying the intimate time before the day stole them away from each other. By the third time they got at it, he realized it was important to keep an eye on the clock. When he became so lost in his wife, he nearly went past sunrise. Becoming a corpse on top of her was not a kink he wanted to explore.

His wanders around the store at night now had a bit of a giddy-up in his step. When Jake was in for a short shift he couldn't help commenting on how happy he seemed. Being turned had been a blessing for his marriage, hands down.

But, as was life, for every plus, there was always a minus, and he was still unhappy with the paltry amount of time he had to spend with Harper. It wouldn't do to see her in passing twice a day. Fixing that would be the next step in his undead plan.

The winters would give him longer nights, he hoped, and that would give them more family time. There was no way to ignore that they would have to make sunset to sunrise work for them somehow. Until then, he would try to force himself to rise earlier in the evening. That morning, he had set the train of alarms he had set out to Nadine's amusement. Blaming his deep sleep on his new medication was an easy lie that she had excepted. It was her requests to speak with the doctor that were hard to push away. Thank god for the distraction of his newly blessed wonder dong to stop her questions. He preferred the effect of that much more than lying.

That night, after dragging himself from bed, he showered, started prep on Harper's supper—spaghetti night again—and was at the door, tucked into the shadows of the foyer, to greet her just before sunrise when her grandmother brought her home. The steady ache in his head was worth the extra time he had with his daughter.

Jeanne handed him Harper's backpack and set her hands on her hips. "So, how are feeling today? Any improvement?" Her toe tapped on the porch, waiting for the answer.

Harper ran circles around them while her grandmother looked exhausted. Grabbing her bag from Martin, she blew a kiss to Jeanne and disappeared into the house, following the sound of Dan's incessant whistling.

"I'm settling into the routine that seems to be working, but the doctor hasn't said much has changed," he partially fibbed, knowing that they were lucky to have her help and that it was wearing her out. As if she could read his mind, she blew a breath against a silver curl that had escaped her coifed hairdo.

"Well, you know I'm glad for my time with my girl, but as I told Nadine, I have my own life to live, Martin. My gentleman friend is starting to forget what I look like, for Pete's sake." She looked over Martin's shoulder when Harper began breaking down her day for Dan Jack. "Who is she talking to?" Narrowed eyes cast suspicion on him.

"That's just Mr. Jack, her invisible friend." At least that was the truth.

"That girl needs more playmates. Drumming up an imaginary man to be her friend, it's telling Martin." Her lips pursed as she lifted a brow, judgement awash on her face. "You need to make time for her if your doctor is going to insist you live like a ghoul in the night."

"I know Jeanne, thanks again," Martin said quickly, shutting the door to his mother-in-law's face.

He knew it was rude and uncalled for with all the time she had sacrificed in the past few weeks. That didn't change the fact that he was already doing the best he could with the situation he found himself in. Jeanne's nagging, as always, fixed nothing, so he wasn't about to waste the time he had with Harper to listen to her gripe that he should be doing exactly that.

"They're green! How funny is that? I wouldn't eat eggs that look like that!" Harper was pointing out pictures in the library books she had filled her bag with, bouncing up and down with the sugared energy of a child who had spent time with a grandparent.

"Wow, that's crazy, Harps. We'll have to read that one later," Dan agreed with a gentle laugh, and looked to Martin. "Actually, why don't you read it now with your dad? I don't know if he's read this one."

He was glad to oblige and sat on the couch beside her to dig into the rhyming story. Reading to her made his cold, still heart almost feel warm. Dan hovered beside them, watching the two finally enjoy some bonding time. They made their way through to the end of the first book after two bathroom breaks, a request for juice, and a pause for Harper to sing a song she remembered. By the time they reached the last page, Harper had settled on the couch beside her dad, her little arms wrapped around one of his.

"I think that's what your dad made for your dinner," Dan teased, floating on the empty cushion beside her.

"No!" Harper giggled. "I don't want that! So gross!" She laughed harder when Martin tickled her tummy.

"You know I wouldn't make you that. I have your spaghetti ready to go when you're hungry." Martin set the book aside and flipped through the others she had brought home. They were mostly the same ones she always checked out. A creature of habit like her father.

"I miss eating good food. I swear I can still taste it sometimes. Watching her slam back spaghetti makes me so jealous," Dan lamented with the cover of humor. He rubbed at his stomach. "That wife of yours can cook a mean meatball."

"I hear that," he concurred. Leaning behind Harper, he lowered his voice. "It hasn't even been a month and I miss it all. Even though the smell of most of it makes me wanna puke now." Martin grimaced at the thought of anything solid in his stomach.

Dan nodded wistfully in agreement. "I'd be happy just to be able to smell it, man. Even gnarly food like brussel sprouts would be a nice change from nothing."

Harper leaned back between them. "Those sprouts smell like toots." She wriggled her nose with distaste and the two laughed on either side of her. Pride tickled her face at their enjoyment of her joke.

"I'd have to agree with that, Harps," Dan acknowledged. "Stinky little things, aren't they?"

"I'm with you both on that, too." Martin nodded in agreement to Dan. Harper looked up between them in a new fit of giggles.

"Hey guys," Nadine said, startling them when she appeared around the corner into the living room. "What do you have going on in here?" She gave the two a crooked look.

Martin looked between Dan Jack and his wife, causing a heavier look of confusion on her face. "We're just reading some books before supper." He jumped up to walk to the kitchen to put the pot of water on.

"It sounded like you were talking to someone else." She looked back and forth between Martin and Harper before trailing him into the kitchen.

"Oh, that. Yeah, I was just pretending to talk to Dan." He kept his eyes on the sink as he filled the pot.

"Who?" she questioned, looking puzzled by his answer.

Martin grimaced at his slip up. "Oh, uh, Mr. Jack. Her friend. We were pretending he was reading with us." He popped the lid on and bumped his hip to hers to move her.

"Did you call him Dan?" she laughed, giving Martin a shred of relief that she seemed to take the answer with a grain of salt. "He has a first name now?"

"Yeah, I guess so," he shrugged and set the pot on the stove. "You know, Giggles. Always creating something in that little head of hers."

They worked in unison to get dinner started, with Martin declining repeatedly to eat, telling her that his stomach was a little off and he had leftovers he left in the fridge at work if he got hungry. Sitting with his family as they ate brought a smile to his lips before he had to leave, once again, for the night.

On the drive to work, he found himself lost in thought, thinking of what their world would be like if he could hypnotize his way through life. If he didn't have to go to work for pennies just to keep a roof over their head. They could live in a castle on a cliff, with a tall stone tower filled with books for Harper, and he and Nadine would make love every night under the soft light of the moon. No one would work, no one would worry, and they could be together, happy as they had found themselves in the past few weeks.

A blaring horn behind him brought him from his fantasy and to the green light that ushered him even closer to Beaumont's. Every turn of his tires toward the store soured his mood more.

From what he understood of vampires, Harper would be an old lady before he had any semblance of supernatural powers that mattered. The pipe dream was delightful to picture, but difficult to let go of. He wondered when the world would lose the newfound feeling of strangeness that touched every minute of his days and nights. When he would feel like he was truly a part of something other than a dead HR rep hiding in a department store, who spent his downtime lying to his family.

The bad mood that insisted on sinking in had smothered the happiness of the time around the dinner table. Pushing himself on, he reminded himself that as far as his family life was going, he was still alive and that should count for something. He had already called time of death on his work life long ago, and like he now was, a lack of a pulse stopped nothing.

Now that the elders seemed to have forgiven Lyla's drunken blunder, he had forever to try to sort things out; and forever to try to find the money to do it. If only he could sue the vampires for the pain and suffering of Lyla's actions.

Even better: *wrongful death!*

Laughing at what a vampire small claims court would look like, he slipped his key into the back door of Beaumont's and then another into his office. More files sat on his inbox. At first he was excited to think that maybe the business was turning around and new hires would be mean a pick up of sales. When he flipped through them, he saw they were all employees to exit process. NO SHOW was scribbled in red pen across each one.

At the rate everyone was leaving, there wouldn't be enough staff left to open the doors. A sense of foreboding crept over him. If Beaumont's closed, how could he find another job? It's not like he could show up bright eyed and bushy tailed for a job interview in the middle of the day. His hand went quickly to his cell and dialed Lyla. His job security needed to be next on the list of getting his life in order. Beaumont's was hell, but it had been a steady income. If he lost that, there was a good chance his undead life would unravel further just as things were looking up.

"What's up, Marty? I'm in the middle of something." He could hear soft music in the background. The apology tour seemed to be ongoing.

"I really need to talk to you. Do you think you could swing by the store tonight?" He wasn't about to start a life of stealing like she did to support his family, and hoped she could give some sort of advice. Even though it felt like asking a tween the best mortgage rates, she was all he had.

"I dunno Marty. Can it wait? I'm tied up right now," she snickered, and he heard someone else in the background do the same.

"I'm having a bit of an existential crisis over here. I could really use someone to talk to other than Jake." He could hear her cover the phone, her voice turning to smothered mumbling until she returned with a dramatic sigh.

"Alright, keep your wig on, Marty. I'll finish up here and meet you soon, okay? You're going to be at the store?"

"Where else would I be?" he asked shrilly and instantly felt bad for his attitude. "I'll see you soon?"

"Yeah, Marty."

He looked at his phone when the line went dead and hoped she meant it.

Distracting himself with the exit files did not take as long as he's hoped. There had been so many as of late he could practically do them with his eyes closed. His typing speed had even caught up with his vampiric pace. Looking over the staffing list, it was a dire as he expected. He considered trying to access the front office for a look at the books, but he knew that there would be no truth in those.

The cavernous store around him was quiet when he stopped typing. If his mind wasn't racing with what ifs and worst-case scenarios, he would have found it peaceful. His mind drifted to the safe in the manager's office. It was a fruitless fantasy to think he could find it in himself to rob Beaumont's, even after how poorly they had treated him over the years. He just wasn't a thief. Even if he was, he would probably find the safe empty, anyway, with how Chance Beaumont drained the business.

A financial vampire of sorts, he thought to himself. It seemed almost worse than what Lyla had made Martin into.

The soft thump of a heartbeat appeared and made its way into the building. Jake, it seemed, was working after all, and a nice snack was just what he needed to clear his head. Pushing back from his desk, he nearly licked his lips, thinking about how long it had been since he ate. Jake had been off for a few days and Martin was surprised that he hadn't been famished, considering the appetite he had been working up with Nadine.

"I know, I know! I hear you. I swear, I hear you."

Martin froze in place when he heard the distressed voice. Speak of the coked-out devil; Chance Beaumont was in the front office.

"I don't think you do, you little shit," a slithering voice spat. "You're only good for what you give me and lately you haven't given me anything, have you? Give me one reason to keep you around."

The voice that he didn't recognize was dripping with threat. Martin kept his body as still as ice, listening to what sounded like a dangerous mess that Chance had gotten himself into.

"I can get you more. Whatever you need. Everything is just running thin right now. I just need a few more days and I can get you something." Chance made a gurgling sound and his heart rate audibly quickened.

"I have been more than kind to you, Beaumont. I've let you live, for one. Now my patience has worn thin." Chance's throat choked at what Martin assumed was a hand around it. "What exactly can you offer me for extending my time?"

"I can double the money if you give me more time," he gargled. "I need to hit the tables."

The thud of a body hitting the floor boomed from the office.

"And what, pray tell, are you going to offer as interest this time?"

"I can get you more." Chance's voice was winded and filled with the begging of a desperate man.

The predatory voice snarled at the offer. "I can get my own fucking blood, you little dipshit. We're beyond you getting me a little extra here or there. I want my cash, not the trash you've been bringing me!"

Chance whimpered and Martin could hear his heart rate nearly become one steady hum it was so quick. "That last guy wasn't good, I know. I can get you better ones. I swear!"

"That last guy was disgusting. He tasted like weed and mop water. You should owe me more for thinking that skinny little bitch was worth anything at all!" A crash slammed within the room and Chance began a stream of apologies.

Weed and mop water? It made Martin picture Jake's goofy smile. It was then that he realized there was only one heartbeat in the building.

Chance's.

The threatening man in the office with him was no human. With his limited knowledge of which beings were real or not, he assumed it was a vampire. He hoped. Other possibilities were even more frightful to imagine.

Was there anyone in that damn town who hadn't gotten themselves mixed up with the vampires? He didn't want to think how much had been going on around him while he had walked through the world with his head in the storm clouds of daily life.

"I swear I'll get the money back to you," he stopped to scream when another crash erupted.

Martin didn't know if he should run or stay put. The only other vampire he had met was Lyla, and this one did not sound like he wanted to make a new friend. It was very on brand for Chance to get into trouble with bloody supernatural beings in order to score some quick cash. If anyone would sell their soul in that town, his name would be at the top of the list.

The names of all the people who had up and quit that had crossed his desk spiraled into his mind. If Jake could easily set people up to be snack packs for Lyla, Chance would have no qualms about letting people die for his debts, let alone to make some quick cash.

Could the coked-out brat really be dealing his employees to a vampire psychopath? He knew he could and knew that the weed scented mop-bucket was most likely Jake.

Chance Beaumont, that monster, would do anything for some quick cash, regardless of the cost.

Lyla had done a wonderful job of sheltering him from the underground world around him in the short time he had been a part of it. He felt naïve, foolish, and ultimately terrified standing with just a wall between himself and whatever beast was at Chance Beaumont's throat.

"You have two days, you little fucking weasel, and then I'm going to take a whole lot more than this."

Another strangled sound gurgled from Chance and the smell of his blood drifted out around Martin, who did his best to ignore his fangs when they dropped down with want. He closed his eyes, willing himself to calm his watering mouth.

"Who the fuck are you?" The voice shouted, too close for Martin's liking.

Opening his eyes, he found the man, fangs still dripping with blood, staring back at him in a leather jacket that reached the floor. Rage would have been a kind look compared to what he found in his fiery eyes. If panic hadn't consumed him, he could have found amusement in how cliched the man's appearance was, from his black-painted fingernails to his inky black widow's peak, as sharp as glass.

Instead, he only saw someone who would have no problem ending his undead life where he stood, shaking in his khakis.

"I, I'm, I'm…" Martin swallowed the rest of his words and ran for the door.

"Who the hell is that?" The cartoonish murderer demanded. "Get up, you human waste bag! Are you dealing with other vamps?"

Martin's feet blazed against the floor and out the door, shattering the glass when he slammed it open.

"Jaysus! What's wrong?" Lyla asked when she saw the state of him barreling toward his car, digging out his keys to hit the unlock button.

"Get in the car! Get in the fucking car!" he screamed. No matter how fast he could move, he didn't know if this guy could run faster. The steel in his old sedan would be an attempt at armor against whoever was currently on his tail.

Lyla matched his pace, jumping into the passenger side beside him. "What in the world is going on?"

"Vampire! There's a fucking killer vampire in there!" Martin fumbled to put his key in the ignition.

Lyla barked a laugh through her confusion and gingerly opened the door. "And there's two in this car. What's your point?" Her laughter stopped when she caught sight of the cause of his terror coming through the broken door in a blur and stopping to lock eyes on them.

"Oh, feck me sideways! That's Bloody Enzo! Drive, Marty!"

Chapter Twelve

Ah, feck.

The car pulled out onto the road, tires screeching as he turned down the main road. Martin flattened his foot on the gas, his eyes scanning the mirrors for any sign of him. Just the sight of him had left Lyla shaken, which could only mean very bad news.

"Who is Enzo? Is he one of the elders?" he demanded, trying to keep all four wheels on the road.

Martin twisted the wheel to pass a dented mini van that was taking its time. The driver, not understanding a killer could be on their tail, wailed his horn at the erratic driving.

"He is in no way an elder. He's just bad news," Lyla replied, her voice quivering. "That guy is not someone to mess with."

Martin was now completely unsettled seeing her reaction. She was able to keep her cool when there was a chance she was fighting for their lives more than she was just being near that man. A feeling of helplessness crept in and heightened his fear when she turned in her seat to look behind them.

Horns blared as he weaved through traffic at top speed. He didn't know if a vampire could keep up their inhuman speed for as long as a car could run. He looked down and found his car was down to less than a quarter tank. If they were being followed, he would soon find out. That was if his old clunker could even be faster than a pissed off vamp.

Lyla looked at the dash when he cursed and pointed to a tree covered carpool lot up ahead. "Go in there. We don't need to cause a pile up running from him."

Pulling the car into the near empty lot, he picked a spot along the edge away from the glare of the high mounted lights and switched off the engine. He couldn't stop himself from scanning the dark corners from which the vampire could jump out of at any minute. His eyes played tricks on him with every rustle of the trees in the breeze. If he still had the ability to do so, he was sure he would have pissed his pants already.

"What is going on? Who is Enzo?" Martin demanded. At the start of the night, he was worried about losing his job. With another stranger's arrival into his life, he was once again worried about losing his life.

"I didn't even know he was in town. He's been gone for years," Lyla remarked, her fangs nipping at her fingernail and her gaze a million miles away, lost in whatever terrifying memories she had fallen into. She finally looked at Martin to find him staring back with a wide-eyed look of expectation between glances to the road and the surrounding trees. "Enzo is a sort of fringe vampire. He's a do-what-he-wants sort of guy who has no problem killing anyone or anything, including other vampires."

"He's like one of those hive vampires you were talking about?" The thought of being taken away from his family and forced to live with people like that monster made Martin shiver. He had spent his childhood moving house to house with some humans who could be considered less than kind. A vampire version of that cruelty was unimaginable. Death would have been a better option. He shook away the thought. Death was not an option that night. He needed to stay focused and get them to safety.

Where that was, he didn't have a clue.

It felt like they should be moving somewhere, and fast. He tapped his fingers on the steering wheel with nervous energy.

"No, he's not what you'd call a *hive guy*," Lyla replied and barked a nervous laugh. "No, there is no hive in the world that would accept him. If he didn't kill them all first."

The isolation of where they were closed in around him. He considered turning the car back on until he realized he had nowhere to go. If a deranged murderer was looking for them, there was no way he would lead him back to his house. Beaumont's was a no go.

Where could you go to hide from a vampire that other vampires cowered from?

His nerves got the better of him and caused his fangs to pop right into his lip. He was so overwhelmed; he felt himself trying not to cry. What exactly was possibly chasing them down?

"Is he a super powerful vampire or something?" He wiped at the drop of blood on his lip as he spoke.

Lyla slowly shook her head from side to side. "No, he's just a psycho. He was when he was living and he's worse now. The last thing a narcissistic wanker needs is super strength and immortality, as you can see by him."

A rustle in the bush in front of them caused them to jump in their seats. A branch snapped loudly when a squirrel scurried out and across the dimly lit asphalt.

"Do you know him? Don't tell me you turned him too?" Martin cringed.

If Enzo was the result of an inexperienced maker, was there was a chance that would be Martin's future as well? It didn't suit his lifestyle to turn into a feral killer roaming the streets.

"No! I told you. You're the only one I've turned," Lyla insisted. The idea that she could be Enzo's maker appeared to turn her green. "A good friend of mine knew him before he was turned. He was a real piece of work even back then. One of those kids that play fancy dress as vamps, pretending to drink blood and dressing all in black, trying to creep out their school mates. The difference between the regular kids that did that, and him, was that he believed his own hype, you know? Most kiddos grow out of those phases, but he became obsessed with the idea of really being a vampire by the time he hit his twenties."

They scanned the tree line and back to the road.

"You're telling me he's just some goth guy that has you so scared?" That didn't add up to him.

"He was never just some goth guy. He loved inflicting pain on people, even hurt animals, before he even became a vamp." She shook her head at a thought she didn't share. "A guy like that should have never been turned. The one who did it was hoping to make a play for a spot among the elders and thought she could use him as a weapon, since he didn't give a damn about anything or anyone except getting real fangs. She was a real bloody cabbage, so of course it didn't work," she scoffed. "As soon as she did the deed, he took off on her to let loose his chaos and no one has been able to catch him since."

"You're telling me this guy has been on a murder streak for decades and the all powerful elders can't catch him?" That seemed impossible.

"That's the funny thing: he's only, like, a decade old. If that!" she snorted. "I'm older than him. I guess it's just that no one is as crazy as him. Not as cruel as him, that's for sure. He's a slippery bastard, that's a fact."

Where could anyone hide from someone that centuries old vampires could do nothing about?

"So, he doesn't have any of the extra powers that the old vampires have? He's just out there destroying the world with what *we* can do?" In as much as that was impossible to believe, it gave him a glimmer of excitement that he wouldn't have to wait a century before he could have some vampiric pull.

If he wanted to be like Enzo. A monster. The glimmer fizzled out.

"His super power is that he's a sick and twisted arsehole." Lyla rubbed her hand across her cheek and pulled her sweatshirt's hood over her head as she looked out the window. "How many regular humans have you heard of, or really, how many have you met that are nothing more than pure evil? He's not the only one out there. Billions of people in the world and evil just keeps spreading. None of them know how to stop *them*, either, do they? Evil is as is evil does. It's never ending."

Martin stewed over that idea before he answered. "I guess you're right. Although, couldn't the vampires take out all of the evil humans? Even just do the mind washing tricks and make them be better people? Isn't that the least we could do since we eat them?" The idea of helping the world as a vampire made it all seem at least a titch worthwhile. He would have appreciated it when he was human and it would make for a better world for Harper to live in.

"Nope. Not our business." Her expression was steadfast. "Vampires don't live the same way, Martin. We can't start controlling how they choose to. You have to remember that we have members of our community that are more powerful than us. The ones you want to do that. They're not only busy trying to keep us in check, and the ones like Enzo, but what about the more powerful people in the human community. Should they get to decide how you and I live because they can. I'm sure they'd be happy to thin the herd of vamps eating their way through town. Even animals have their own codes to live by. It's not like we're their judge and jury in the end. That's why we don't drain people." She let out another cynical snort. "At least we're not supposed to. I suppose vamps can be just as evil as people. The vamps like that - like Enzo - I stay the hell away from, and the humans with that streak, I just don't eat. Evil tastes like shite."

Martin hadn't tasted many didn't blood types, so he didn't know if that was true or not. It did make sense. One's energy had to materialize in one way or another. As a flavor would make as much sense as their health. Thinking of blood had him whipping his head to Lyla, who sat holding her legs to her chest in the seat beside him. In the confusion, he had completely forgotten what Enzo had said.

"When was the last time you talked to Jake?" He pressed on when Lyla merely shrugged. "Enzo had something that makes me worried he may have gotten himself into trouble."

She reached into the bag slung across her chest and pulled out her phone to tap through until she was dialing his number. "He knows better than to not pick up for me."

Martin could overhear the continuous rings until he was finally relieved to hear Jake's voice on the other end of the call. His stoned vibrato called out.

"Hey buds, you know what to do."

A loud beep followed. It was the answering machine. Lyla redialed and the same message repeated.

"Feck! Jake, call me back NOW!" Lyla shouted into her phone and tossed it up onto the dash with frustration. Her force left a small crack in the windshield before it landed with a thud.

"Do you think Enzo may have done something to him?" Martin knew the answer. He did not want to be the one to speak it.

"I knew that fecker would get himself in too deep." She punched her fist into the center console of the car, cracking it down the middle. "If anything happened to him, it's all my fault," she whimpered through gritted teeth, her head gripped in her hands. "I just can't stop messing up! This is all my fault."

Martin's still heart broke for her, even though he was one of the missteps she had made. When it came down to it,

Lyla wanted the best for everyone. She just couldn't find her footing, even after all her time as an immortal.

"No, it's not. If anyone, I'm sure Chance Beaumont is the one who got him involved. He's the cokehead owner of the store and the one Enzo was pissed at tonight. He'd sell his grandmother for a buck and speaking of which, let's not forget about Enzo. That guy is to blame for all of it. Not you." He prayed Lyla's phone would ring and Jake's clueless voice would fill the car.

Lyla turned to him, her head tilted with gratitude until the slight smile slipped from her face. "Did you say that guy is into coke? As in cocaine?"

"Yeah, he's a real piece of work. Spent almost all of his daddy's money in the first year he took over." Martin looked quizzically at Lyla, who sat motionless except for her jaw that slowly dropped. "What?"

"Remember what I was like when I drank blood that had beer in it?" She slowly blinked, waiting for him to answer.

Martin thought back to her tipsy behavior. "Yeah, you were…" He instantly understood her concern.

"If Enzo is drinking from someone high on cocaine, that means his already unbalanced mind is as high as a kite! High as the damn moon!"

Martin dragged his palms over his face to the back of his head and gripped his hair, willing himself to not flip out. This guy just got worse and worse. He started the car, wanting to get as far a way as he could. There was nowhere to go. Regardless of that, they would have to decide on somewhere before sunrise or his sedan would quickly turn into a vampire air fryer.

"Maybe he didn't follow us. He seemed pretty focused on Chance. We're just two lowly baby vampires. If he is high, maybe he forgot about us and went back into the store. I think he was just wanted us gone." As fast as vampires could move, there was no way that he hadn't caught up with them yet. High on cocaine, he would probably be even faster. Martin came up with as many reasons as he could as to why Enzo had already forgotten about them until his nerves began to calm. He was a problem, but one for another day. Getting to safety before sunrise and under the same roof as his family were the things to focus on. He was Chance's problem, not theirs. There was no reason for him to give a damn about them.

Lyla broke the comforting silence of their thoughts when she turned to face him in her seat. "His name isn't even Enzo, you know? That's just the name he took on even before he was turned. The fecking guy's name is Kyle. Can you believe that? Fecking Kyle. My friend who went to school with him said he was just this dorky kid who was fifteen before he switched from Velcro shoes to shoelaces. Fecking *Kyle*!"

Martin choked out a laugh, which surprised him. It did make him a lot less intimidating picturing him in his tough guy leather duster jacket trying to make bunny ears with his laces.

"Fecking cokehead Kyle." Lyla exclaimed. She pressed a tight smile and nodded when he laughed again.

"You should never underestimate the nerdy kids, I guess. Most of them turn out to be geniuses or su-pervillains," he acknowledged, looking toward the road. "Where do you think we should go? We can't stay here forever."

Their hands went up over their heads and they shrieked in unison when the rear windshield's glass shattered forward and covered them in tiny, sparking bits.

Enzo was wickedly smiling in the rearview mirror until Martin slammed the car into reverse. The front of the car lifted when it didn't totally clear the attacker, and they watched him tuck up into a screaming ball as they tore out of the parking lot.

They both left a trail of expletives in their wake as they tried to put as much distance between themselves and Enzo as they could.

"Do you think we killed him?" Martin shouted with desperate hope.

"You ran over his leg, Marty. Even without the drugs, that's not going to stop him."

The roads had become empty, giving him a chance to race faster to an unknown destination. A blur behind them bumped the top of the trunk and Enzo's face appeared in a mist. The same thirsty smile twisted on his lips.

"Dammit! Drive, Marty!" Lyla demanded, as if he were driving slower than he could. The blur of the vampire moved to their right and up along the passenger side. Lyla slammed the lock down as if that would have any defense against the invasion.

Enzo stilled, all but his long jacket whipping in the wind, and was in full focus when he grabbed onto the side-view mirror, jockeying his legs up to kick in the window that protected her. One swift kick and the glass shattered across the front seats.

His hand grabbed at Lyla, missing her arm and snaking instead around the loose strap of her bag, causing him to slip further from the door in mid air. A wail cracked out into the dark sky when Martin swerved the wheel, forcing the car to slam Enzo into the broadside of one of the sky high oaks that were whizzing by. The shadow of his body tumbling into the ditch darkened their mirrors.

"Thanks," Lyla sputtered.

"Where are we going? We can't go to my house. Where's yours?" Martin looked from the road to her and back, expecting her to answer quickly.

"We can't go there either," she mumbled, her eyes on the side mirror.

"What do you mean, we can't go there? Is because it's a vampire's house? He can get in?" Martin had a very low tolerance for the eternal argument she was struggling with. "I'm running out of gas here, Lyla. We need somewhere to go! Can we go to Owen's?"

"NO!" she yelled louder than needed.

"Why? You have to know somewhere we can go?" Martin struggled to keep the wheel straight as he looked obsessively in his mirrors.

A flash in the rearview caught his eye and they could see that Enzo was again on their tail, albeit slightly slower than he had been.

"Oh, shite! That's some good coke!" Lyla exclaimed and sat forward in her seat looking from side to side at their location, which was quickly changing by the second. "Here! The next left, turn there," she directed.

The tires squealed as he barely made the turn. "Where now?" He banged his palm on the wheel when he saw the shape of Enzo following them down the blackened dirt road.

"Watch it! We need to keep some of this car in one piece!" Lyla blurted, pointing to the steeling wheel.

Martin had hit the same spot he had out of frustration in the Cluck Hut parking lot, bending it even further in.

He worried as the street became more and more narrow. "Where are we going?" The lights of the sedan did little to brighten the brush lined road as they bumped along at top speed.

"Keep going straight. We're going to my place." Her head bumped the roof when Martin hit an especially wide dip in the road.

The few minutes felt like hours before a building appeared to rise up into the moonlight at the end of the road. As they approached, he could make out the shape of a large barn.

"Where do I go from here?" He slowed the car just slightly.

"No! Keep going, don't slow down!" She flashed her attention back and forth between the quickly approaching barn and the psychopath who had no signs of stopping.

"How do we get in?" He slowed further until Lyla smacked his arm, pointing at the side of the barn that was now only a few yards away.

"Floor it Marty! We're going through!" She pointed to the barn wall, bobbing her head with encouragement, her face tight, and braced for the impact.

There was a good chance they were just going to leave themselves in pieces for Enzo to pick at.

"What are you crazy?" he yelped.

There wasn't time to get into that weighted question, nor was there time to change direction. He pushed the peddle to floor again and pushed back on the twisted steering wheel just before the car splintered the wood around them into an explosion of old timber.

When the vehicle came to a stop, he could see they had landed within a space set up as a home, mere feet from a bright green velvet couch. A woman with short blonde curls, dressed in cozy sweats, jumped up from her seat, startled to her core at the sight of them. She squinted her eyes through the dust that plumed around them until a look of recognition and then annoyance settled in her deep brown eyes.

"Dammit, Lyla! Again?" she fumed. "You've got to be kidding me!"

"Yeah, yeah, I'll apologize later," she interjected, climbing quickly through the passenger side window. "Right now, we need to move!"

Martin followed her lead and jumped from the vehicle, sprinting further into the barn's living room.

Enzo had arrived and was standing at the edge of the building, unable to cross through the wide hole they had made. The string of twinkle lights that now hung loose from the barn's roof glimmered on his fangs when he yowled with frustration.

"What have you gotten yourself into now?" The young woman gestured around at the massive damage they had just caused. Martin could see she had been in the middle of a chef competition show that still blared from the now rubble covered tv, when they had unceremoniously arrived.

When the woman stepped forward to get a better look at the raging vampire, Martin reached out to stop her, only to have his hand shaken away. She planted her feet aggressively and crossed her arms when the dust settled enough to see Enzo clearly.

"Oh hell, no! Is that fucking Kyle?"

Lyla stepped to her side, the security of the barn now calming her voice. "Yeah, sorry, babe. It's fecking Kyle again."

Chapter Thirteen

Barns, bobbles, truths, and troubles.

No matter how surprised the woman was with Martin's car now sitting in her living room, she seemed to know how to handle Enzo stalking them along the gaping hole in her house.

"Dark room, Lyla. Now!" she ordered, heading toward a large power switch on the wall.

Lyla grabbed him by the arm and raced to a dry walled structure that stood awkwardly in the middle of the barn. Whipping open a heavy metal door, she shoved Martin inside just as a burn creeped up his back, scorching the skin under his shirt. He shielded his face against a bright light that threatened to melt his eyes until the door slammed shut behind them, locking them in a blackened space of about six by six feet.

"What the hell is going on, Lyla?" Martin demanded, stretching his back to relieve the tightness that had overcome his skin. "Who is that? Where the hell are we?"

The space reminded him of where he thought he was the day after he was lucky enough to meet her. Although it was warmer and it smelled of vanilla. He was more worried about what lay outside of their little box.

Lyla slid her lids closed against the barrage of questions. "Give me a minute, Marty." She pressed her head against the wall, listening. Apparently, she had the same worries.

A high-pitched wail crackled in the air outside of their shelter.

Martin covered his ears until it stopped. "A minute? Are you kidding me? What the hell is going on?"

Death was officially too eventful.

"All clear," the woman on the other side of the door called and gave it a knock.

Lyla opened it quickly and rushed toward the hole in the barn's wall, looking out into the moonlit woods around them. The space was now only lit by the strings of twinkle bulbs and the television still showing the cooking competition that now turned his stomach if he focused on the screen. There was no sign of Enzo pacing about outside or whatever had set the barn ablaze with intense white light.. Now that he could get a better look at the space, he could see that all the walls, not just the strange windowless room, were dry walled and painted in a soft beige. The dust from the damage covered the squished front end of his car and splayed out into the room. The décor of the building was soft and homey, not what he would have expected inside a broken down looking barn in the middle of nowhere.

"The UVs take care of him?" Lyla asked the woman.

"In less than a second. He booked it pretty fast after it hit his face full on. I doubt he'll be back tonight." She looked over Lyla's shoulder.

"Thanks, Laine." She looked bashful when she moved to kiss her cheek. The woman seemed familiar enough with her to lean in for it. "Sorry about the wall. I'll have it fixed ASAP."

She frowned at Lyla with narrowed eyes. "You bet your ass you will. It better be fixed by tomorrow. I don't want critters making a home in here again."

Martin looked over the damage to his car. It didn't look like it was about to get them anywhere in the shape that it was in. He hoped that wherever they were, they would be safe until they could find a way back into town. "Lyla, where are we?" he asked, wondering if he'd make it home before sunrise.

"This is my safe house," Lyla answered, picking up a piece of barn board that had landed on the dining table.

"Excuse you? Uh-uh, Ly! This is my house, not some vamp hidey-hole." The young woman picked up a piece of timber and tossed it in a pile that had been made beside the car, and wiped a hand on her track pants.

"Sorry, it's Lainey's house, but I have it rigged up as a safe house," she corrected herself. It wasn't enough for the woman's liking and she stared back at Lyla with a perfectly groomed brow tipped up. "What? It is."

"I said you could do the UV lights and such to keep you safe, not to be used as a safe house for you and your vamper friends to hide out in every time you get yourself into trouble." She tossed another board. "Preventative, babe. Not a backup for the shit you get into. Shit you said you were done with."

Lyla gave her a shy smile. They shared a quick, silent conversation with their eyes. "You're right. I'm sorry."

The woman she called Lainey saw something in her face that was enough to soften her edges.

Martin stood silently, wanting to scream.

Even though it felt wrong to interrupt their apologetic moment, he couldn't help interjecting himself.

"Lyla, I thought you said I couldn't go into someone's house without an invitation." He wondered if it being a barn made a difference. It was nicer than his own house, so that made little sense to him.

Like everything else in the damned world, anymore.

"I was invited in a long time ago," Lyla answered, putting her attention back to the wreck of a room.

He retraced their unannounced entrance with his eyes. "But she didn't invite me in. How am I able to be in here and Enzo couldn't?"

"I guess because we share blood." She looked in the passenger window, pushing some of the broken glass onto the floor of the car.

That answer was not reassuring. "You *guess?* You didn't know if I would be able to pass through? What could have happened to me?"

"You're fine, Marty. It all worked out. Can we deal with the problems that we have instead of ones that we don't?" She turned her attention back to the damage to the house.

If he hadn't been able to enter when they hit that wall, he could only image what would have happened to him with the momentum of the car.

Smooshed was the word that came to mind.

Since he was still in one piece, he decided to come at Lyla about that possibility later. She was right. They needed to sort out their current crisis. Nadine and Harper alone in the house was enough stress to add to the mess of being chased by a psychotic, drug-fueled vampire. Their ghostie roomie wouldn't be able to offer much in the ways of security if he couldn't make it home before the sun. Nadine would worry herself silly if he wasn't there when she woke. Especially if he was dead to the world and unable to answer his phone. He jumped out of his thoughts when the woman shouted.

"Why is Kyle creeping around my house again? I thought you stopped messing with him a long time ago."

"I swear it's not my fault this time. I was just going to see this guy," she pointed to a shaken Martin, "and that freak was there. He started chasing us and we didn't know where to go. Marty's got a wife and kid at his place, and it's not like it's done with the traps we have here. Where else is there?"

Lainey looked at Martin, who stared back at back at them, his foot anxiously tapping at a speed that caused it to blur. "So, you're Martin, huh?" She looked him up and down and then turned a stink eye to Lyla. "You gonna introduce me?"

"Sorry, Lainey, this is Martin. Martin, Lainey." Lyla tensed with a knowing of what was about to be said.

Lainey held out her hand, and Martin shook with trepidation. "The famous Martin. The one worthy of being turned," she replied bitterly. "I didn't know if I'd ever get to meet you."

A warm palm and audible heart beat confirmed to Martin that she was human. He nodded with an attempt at a friendly grin, unsure of what he should say, or who she really was.

"Please don't start with that right now. Enzo is—" Lyla stopped when Lainey interrupted.

"Kyle, Ly. His name is Kyle. Stop making it seem like he's some all-powerful creature of the night." Lainey scratched a manicured nail to her curls, surveying the destruction to her home.

It was baby vamps who had caused that, after all; not Enzo. He could see why she was more concerned with Lyla than him in that minute.

"Yeah, well, *Kyle* is all hopped up on coke blood and has been eating his way through Marty's job. I've done my best to hide from him, but I never expected to come face to face with him in the Beaumont's parking lot! I didn't even know he came back to town!"

"Are you serious?" Lainey lost the frustration in her voice and tensed with concern.

"As serious as a heart attack. I wouldn't have come here if we had any other option, but I'm pretty sure he's still wanting to kill me. I honestly have no idea when he got back in town or I would have done something about it." Lyla nibbled at her fingernail, waiting for a reply.

Martin stared back wide-eyed at the women. Enzo wanted to kill Lyla? What could she have gotten herself into? Thinking the freak had been chasing him for eavesdropping, he should have known it was Lyla that he was after.

Lainey's face flattened with the seriousness of what she said, her jaw flexing as she reeled in her composure. "Call Owen."

"No, I'm not calling him. I can handle this," Lyla grumbled, digging in her heel like a child.

"Lyla, call Owen," she repeated, with one hand on her hip and the other holding a chunk of her wall.

"No, I don't need to call him." Lyla picked up the mess again, not setting her eyes on anyone. "I can figure this out on my own. He's still pissed about me and you, let alone him," she directed her thumb toward Martin. "He'll think I'm pulling the scams again." She looked up to find Lainey look at her with angry questions in her eyes. "I'm not! I swear! I already promised you I wasn't."

Lainey took a heavy step forward. "You need to call Owen, Lyla. Kyle is dangerous enough without drugs pumping him up. You're putting us all in danger if you don't have Owen take care of him. You said Martin has a kid, Ly. Come on."

"It's not that easy. It's not like a vampire can just be arrested by some secret supernatural police force, Laine. You know that. If he gets looked at, I get looked at, and Owen said after Martin to lie low and keep my nose clean." Lyla's eyes reddened with burgeoning tears. "And I was! I've been doing my best, but it's just never enough." She looked down hopelessly at the lack of progress they were making to the mess and pulled a chair from the table to slam herself down on, resting her face in her hands.

Lainey crossed the room to kneel in front of her. "I hate when you talk about yourself like that. You know you're more than enough." She set a gentle hand on her knee.

Lyla smeared blood under her eyes when she dragged the back of her hands against the tears. "I'm sorry I brought you more trouble. I've been trying so hard to live right for you, but I can't seem to do it."

"I know, sweetheart. I know," Lainey gave her leg a squeeze and sighed. "Your cute little ass is dead, though, so that's harder than it sounds."

Lyla snorted a laugh and rubbed at her eyes again. "Love you, Laine." She leaned down and gave her a tender kiss.

It was clear to Martin that Lainey was far more than just a friend. In the world of chaos in which they found themselves, the sweet moment settled over the room like a sedative.

"Love you too, Toofy," she teased and stood from her. "Now, I'm just going to say it one more time and then I'll drop it. Call Owen."

Lyla looked at her fingers, that were tangling together on her lap. "I'll fix this, I promise."

"Kyle is nothing but trouble," Lainey spat and kicked at the pile of broken wall. She blew a long breath that seemed to deflate her and pulled a cell from the front pouch of her sweatshirt. "I'm gonna make a couple of calls and see if I can get this fixed sooner rather than later, and you figure out where we can go in the meantime." She walked to the other side of the barn, leaving the two alone with the mess.

Martin didn't know what to say to Lyla. He had never seen her looking so defeated.

She wiped a hand under her nose and the back of her sleeve over her face until it was nearly clear of the crimson streaks. "Soooo, that's my girlfriend, Lainey." She huffed a quick laugh and stepped away from the chair. "I've been meaning to introduce you."

Martin smiled. "She seems great." He looked over at her and could hear her speaking another language to whoever was on the other end of the phone call. "She's French?" he guessed by what he could understand. She hadn't had an accent.

"No, just insanely smart. She speaks, like, six languages and has about a million degrees." She dug in her bag and pulled out a tissue. "I don't know what she sees in me, but I'm not about to ask."

Not knowing how to reply to that, he decided to pivot. "What did she mean about the trouble you were in? How well do you know Enzo?" It was time to know exactly how deep their situation has taken them.

She ran a hand through her dark hair and shook out the dust that had settled in it. "It's not that I know Enzo well.

I never did business with him, just some people we know in common. Petty shite. Just to keep some money coming in. I'd knick something here or there and pawn it."

"What about that would make Enzo want to kill you?" None of it made sense. Which was the only thing that made sense since nothing did anymore.

Lyla kept her eyes to the floor. "Well, I happened to take something that I didn't know was his and I haven't been able to get it back. Some old amulet crap that he thinks belonged to Vlad, the old stabby guy."

He thought for a blink before he replied. "Vlad *the Impaler?*" Martin blurted.

"Yeah, that's the one. It's totally not. Not nearly old enough, but his goth-arse was convinced by someone that it was, and he wants it back." She rolled her eyes dramatically.

Martin didn't care if it was a prize from a gumball machine or the crown jewels. Its worth was currently their lives. "Can you get it back?"

"That's the thing. When I brought it to my guy, he told me it was early twentieth century at the oldest and was only good for the gold bits in it." Martin didn't like where that was headed. "So, he melted it down, and I took the money." *Ah, crap.* "I knew he was nuts, but I didn't think he would want to kill someone over a bobble."

"Do you think you could find another one?" If it wasn't old and nothing expensive, there was a chance they could find a duplicate.

"I've looked, but haven't come up with anything. I've searched online, I've checked other pawn shops. Nothing." She dug around in her bag, not pulling anything out.

"So that's the scams you were getting into? Stealing and pawning things?" he asked, and she bobbed her head in reply, keeping her attention on her bag. Her lack of focus on him became irritating. "Why?"

"Why?" she snorted. "The same reason you're still at your crap job, Marty. I need money for things. I may not have a mortgage like you do, but I need things in life, too."

"Like paying Jake fifty bucks a person for your snack?" he scoffed.

That got her attention. "What?"

"The fifty bucks you give to Jake every time he brings you someone to make a meal out of." He grit his teeth when she laughed at him. Being sold like an appetizer wasn't a laughing matter to him.

"I don't really give him the money," she said, looking him in the eye. "I just tell him I do."

"Jake's a moron, but he's not dumb enough to believe that." Knowing he may never see the goofball again, he regretted the name calling as soon as it crossed his tongue.

"Don't I know it?" she attested. "That's why I've been using him to work on my hypnosis abilities. They've slowly been getting stronger and his cooked brain is perfect to practice on. I just tell him I'm giving him money and he walks away believing it. He's a fecking empty sack between his ears. The meals he brings me are just the blood icing on the blood cake." She laughed long enough to get a stare from Lainey from across the room. "It's part of my plan to give up the out-right stealing and such. Hypnotizing folks isn't much better than stealing, but it's more in line with how vampires survive and has been since the beginning. Our laws and the laws of man are very different, as I'm sure you can understand."

He did. He was using Jake as well. The guy chose to deal with the underworld of vampires, so there was bound to be some blow back on him, but he had been using him as a snack and justifying it to himself. He really wished he knew what had happened to him, and he could tell that Lyla was sharing the thought when her laughter stopped and sadness clouded her.

"Do you think he's okay? Jake, I mean." Martin could hear his smoky laugh as if he were in the room with them.

"Honestly, no," Lyla answered, barely above a whisper.

Martin knew that would be her answer, yet hoped he was wrong. He could only shake his head in reply.

"So, what are we going to do? Do you think he's going to come back? We have a few hours before sunrise." He knew they needed to decide their next move before they both dropped dead for the day.

"Well, we can't stay here. Enzo has bought off enough people in the past that we would all be sitting ducks with that hole in the wall."

"My house is a no go, too. There's no way that Chance wouldn't tell him everything about me if it could buy himself some time." He would do that in a heartbeat.

Martin felt the pressure of that realization suddenly push upon him like his car had that barn. "What if he does go to my house? Oh, my God. Lyla, what if he has someone that can get in and hurt them?" He wanted to say because of you and swallowed the words. Blame and finger pointing would keep no one safe.

"I hadn't thought of that," Lyla admitted and started for Lainey. "Hang up! Is there gas in the van?"

Lainey advised in english that she would call back whomever she was chatting with and dropped the phone from her ear. "Of course, but where did you want to go?"

"We obviously can't stay here and Marty's wife and kid are alone in his house." There was no reason to explain the crisis any further. Lainey's face dropped.

"*Fuuuuck*," she acknowledged, drawing out the word. "How about Owen? Did you send out your feelers to him?"

Martin assumed she meant the same way that Lyla had sensed him and hoped she had. They definitely needed someone older and more experienced to take over.

"I will, I promise. Right now, we need somewhere safe to go where he can meet us."

The trio looked back and forth between each other. Martin hoped they would come up with something fast or he was going to find that van and make tracks home on his own.

"He knows everywhere I can go. What about Suze? Is she in town?" Lyla inquired, optimism lighting her up.

"No, I told you, she sold her place. She's just as sick of this place as we are," Lainey sighed, wringing her hands.

"Yeah, I don't blame her. Not the vacation town it used to be." Lyla kicked at a broken board on the floor. "I don't know of anyone else."

Martin's spirit rose. "We just need a house that isn't owned by a vampire and have someone to invite us in, right?" He had the perfect place!

"Yeah," they both agreed in unison, anticipation straightening their spines.

"My mother-in-law just bought a beach house and my wife has a key! She's on the deed!" He nearly bounced in place. Jeanne's spoiling of his daughter was about to finally pay off.

He was going to get his family, no matter what. He wasn't about to leave them on their own. This way, they could hide out, just outside of town, in a place that there was no way anyone would know about. They could buy themselves some time until Lyla got her sire involved. Based on how she spoke of the power of the elders, that had to be all they would need to take care of Enzo. It was all over a stolen trinket, after all.

"How far away is it?" Lyla asked, sprinting to the fridge.

"About forty-five minutes from my house. It will be cutting it close with the sun, but we should make it. We just need to stop and get them first." The most important thing to Martin was to have Nadine and Harper with him so he could know they were safe. Everything else would work itself out. He had to believe that, if nothing else.

Lainey grabbed a set of keys from a hook on one of the three walls still intact and Lyla snatched two black bottles from the fridge. He recognized them immediately as being like the one she had given him that fateful night in his bedroom.

"Here, drink this," she ordered, tossing him one. "It's loaded with caffeine and will give us a kick in the arse when the sun starts on us."

He looked at the bottle, keeping in step with them when they as they dashed to a rear door. "We can go in the sun?" If she had been keeping a miracle drink from him, he would lose it.

"No, not unless we want to be barbecued. This will just keep us awake a little longer."

The paint-chipped white cargo van that sat behind the barn answered his next question. There was a blackout tint on the front windows, and no others in the rest of the body. It was more or less a coffin on wheels that would transport them to the beach that day.

Lyla signaled for him to join her in the back, and Lainey hopped behind the wheel.

Settling himself on the bare metal floor of the van, he shouted the directions to his house to Lainey and prayed that Lyla was somehow getting in contact with her sire. Gulping down the ice-cold blood, he fought to keep it in his stomach when it churned against the chilled taste.

The only thing left to do was to find a way to tell Nadine what was happening.

To tell her that her husband was a vampire.

Who was now on the run for his life.

Easy-peasy.

Chapter Fourteen

Bat out of Hell.

THE ROAD SLIPPED ALONG below them as the van careened toward Martin's house. He had no idea what he could say to get Nadine to go with them in the middle of the night. Just setting eyes and them and knowing they were in one piece was all he could think about. The van had barely stopped in the driveway when he was out the rear door and racing to his house. The two tandem heartbeats that greeted him did little to slow him down.

"Whoa, where's the fire?" Dan asked as Martin nearly ran clear through him and straight up the stairs.

Peeking in Harper's room, he could see her sleeping peacefully. Dan, who floated along behind him, was asking a flood of questions that Martin ignored and rushed to his wife's side.

"Nadine. Nadine, wake up," he urged, compelling himself not to shake her awake, knowing he could not control his new strength, as upset as he was.

"What's wrong? What's going on?" Her eyes struggled to open against the deep sleep she had been in. "What time is it?" She reached for her phone, plugged in on the nightstand.

"We need to go. We don't have time for me to explain, but we have to go." He tried to help her sit up, wanting to grab her and throw her over his shoulder. That would do nothing but freak her out. There were going to be enough things that shook her to her core. He didn't need to add to it all.

"What in the world are you talking about?" Her eyes started to awaken to the room around her. "What is it? Is it a fire?" She leapt from bed and headed for Harper with Dan, unknowingly to her, and Martin on her heel.

"No, it's not a fire. We just need to go. I'll explain in the van." Martin made every attempt to keep his voice calm.

Nadine stopped with her hand on her daughter's door. "Van?" She was now fully awake and unimpressed at being awoken in such a way. "What are you talking about? What van?"

The knob twisted in her hand and the door slid open, revealing a slumberous Harper squinting against the hall light. "What's going on?" she asked, looking between the three.

"Daddy has a surprise for you guys, Giggles. Grab your bear-bear. I'm taking you there now." A wide, forced smile was plastered on his face.

"We're not going anywhere. It's the middle of the night!" Nadine exclaimed.

Dan moved his face in front of Martin's view. "Have you lost your mind, Martin? What's wrong?"

"Not now," Martin huffed to him.

"You're damn right not now," Nadine barked. "We're going back to bed."

Martin growled with frustration. "No, not you," he replied. As far as Nadine could see, he was fighting with her and a voice in his head.

"Not me?" She was officially past confused and had settled comfortably in pissed off. "What is wrong with you?"

A furious glare to Dan had him evaporating beside them with a quizzical frown. There was no threat to him from the psycho, so he would rather he be upset with him again than hinder getting his family on the road.

Harper was turned around by her mother and ushered back to bed. Martin was grabbing at her blankets before they could settle on her tiny body.

"Have you lost your ever-loving mind, Martin?" Nadine spat through gritted teeth. She tried to grab the blanket from him and found his grip too strong to budge.

"I know I sound insane. I need you to just trust me and come with me, okay?" he pleaded with her. "Trust me. We need to go now." He pulled a sweatshirt from Harper's closet and tugged it over her head to cover her pajamas before he swept her up in his arms and down the stairs to the kitchen.

Nadine followed, taking in the seriousness of his eyes as he passed and looked down at her flannel pants and oversized t-shirt. "Can I at least change first?" Her annoyance gave way to unease.

"No time for that. You're dressed fine for where we're going." He took her hand before she could have a second thought of it all and tugged her along down the stairs.

Throwing open the drawer, he grabbed the key ring that Jeanne had given her, shoving the keys to the beach house in his pocket.

"The beach? Seriously, Martin? What is this?"

He grabbed her hand and headed for the door; not slowing a step when she tugged a jacket from the coat rack as he stepped out onto the porch.

Seeing the van with its blacked-out windows, she went stiff as a board. "What in the world is that?" she gasped. "I'm not getting in that!" She reached for Harper, trying to get her from his arms.

Before she could get a hand on her daughter, a blur circled them, whisking Nadine up as if a tiny tornado had appeared on their porch. Martin followed, hopping in the back of the van with Harper in his arms and Nadine in Lyla's.

"Head south on nine toward the beach and I'll get you better directions when we're closer," Martin yelled up to Lainey as she threw the van in reverse. He settled on the floor of the van; Nadine and Harper across from him, Lyla to his side.

Shock locked Nadine in place, her arms now around her daughter, whose own look of amusement was the polar opposite of her mother's.

"Wow! How cool was that, mommy?" she cheered, looking up at her frozen mother. "Zoom! Zoom!" She spun her hand in front of her.

It appeared as if Nadine's brain had officially been broken by what had just happened until she began to tremble. "Martin. What the hell is going on?" Her voice vibrated in time with her body, her eyes not leaving Lyla and her arms tightening on Harper. Martin and Lyla listed toward them when Lainey took a corner a little swiftly. The terrified woman pulled her daughter back away from them further.

The look of fear that his wife had set on him broke his heart. He knew he couldn't keep his secret forever. It would have been nice to have time to come up with a better way to show her what he now was. At least give her some wine and flowers before dropping the bomb that her husband was now a blood-sucking creature of the night.

"Okay, sweetheart. I need you to listen to me, and more than anything, I need you to believe what I'm about to tell you," he started quietly and slowly. Nadine regarded him with distrust. He held up a hand when she tried to speak. "I need to just get this out and over with."

She sat back against the van's cold metal wall; her entertained daughter wrapped steadfastly in her arms and narrowed her gaze at her husband, waiting for whatever he was about to spill out.

"We're vampires," Lyla said flatly and dropped down her fangs with a grin.

Nadine screamed bloody murder, her mouth wide enough to nearly dislocate her jaw, as her daughter's face lit up, clapping at the trick she had witnessed.

"Lyla!" both Martin and Lainey bellowed.

What in the world was he going to do with her? It was as if she was unable to do anything with a gentle stroke.

"What? Rip the band-aid off, mate. Just like I did with you?" She looked back at him with a look of bewilderment at his anger.

Nadine continued to scream, pushing herself against the wall as she could press through to freedom.

"Sweetheart, it's alright. Calm down, you're safe," Martin attempted to coo her into a more placid state. She was hearing nothing he said. "Lyla, can you hypnotize her or something? A little help would be appreciated!"

Harper shifted in her mother's arms, the happiness on her face turning to worried fear of her reaction. "Mommy, don't be upset. Daddy's just like *Veromika* now. Don't be scared." She twisted her little body in her mother's arms to wrap hers around her. "Please don't be upset."

The sweet actions of her daughter seemed to set her back into mama bear mode and she pulled herself together as best as she could, panting from the excitement. The rush of adrenaline had her heart racing. Before he could stop himself, Martin's fangs dropped, and he slapped a hand over his mouth to conceal them.

Nadine's eyes widened to the point Martin was sure they would fall out of her head.

"It's true," he mumbled through his palm. "I'm so sorry I didn't tell you, but it's not a simple thing to bring up."

The van sped up as it merged onto the highway, bumping them along in the back.

"You're serious?" Nadine asked, still trembling from head to toe. "You can't be serious! Vampires aren't real!"

"I can assure you they are," Lainey called out from the driver's seat. "Real and nothing but trouble, if you ask me."

"Not helping Laine," Lyla grumbled.

"And you announcing it like that is?" Lainey turned to glare at Lyla before looking back at the road and jerking the wheel when a car's horned blared beside them.

"We have bigger fish to fry than one scared woman, Laine. This is an undead or dead situation. You know who we're running–" she stopped and swung her head to Martin when he grabbed her shoulder.

"Please, Lyla! Just stop fucking talking. Please!" If she made one more declaration of danger, he was sure that would be the end of his wife. Things were going from bad to utter disaster with every passing second. The caffeine in the blood had made his body buzz, and the jitters were not helping.

Lyla's mouth pouted down at his outburst, and she pulled her knees up to her chest, miming a zipper on her lips.

Nadine had paled to the point that she now shared a complexion with Dan. She stared at his fangs that framed his mouth as he spoke. He could hear her heart rate increase to a level that he was sure he would be able to hear it even without his vampiric ears.

Attempting to take Harper from her smothering arms only made her breathing shorter and more shallow. Martin was sure he was giving his wife a heart attack. His panic grew along with hers until Harper's lip quivered with upset and she whimpered.

"You guys need to chill the hell out," Lainey demanded. "You're scaring the life out of that poor child."

As if the air around him had slapped him cold across the face, Martin snapped out of his own fit of hysteria and turned to Lyla, who remained silent at his side.

"You said you've been practicing the hypnotizing thing. Please do something," he begged her. If Nadine stayed in such a state of shock, he was sure she would keel over before their eyes. "Just try, dammit!"

"I don't know if it will work. I haven't had a lot of success and I'm sure her mind is stronger than a stoners." She moved to sit on her knees, slightly closer to Nadine, who had spiraled into a dangerous level of hyperventilating, still trying to hold on to her daughter. "What if I melt her brain or something?"

That comment had Nadine attempting to pull her daughter toward the front cab of the van.

"Try!" Martin insisted. He would not let anything happen to his wife. Not after all he had been through to stay alive in his own way, to stay with her.

Lyla leaned forward, stopping Nadine in place. She gave her body a shake to psych herself up before she began. Her words were nearly silent when she moved closer, her eyes soft and unfocused. "Nadine. Listen to my voice," she purred. "All is well, all is grand, Nadine. You're safe. We're all safe."

When her breathing slowed to a reasonable pace, Martin wanted to sweep her into his arms, but he kept his distance to let Lyla do her work. Even with the chaotic situation they found themselves in, it was fascinating to watch the way Lyla could take his wife's mind under her control and quiet it like a sedative. Nadine's eyes matched the cloudy, dreamlike look that Lyla projected to her.

"Mommy? Are you okay?" Harper asked when her mother's arms went limp around her.

"Mommy is fine, Giggles. She was just upset," Martin said soothingly, his arms out to her. "Come sit with daddy."

She wiped at her nose that had grown damp with her watering eyes and scootched across the van's floor to sit on her father's lap. The distress that had been building within her lessened along with her mother's.

"Where are we going Martin? Am I staying on nine or should I be looking for an exit?" Lainey questioned.

That's when he realized he had no idea what the address was. "I have no idea. She never told me."

"Who? Her?" Lyla asked, pointing at his wife.

"Yeah. I just know it's along the beach. She never told me exactly where." Martin felt foolish that he hadn't thought his plan through far enough to get the damn address.

"Nadine," Lyla started again. "We're going to the beach. Doesn't that sound nice?" Nadine gave a small nod of her head, a contented smile growing. "I need to know where the beach house is, Nadine. Then we can all go and relax. Doesn't that sound nice?"

She bobbed her head again. "It's in Lapis Bay," she slurred.

"Good, that sounds lovely. Now what's the address, love? Tell me the street address," she prompted.

"It's 23 Arcade Way," she smiled. "Right on the beach."

"Did you get that?" Lyla called up to Lainey.

"Got it. Mapping it now," she replied, the van swerving back and forth as she tried to keep up the speed and enter the address into her phone.

"Perfect. Now sleep," she ordered to Nadine who slumped down, her head lolling to the side. Lyla shifted her to a more comfortable position on her side and turned back to Martin. She had a look of pride that she was trying to swallow. He couldn't blame her. It was a really impressive display of skill. Having his wife sleeping peacefully instead of doubling over and dying from fright was an added benefit.

Harper watched her mother, a muffled snore now slipping from her nose, and then to Lyla. "You're magic, aren't you?" she asked her with a sparkle in her eye. Lyla answered with a wink and a finger to her lips.

"Thank you, Lyla. That was a mess." He shook his head and put an arm around his daughter. "Not that I thought she would take it any better."

They all stared at Nadine. The only noise was the van rumbling along the road until Harper piped up. "It's not an arcade, just so you know." She yawned and set her head on her father's lap.

Martin looked down at her. "What do you mean, sweetie?"

Another yawn had her mouth gaping before she began again. "The house at the beach. It's just the name of the street. No games or nothin'." Her eyes drooped as Lyla and Martin quietly chuckled at her disappointed observation.

Soon she had joined her mother in peaceful slumber.

"So, what happens to her now?" Martin nodded to his wife. "Will she just wake up normal and fine with it all?"

"Sure," Lyla asserted and stretched her legs out. She looked to the front window of the van, the signs above whizzing by.

Martin waited for her to elaborate. She didn't.

"Sure? Just like that? It's all good now?" If it was that easy, he could have let her know right from the start. Nothing was that easy.

"Well, to be honest, I don't really know," she admitted and gave him a grimaced frown. "I've never gotten that far with Jake."

He should have known it wouldn't be that simple. Nothing ever was. Closing his eyes, he tilted his head back until it bumped on the side of the van. He bumped it again, harder, and then again, even harder, until Harper mumbled in her sleep from the disturbance.

"At least she's good for now," he acknowledged. One step at a time. "Do you know if Owen knows we're in trouble? Is he going to meet us there?"

The sooner they had help, the better.

"I'm sure he felt something tonight," Lyla snorted. "I haven't been that freaked out in a while."

"So, he knows?" Martin pushed. She was dodging every question he asked.

She remained silent, her attention on her fingernails.

"Ly," Lainey pushed with warning in her voice. "He knows, right?"

"He'll reach out, don't worry."

"Don't worry? Are you kidding me right now, Lyla?" Martin tried to keep his volume in check so as not to disturb his sleeping family. "I'm pretty sure we need him now, not when he can get around to it. Did you tell him how bad it is?"

Being connected to her made him sure that he would be one of Enzo's targets. Which made his family targets. The powerless feeling sunk over him. All he wanted, more than anything, was to keep his family safe. The bumbling duo of baby vampires wasn't the ideal team he would choose to accomplish that task.

"It's not like he reads my mind. He'll know something is wrong and will know where to find me." She chewed roughly on her thumbnail with her fang. "It will be fine."

Martin groaned. "That's the only way you know how to get in touch with him?"

"Yep," Lyla stated as Lainey said no.

"He's not some mystical being in a cloud, Ly," Lainey scoffed. "I know damn well you can call him on the phone. Just as much as you know, that's one of the main reasons I made you get that cell. Call him now! Give him the address and tell him everything that is happening. So, help me, Lyla. I will pull this van over and walk away."

Martin wanted to scream at them both. Instead, his fang dug into his tongue. He was getting mighty sick of one step forward, three clumsy, neck-breaking steps back with the choices they made.

If they were abandoned on the side of the road, with the sun trapping them inside, Nadine and Harper would be without anyone to assist them once he and Lyla fell unconscious for the day. He couldn't believe that Lainey would do that to them. A semblance of relief came when she kept the van racing along the road.

"Please, Lyla. Call him. We need him," he beseeched, looking at his sleepy daughter. "We need help." He wanted to add that it was all her fault. That everything was her fault. All the troubles and danger they all had suffered had been because of one grave decision after another on her part. Again, he pressed his fang into his tongue. Having her shut down would just make things worse. He swallowed the critical words.

Lyla finally looked at him. "I know! You don't think I know that?"

"Then call him!" Martin ordered.

"It's not that easy!" Lyla buried her face in her hands. "He doesn't bloody know about you, okay? I don't know what he'll do when he does."

He felt as if he had been punched in the gut as the world around him slowed. "What does that mean? How can he not know about me?"

"Lyla! You told me you told him," Lainey blustered. "You said it was all sorted. You promised me no more lying!"

"I did tell him about Martin. I just sort of made him think I took care of him." Her face remained hidden from the judgement that filled the van.

"Took care of me?" He knew she didn't mean in a maternal sort of way.

Lyla left the question in the air for a minute before she answered quietly, "I may have implied you were dead."

"Oh, Lyla!" Lainey sighed deeply. "You didn't!" The van rocked as she zipped around the vehicles at top speed.

"It's not completely untrue! It's not like he has a pulse anymore." She raised wounded eyes to him. Yet another line of fire that she had pushed him in front of. "I tried to tell him. He was so mad, and I had been trying so hard to fix all of my feck ups."

She punched the floor of the van, leaving a dent and briefly waking Harper. When she mumbled about bunnies and then started to snore, Martin leveled a rage filled scowl her way, wanting to reach out and smack her silly.

"I'm one of your fuck ups, Lyla!" he hissed. "You haven't fixed much for me!"

Lyla pulled at her braid. "Well, when I could see he didn't have any sort of blood link to you, I lied, okay? If I hadn't, I don't know if he would have killed you himself."

That possibility hung between them. If she asked Owen for help, he would know the truth about Martin. Then they might have two angry vampires coming for them. The white knight of Owen lost its sheen. If he wasn't an option, no one was. There was no one coming to their rescue.

They didn't speak another word until Lainey pulled up to the beach house.

"Okay, I made good time. The sun isn't quite up yet. I'm going to set up a room for you guys. Stay here until I come and get you," Lainey ordered, jumping from the seat. She leaned back over and looked at Martin. "Keys?" He reached into his pocket and threw them to her. "Try not to kill my dumbass of a girlfriend until I get back, please."

They listened as she jingled the lock open, and the door shut behind her. The exhaustion of the night and coming sun wore on them both.

"He's really gonna kill me if he finds out you didn't do it yourself?"

"I don't know," Lyla whispered weakly.

"I thought you were his favorite little vamp?" She had called herself a sort of daddy's girl. If she was, there had to be some sort of consideration for them both.

"I am. That's why he didn't kill me for what I did." She looked up with a smile, saying it as if she had merely scratched his car. The humor that she used to cover up her discomfort was gnawing at his nerves. Court Jester Lyla seemed more in control than spiraling Lyla, so he gave it a pass. If they were on their own, they needed their wits about them.

"What are we going to do, Ly?"

"I'm gonna fix it. I'm gonna call him and I'm going to come clean, and I'll take what I get. He won't hurt you, Marty. Any of you. I won't let him." She looked down lovingly at Harper, who was now scratching at her wiggling nose like a rabbit, drool trickling down onto Martin's khakis. "I promised you only the truth from now on, and half-truths aren't truths at all. I know that now."

With the earnest words, she lowered her face, the weight visible on her shoulders.

A crack of hope returned that Owen may still be a possibility of helping them. Someone, or something, was better than nothing. They waited until Lainey knocked on the rear door and swung it open. The sky was still dim against the faint line of light along the horizon.

Martin passed Harper to Lainey and picked up Nadine's limp, sleeping body. Lyla hopped out and started digging in her bag. He hoped for her cell phone.

Approaching the house, she turned her attention to Nadine who began to stir in Martin's arms. "Can you hold her so her head or her feet are through the door?'

"Are you serious?" It seemed like a silly necessity to gain entrance.

"I don't make the rules, fella." She waited while he stepped as close as an invisible barrier would allow him and held her feet over the threshold. "Nadine? I need you to invite me in. Me and Martin, yeah?"

"Come on in," she mumbled.

It was enough to break the barrier and Martin stumbled forward, nearly dropping his wife.

Worry creased Lyla's face when she went back at her bag to pull out her cell and moved with a flash into the house.

"She's calling him?" Lainey asked as they crossed into the living room.

"I think so." He lay his wife on a long pastel pink sofa that faced the rear of the house. Lainey gently placed Harper beside her and her sleeping arm snaked out and snuggled her daughter.

As he looked around the high-ceilinged room, he found it impressive how palatial it was. Of course, since it belonged to Jeanne, he shouldn't be surprised. Under any other circumstances, he would have kicked his feet up with a drink and enjoyed the view of the white sand beach beyond the broad back deck.

"I have the first room on the left blacked out for you guys," Lainey advised.

And there was reality kicking him in the ass again.

He supposed moonlight in lieu of sunlight would still be a remarkable view. Once they dealt with all of their fellow vampires who wanted them dead.

He checked on Nadine and Harper, giving them each a kiss on the cheek when he found them sleeping peacefully. When she woke up, there was a good chance that she would raise holy hell again, finding themselves another town over, with a stranger, and her husband in the next room, pulseless and side by side with another woman. Not exactly an ideal family getaway.

As if she read his mind, Lainey stepped to his side. "She'll be fine, don't worry." She rested her warm hand on his shoulder. "I'll be able to handle her."

Martin nodded, knowing that no one could handle his wife when she didn't want to be handled. Not that there was much he could do about it. The caffeine in the blood he had chugged wasn't as effective as he had hoped. The buzz of the rush in his veins was already wearing thin and as the sun slowly began to appear for the day, his body grew heavy.

"What are the chances that Enzo will just move on to something else and leave us be?" he asked her. She seemed to know more about him than he did.

"First of all, that little snakes name is *Kyle*. Don't feed into his self made image and give him that power." She took the blanket she had slung over her arm and covered the two on the couch. The gesture touched him.

"Fair enough," Martin replied wearily.

"But, with how he is so erratic, who knows? There's a chance he will. He left Lyla alone for quite a while before he popped up again. Kyle is a piece of work." She pointed to the hallway that led to the dark room she had set up. "He won't be a worry for the rest of the day, so go do your dead to the world thing and we'll deal with what happens when it happens."

"How are you so calm about all of this?" Having known Lyla longer than he had would desensitize her to a certain extent, but she was somewhere beyond that. She seemed to just jump in and deal with whatever was in front of her. Martin already had a great respect for her in the short, insane time since they met.

"You can't help who you love, right? I fell for someone who lives in a crazy, unimaginable, supernatural world. For that love, I make it work." She pointed again toward the bedroom, trying to usher him along before he became a dead weight in the middle of the living room. "I also believe everything happens for a reason. The universe has a plan. Maybe Enzo is here to force Ly's hand about being completely honest about you to Owen, or to bring you to a place that you can some clean to your wife. Honesty, love, and kindness make the world turn, Martin, and the universe takes care of those who mind that."

Martin fought the heavy droop of his eyes as he shuffled his feet in the direction of the room she prepared. "That sounds like an ideal world, doesn't it?"

"Life is as wonderful as you make it, Martin. Never forget that."

Her echoing voice sounded far away as he crossed the threshold to the darkened room. Two twin beds lined the walls with ruffled blue covers and fluffy, thick pillows. The window in between was covered with thick, plastic garbage bags which had been tightly and thoroughly taped to the frame, keeping out all the light from outside. It was not the night that Nadine had described as their first romantic trip to the beach. Not the wonderful life he wanted.

Tossing himself face down onto one bed, he noticed Lyla wasn't in the other. He strained to hear her, hoping she was somewhere safe, and he could barely make out her voice whispering to someone. As the world turned black, he hoped she was talking to Owen.

Chapter Fifteen

Ashes to ashes.

"Marty. Hey, Marty. Wake up," Lyla's voice called out from the darkness.

Opening his eyes, he turned to find her sitting cross-legged on the opposite bed. The pressure of sunlight had left his body, telling him the day was over and the sun had begun its descent into night. He shot up to his feet.

"Did you call him?" he asked while his attention went to the living room. Nadine, Lainey, and Harper's voices sounded at ease while they chatted about what he assumed was a talent show on television that hummed in the background. It was more than he could hope for.

"I did."

Martin sat himself back down, readying himself for what could possibly be devastating news for him. As long as he could protect his family, he didn't care what happened to himself. He had said it over and over again in his mind and it was now more of a fact than that he did not have a heartbeat. His choices and the outcome of those choices had led them all to the predicament they found themselves in. When it came down to it, he had been living on borrowed time since the day Lyla chose not to end him. He leaned forward and locked his eyes on her. "And?"

"He was pretty pissed and ate my head off at first, that's for sure," she said, scrunching up her nose.

Martin didn't know if her light mood was good news or to cover very, very bad news. He braced himself for whatever she shared next.

"In the end I think we're good," she gave a relieved smile, to his surprise. "I think it helps that I called just as he was tucking in for the night. He's always more forgiving when he's too knackered to be angry."

"So, I'm good? He's not going to…," Martin's face rumpled, not wanting to finish the sentence.

"Send you on your way? Give you the big adios?" she snickered, clearly as relieved as he was. "Send ya to the farm?"

He held up his hands in surrender. "Yes, all of that."

The joy in her eyes and the release in her body told him all he needed to know. One chance of death down. Now to sort out the other vampire that wanted them dead and to get on with life.

At that moment, he was more terrified of the conversation he had to have with his wife.

"I just spoke with him again before you woke up," she announced with a grin. "He says he'll help us. Put me a little lower on his list of favorites, but we should be good. Later tonight he should be here and we'll sort out what can be done."

"Any idea of what that is?" he asked, hoping it would be quick, easy, and a way back to their dull, immortal lives, yet knowing it wouldn't be so simple.

"If Enzo is dumb enough to show up while he's here, I know Owen wouldn't think twice about *shunk!*" She dragged her thumb across her neck as she made the sound.

Having something to do with someone's death wasn't a comfortable idea to sit in, even as a blood-sucker. That being said, if it came down to Enzo or those he cared for, it became an easier pill to swallow.

"Any idea how they're doing out there?" He bobbed his head to the living room. "Is Nadine alright?"

That he could hear her having lighthearted conversations was more than he could hope for. The slur in her words told him that Lainey had found Jeanne's stash of expensive French wines, which would be an added touch. As long as it kept her from flipping out, he would move heaven and earth to keep those bottles stocked if he had to.

"I haven't been out there yet. I didn't know if it would be wise before you were up," Lyla admitted, her head tilted to listen to the conversation in the next room.

"Lainey said she's doing fine. Not quite believing it, but the screaming has stopped."

"She's taking it better that I did when I found out, and I'm the one with the fangs," he said with awe to the strength of her.

"Look how cool your daughter is about everything. She's got to get that from someone, and we both know that's not you," Lyla observed.

"Fair enough."

Harper was very excited about a young dancer who had just received the judges' votes. A woman's voice that he didn't recognize answered her. They stood in tandem when they heard her.

"Who the hell is that?" he questioned as he moved to the door. Lyla pulled him back to listen more.

"I have no idea. Is it your mother-in-law?"

They peeked around the corner of the doorway, unable to see the length of the couch. "No, that's not her."

Even with the friendly tone to her voice, it didn't bring him comfort to find a stranger was under their roof. They booked it to the living room and stopped in their tracks when they laid eyes on Harper's new friend.

Sitting on the couch beside her, with one leg tucked under the other and her head resting on her fist, was a woman in full Woodstock-style regalia of bell bottoms and halter top, from what they could see of her translucent body.

"Oh, *Jaysus!* That's a bloody ghost!" Lyla blurted in a hiss. She jumped back behind the wall, leaving just her nose up visible to the room.

Seeing them lurk at the entrance to the living room, Lainey regarded them quizzically and then motioned for them to come in. They walked slowly, side by side, into the room. Nadine and Harper, still in their pajamas from the night before, watched them. It took a second to take his eyes from the phantom stranger and look to his wife, who appeared nervous yet more even-tempered than before Lyla had stepped in earlier. He stole a few glances at the ghostly woman who smiled back at him, not wanting to his attention to linger and alarm Nadine with their newest *WTF* revelation.

"Hi Daddy!" Harper greeted him with an excited grin, jumping from the couch to wrap her arms around his legs.

Nadine started to reach out for her and stopped herself, her eyes on Martin. "Did you have a good sleep?"

"I did, Giggles," he replied, ruffling her hair.

The room stilled, waiting for Nadine's reaction.

"Hi," she whispered.

"Hi," he returned.

Silence again fell. Lyla sat beside Lainey, who slapped a hand over the vamp's mouth when she tried to speak, scolding her with a heated look.

"So, I guess it's not just allergies, huh?" Nadine finally said, her tight frown tipping up into a tiny smirk.

Martin barked a reassured laugh at his forgiving wife's seeming acceptance of some of the most inconceivable news anyone could receive. "No, not allergies."

Nadine swigged the last gulp of her wine and clinked down the glass on the coffee table in front of her. "Well, I'm going to have a pee, grab another bottle of this good stuff, and then we can talk, alright?" She stood, wavering a step from the liquid courage she had imbibed in, and released a tiny burp as she wandered down the hall.

He watched her tip-toe away, not knowing what else to say to her. "Is she really okay with this? Is she still hypnotized?" Martin quizzed the two women as Harper curled back up on the couch with their guest. "And who the hell is that?"

Lainey followed the finger he pointed to the couch, "Who? Your daughter? You good, Martin?"

"She can't see her," Lyla advised with her eyes on the specter.

"See who?" Lainey asked just as realization brightened her expression. "Oh man, there's someone here, isn't there? I knew I felt something."

"What do you mean, you *felt* something?" He didn't like the idea of the ghost being seen by his daughter any less than he liked to the possibility that she may have made Nadine feel something else strange. She had enough on her metaphorical plate dealing with his nonsense.

"She's an ice pack, Daddy!" Harper declared, pointing to Lainey.

Lyla laughed at the bewildered look that sank into Martin's face. "Not an ice pack, ya wee mucker," she managed through her chuckle. "An *empath*. Lainey is an empath."

She pointed down the hall. "One of the reasons that your wifey down there isn't popping her top at all that's been revealed."

"Popping the bottles has helped too," Lainey added, picking up her own glass of wine. "Her mama has great taste in wine."

Martin didn't know what empath meant exactly. He had heard of psychics and the lot. Empath was a new one to him. Since Lyla seemed fine with it, and it was helping Nadine with acceptance, he would save those questions for another day. "Sure, great, but what I want to know is who is that?"

"You know I can hear you, right?" the woman snickered, sliding her fingers along strands of her long, honey-hued hair.

"This is my new friend Agatha, Daddy. Isn't she pretty? I wanna grow my hair that long!" she beamed. Her signature giggle escaped her when the woman dangled a lock in front of her and her small hands passed through without a touch.

"I didn't mean to freak you out, man," she apologized. "People don't normally see me around here. This little chicky was waving out the window at me, so I thought I'd come and say hello and have some company for a little while, you know?"

"So, you don't haunt this house? You can go outside?" Martin wondered aloud. Dan Jack couldn't pass through the exterior walls of their house, but this gal could cruise the beach?

"Haunt? Ah, no, man, I don't haunt anyone. I don't wanna be bothering people. I'm just doing my thing, you know? Like that cat, Emerson, said: Life is a journey, not a destination." She snickered, "Well, my afterlife is."

"A cat said that?" Harper looked up at her with wonder.

"Oh, man. You're too much, little babe," she reached out for her, and when her hand passed through her petite head, she set it behind her on the couch, pushing away a frown that tried to settle on her face.

Lainey's attention bounced between Martin and the empty spot on the couch as if she were watching a high-paced tennis match. "What's it saying?"

"She. *It's* a she," Lyla filled her in. "Name's Agatha and seems like a crunchy hippy type."

"That makes sense. She had a really fun energy," Lainey smiled at the void beside Harper. "Nice to meet you, Agatha. I'm Lainey, this is Lyla. I'm assuming you already know Harper, and this is her dad, Martin."

"Far out, man! You can all see me except her and even she can, like, feel my spirit?" Agatha grinned. "This is wild!" She pointed back and forth between Martin and Lyla. "Even more wild that you guys are, like, actual vampires. That's so heavy, man."

Martin attempted to reply when he heard Nadine's footfalls in the hall moving toward them.

She held up a wine bottle in one hand and a corkscrew in the other when he wandered back to the couch. "I think it's time for us all to have a little chat."

They all turned to a rap on the front door.

"Perfect timing, as always, Owen! He'll be able to answer a lot more questions than I can and we can finally get things sorted." Lyla leapt from her seat and to the door. "Nadine, I'm gonna need your help for one second. I just need you to invite him—" She jumped back as she opened the door.

Enzo stood on the front mat, his grin as slithering as a slug. "That would be very helpful. Thank you, Lyla."

Taking one look at the fierce-looking guest at the door, Agatha left in a mist, leaving Harper pouting on the couch.

"And now who's this?" Nadine asked, stepping forward. "A werewolf?" She snickered at her question until Enzo turned his attention—and his fangs—to her. All humor left her, and she jumped to grab Harper from the couch.

"Get her out of here," Martin ordered, trying to keep his voice calm and even. "Go into the bathroom and lock the door."

It would be better than nothing, even though a flimsy lock would be no match to a vampire's strength.

"Go!" Lyla demanded of her.

Holding Harper in her arms, fright held her feet in place and sobered her eyes. Lainey rushed to her side and ushered her down the hallway and out of sight.

"It would be smart of you to leave her, Enzo," Lyla challenged, her feet planted firmly within the house's safety.

"Are you threatening me, you little bitch?" he spat, his body pushing against the power that held him at bay.

With those words, something broke in Martin, this time for the better. He was sick of being pushed around, having his life determined for him, and he was damn sick of bullies getting away with whatever they wanted. No one called his sire, his friend, a bitch.

"No, fucker. We're threatening you." Two against one had to matter for something. Especially with Lyla's newly developing abilities. "There's nothing here for you. Go cry about your missing necklace somewhere else and leave us be...*Kyle!*"

As if the name was poison, Enzo recoiled a step before blazing forward against the home's hold. "My name is Enzo, you little puke!"

Martin ignored his body that shook and stood side by side with his sire, no longer the man cowering in his office, eating the same old ham sandwich and being stepped on and over at every turn. He was now a vampire; and he would not let a fool in a leather duster hurt one hair on anyone's head.

"Get out of here, Marty. This isn't your fight. Go look after your family," Lyla insisted, trying to push him back from the door where he was now nearly nose to nose with the brute.

"No, I'm not leaving you here, Lyla. If anyone is going to leave, it's this punk." He rolled his shoulders back and doubled down in his stance.

The lack of fear he was being shown gave Enzo a falter in his glare. An obvious narcissist who had gone most of his life, alive and undead, didn't seem to know how to respond when violence wasn't an option.

"How long do you think you can last in there? You can't out wait me and you know it. Eventually, you're going to have to eat. Which one do you think you'll have first? The hot piece of ass or that tasty little nugget she was holding? Maybe Lyla's little play thing? Have you been using her as a blood bag already, or will this be your first taste, you little bitch?" Enzo smiled at the anger he was seeing reflected back to him.

"We can wait as long as we need to," Lyla sneered, stepping up to stand shoulder to shoulder with Martin, even though her shoulder was closer to his elbow.

"Oh, did I hit a nerve?" Enzo pressed. *"Brainey Lainey.* She was always such a know-it-all in school. Stuck-up cunt, always looking down her nose at me. I'd love to have a little taste of her to see if she's as bitter as I expect."

"You'll do no such thing, you sad little wanker," Lyla countered. "The only thing you're going to do is get the hell out of here. Now."

"Who's going to make me? The two of you?" He stepped half a foot back. "Come on out and do it. No one disrespects me and gets away with it. Why don't you come out here and show me who's in charge, you pathetic leprechaun?"

Neither of them stepped forward. Name calling wasn't going to be enough to make them foolishly walk outside of the only armor they had.

"This is crazy. All of this over a necklace?" Martin shook his head. "You're a fucking immortal being and you're spending your time on a vendetta over jewelry?" He could see the rage building in the man before him the more he was being minimized and pushed further. "You act like you're some movie-worthy villain, as if you have some kind of bass-heavy soundtrack playing with every fucking step you take, but you're here wanting to beat up a girl over a necklace!"

"I'm not going to beat-her up," he condemned. "I'm going to kill her." The flat statement brought Enzo back to a steadier stance, nearly foaming at the mouth.

"Not gonna happen, *Kyle*," Lyla seethed. "You can stand there and meet the sun before you put a chipped, manicured finger on me." He flexed his fists as if hiding the black polish and Lyla nearly laughed. The empowerment that pushed Martin on seemed to be contagious. "I'm not coming out there, and there's no way you'll ever get in here." She crossed her arms, pressing her lips into a half-smile. "So, feck off or put on some sunscreen."

Enzo's lips twitched, and he narrowed his glare to her. "You won't be so smug when I get a human to cross that doorway. Maybe grab that little girl and bring her right here so I can dine alfresco."

Martin started for him until Lyla slapped her hand back to his chest to stop him. "Do it," she dared the challenger.

He couldn't believe she would taunt that monster when he was threatening his daughter. That was a threat too far. He tried to ignore the whimpers and cries he could hear clear as day coming from the bathroom.

Enzo took a step closer to them. "You think I won't?"

"I know you won't," Lyla confidently leveled at him. Enzo opened his mouth to speak and stopped himself. "You think you can just walk up to stranger and ask them to kidnap a child? Not everyone is a psychopath like you, moron."

"You think I don't know that? It's called mind control. I could have this whole little town climbing on this house in a minute if I wanted to."

"Then do it," Lyla shot back through gritted fangs.

The uncertainty that blinked in his eyes told Martin what Lyla was getting at.

"You don't know how to do it, do you?" Martin scoffed.

"No, he doesn't." Lyla replied as Enzo boiled over. "He wants everyone to think he's this ancient, all-powerful vamp and really, he's just a wee areshole of a baby still."

"That's not true!" Enzo almost whined, his outburst turning to tantrum. "I was able to track you down, wasn't I? Smelled your fear all the way from that busted barn."

Lyla tsk'd, shaking her head. "That's not the same as hypnotism at all, ya damn gobshite!"

Enzo visibly attempted to rein in his temper to reclaim the upper hand. "If you think I can't, you're a bigger fool than I thought."

"Then do it, *Kyle*. Go hypnotize the town and get back to me," Lyla dared and had the door halfway to slammed in his face when he let out a shriek.

"I will burn this house down around you, Lyla. So, help me, I will destroy you all!"

That was a threat he could follow through on.

She again opened the door wide. Martin tried to think of how to get his wife and daughter out of the house and as far away as possible, as quickly as he could.

"That's right, bitch. No one talks to me like that and lives to say another word." Enzo reached into his jacket's pocket and pulled out a metal lighter.

Before she could attempt to say another word, Enzo's head turned to the side in a blur with a sickening snap. When his body fell to the welcome mat at his feet, they found a young man, no more than thirteen, standing behind him, cracking his knuckles.

"Owen!" Lyla gasped. "*Jaysus*, I have never been happier to see you!"

The boy, dressed in a pristine silk suit which looked as if it cost more than Martin's mortgage payments, pressed a groomed lock of sandy blonde hair back into place and then fiddled with the gold cufflinks on his wrists.

"That is Owen?" Martin sputtered, looking him up and down. He didn't know what he expected, but it was not someone who looked as if they weren't old enough to drive.

Enzo lay on the ground, his neck twisted unnaturally, yet still alive, moaning and casting insults to the boy, who looked down at him with disgust.

"Excuse you, young man," Owen chided. "That is not how you speak to your elders."

Lyla bounced in place, joy nearly causing her to float. "I told you that you should have fecked off, Enzo!"

"Enzo?" Owen asked with a newly bloomed interest. "This is *the* Enzo?"

Lyla raised her brows as she nodded. "That's him, sir."

"Right then." Owen reached a hand into his double-breasted suit.

Ashes and a peppering of embers floated into the seaside breeze where Enzo had lain before Martin could register that Owen had pulled out a polished wooden stake and plunged it into his chest, disintegrating him instantly.

"Oh, shit!" Martin exclaimed, trying not to let the drifting remains of Enzo get into his mouth.

"Language, please," Owen playfully reprimanded. "You got a tongue on you like my Lyla here, don't you? And with your own little one inside, at that."

Martin could only mumble an apology, staring down at the pubescent looking boy.

He smiled back, clapping his palms and giving them a brisk rub. "Now, if someone could invite me in?"

Chapter Sixteen

Turn around.

LAINEY HAD TO HELP Nadine out of the bathroom, with Harper held tight. The lubrication of the wine had worn off from the rush of adrenaline, and she struggled to stay calm for the sake of her daughter. Martin walked to her, hoping she wouldn't be afraid of him. To his relief, she welcomed his arms around her.

"It's over, sweetheart. You're safe," he whispered in her ear.

Harper sniffled and tucked herself under his chin. The three stood in the embrace until Nadine finally pulled away and set Harper on her feet beside them.

"What a lovely sight," Owen observed from the doorway, causing Nadine to spin around to find the well-dressed tween watching them with a serene smile. "I hate to disturb, but I'll need an invitation, dear."

She looked to Martin for direction.

"It's fine, Nadine. Lyla knows him," he said and was met with a look of uncertainty from his wife. "Oh, yeah, sorry. This is Lyla," he introduced. "She's my, uh…she's— "

"I'm the one who caused all of this shite," she finished. "If you invite him in, we explain everything and I can get on with my apology tour."

Nadine watched each set of eyes that waited for her response. She sat Harper on the couch and turned to Lainey. "This is okay? He's not going to hurt anyone?"

"He's cool. He won't do anything to anyone in here. I can vouch for that," she replied.

Owen smiled at her. "Thank you for your trust, Lainey. You're a good egg."

Harper's mood improved with the comment, shimming across the couch to get a look at him. "Good egg," she giggled with a sniffle. "He's funny."

Martin's pride welled with what that child could handle. Lainey may be a good egg, but his girl was one tough cookie. He made a mental note to tell her that later, knowing it would tickle her.

"Do I just invite him in? What do I say?" Nadine asked the room in general.

"I can help with that," Owen offered. "May I come in?"

"Yes," she agreed, moving to Harper's side.

"Wonderful," he exclaimed as he crossed the threshold. "Nadine, is it? Thank you so much." He looked over the gathered group with eyes that were uncomfortably wise for someone who appeared to be so young. "Well, shall I start things off or do you have anymore surprises for me, Lyla?"

"No, sir," she said, looking at her feet.

Crossing the room to stand before her, he matched her height. Tipping her chin up with his finger, he gazed into her eyes. "What's happened, my sweet lamb? I can tell you're holding back?"

Martin hoped it was something that he already knew about, but when it came to Lyla, it was anyone's guess.

A smile flickered across her lips. "I was able to completely hypnotize her," she pointed to Nadine.

Martin's relief was short-lived when his wife saw who she meant.

"You what?" she gasped. "Me?"

He sat beside her, putting an arm around her shoulder. "Don't worry. It was for the best." Anything was better than scaring her to death.

Nadine tensed when Owen started for her, a beaming smile on his face. "You didn't! But you're still so young!" He stopped when Nadine put her hand across Harper and pushed them both back against the couch. "I'm sorry, dear. I'm not trying to frighten you. You see, I'm just so impressed with my Lyla." He looked her over, making her squirm more. "Would it be alright if I just have a look in your eyes? Just a peek to see how she did."

Martin remembered Lyla worrying about melting her brain and now worried about the possibility himself. She seemed normal, which, considering what she had experienced that day, could be due to a little mental melt.

"He's safe," he assured her. "Just let him have a look." He hoped he found nothing wrong and hid that thought with a reassuring nod.

Better safe than sorry when it came to mind controlling vampires and their potential side effects. Martin resisted shaking his head to that fact that was an actual thought and scenario in his life. A month ago, a checkup would be blood pressure and maybe blood tests. Now it to make sure the blood suckers didn't turn his wife's brain to goo.

Nadine gave her trust to the trio, who gave expressions of approval. Still holding Harper back, who looked at Owen with the childlike wonder of seeing a unicorn, she leaned forward, eyes open, if not unsure.

After a brief inspection, Owen turned his attention to Lyla, clearing the space between them in a millisecond and tugging her into a loving embrace. "My sweet lamb is a genius!" he declared. Delight danced in his eyes when he looked around the room. "A genius! So young, yet so gifted." He planted a noisy smooch on her cheek.

"I just calmed her down. It's not that big of a deal," Lyla mumbled, as the sly smile she tried to hide said she knew otherwise.

"Nonsense," Owen dismissed. "A genius!" He pinched her cheeks. "Now, Nadine. How are you handling all of this?" he asked her, as if he were discussing nothing more than a makeover. "I can see you have your wits about you, and you haven't run out the door, so good on you."

"I…I'm figuring it out," she answered, to which Owen gave a bawdy laugh.

"Aren't we all, dear? Aren't we all?"

"'*Scuse* me," Harper piped up. "You're a vampire, like my daddy?" The awe spread on her face when he zipped to kneel in front of her small legs that dangled from the couch.

"I am as much a vampire as you are, the bravest little girl I've ever met." He gave a pleased look of approval to her.

Harper lifted her chin, happy with the compliment. "I am, thanks. I'm not scared of 'nuthin."

Owen smiled softly. "I can tell."

"Can I ask you a question?" she posed, putting a hand to her chin in thought.

"Of course." Owen answered with an impish conspiracy in his voice.

"My daddy doesn't seem to do any vampire stuff except the sleeping," she stopped and looked up when the room tittered, giving them a disappointed pout before continuing. "*Veromika* can do lots of stuff, like turning into a bat!"

Owen looked up at Nadine, obviously not understanding who she was talking about.

Martin answered his wordless question when she didn't, "It's her favorite cartoon; a little girl named Veronika, who's a vampire."

Recognition bobbed his head, and he turned patiently back to Harper for her to finish her question.

"It's a really good show. You should watch it. She's so funny!" she insisted.

"I'll be sure to give it a go," he mused. "But what is your question for me, my sweets?"

"Oh, right. *Veromika* can turn into a bat," she repeated. "Can you do that?"

A hearty laugh shook him when he stood. "Wouldn't that be a sight!" he answered without answering. "I'll have to watch that show of yours."

He addressed Martin and Nadine. "You're raising a wonderful spirit here. She's going to do amazing things in this world. I can tell." He gave the girl a pat on the head as one would a puppy. "Now," he spun around to Lyla and Lainey, "As much as this darling isn't afraid of *nuthin'*, as she said, I think it would be best if our warm-blooded new friends leave us to chat for a few minutes."

Lainey motioned for Nadine to follow her, starting for the hallway. "Let's go have a look at that wine collection."

Standing to join her, nervously looking at the others, she held her hand out for Harper, who ignored her.

"Let's go, sweetie," she requested, visibly trying to keep her voice light.

"I'm good," she answered, not budging from her cushion, giving a loud yawn from the excitement and late hour.

Martin tried not to snicker at his strong-willed daughter. It was like looking at a mini version of his wife.

"No, we need to go now," Nadine said more firmly and waited until Harper finally looked up at her.

"Why? I wanna hear the vampire stuff," she whined.

"You can hear about that stuff anytime," Lainey grinned. "Why don't you come with me and let me tell you a secret?"

Harper lit up and bounced from the seat to chase Lainey down the hall in a fit of giggles.

Once again, Lainey to the rescue.

"Thank you so much, dear. I'll only steal your lovely husband for a few minutes," Owen called out when Nadine trailed behind the other two, giving glances over her shoulder to the trio of vampires that stood in her mother's beach house.

She was officially a part of Martin's new *WTF* life.

Once they could hear them settle into the kitchen, Martin sat stiffly, concerned with whatever was about to be said. Now was the time for the blow back, he was sure of it.

"Sit, please," Owen asked of Lyla, who joined Martin on the couch, stretching her arms behind her head before slumping down as if expecting a lecture. Owen sat gracefully in an armchair across from them. "It's so bizarre to chat to mortals," he whispered, as if he had done something naughty. "Anyhoo, where should we start?" He looked back and forth between them. "I suppose with an official introduction?" He gave Lyla a look of scolding. "It's so nice to meet you, Martin. Now that I know you exist." A snort of a chuckle took the edge from his words.

Martin gave a tight smile in return.

"I said I was sorry." Lyla tucked her legs underneath herself and hugged one of the fuzzy, pink throw cushions from the couch.

Owen gave her a long, thoughtful look. His frown was part frustration, part amusement. Martin could tell that this wasn't the first time she had pressed her luck with him, although he could also see the love he had for her.

"I just don't understand why you would keep this from me?" he bemoaned. "You had been doing so well with turning things around and then you keep this weight on your shoulders?" He picked at a piece of lint on his suit pants. "I'm hurt that you wouldn't trust me."

"It's not about trust. I was scared. I didn't know if the others would be as cool about it as you would. They aren't as keen on my feck ups as you are." She rested her chin on the pillow, giving brief peeks to her sire.

"Oh, pish. They're for me to worry about, not you. Trust me. They have their own secrets that aren't so secret. We cover for each other just as I cover for you." He clucked his tongue. "You honestly think I would let them harm you?"

"I didn't know. It's not like it's the first time I've found myself in trouble," she admitted. "They've threatened to end me before and you know it."

"True enough," Owen tittered. "You do keep things interesting."

"I don't know. After everything and I'd already sold the lie, I sort of started to like the guy. It was nice to have a friend." She looked at Martin to find his face soft from her confession and she smacked him with the pillow. "Shut up, eejit," she teased with embarrassment.

With all that had changed, all that had been truly maddening and awful, he too could say he was glad for her friendship.

"You've been so busy and I kind of got attached," she mumbled into the pillow. "And I was worried that if you found out I lied, that you would kill him."

"Of course I would have!" Owen exclaimed in agreement.

"What?!" Martin bellowed.

His outburst startled Owen. "Only if she had wanted me too, Martin. It's no offence to you."

No offense? All the offense! So much for him being any sort of teenaged-grandfather-figure.

"He didn't, though, did he, Martin?" Lyla stated plainly.

Owen smiled, as if all was well again.

Was he supposed to thank him for sparing his life? He stayed quiet and stewed instead. Someone who could so easily take his world away was not someone to complain to.

"I just wanted you to see I could take care of it myself." She turned sad eyes up to him.

"Lyla, you need to stop trying to rush everything. One night at a time, my girl. I see you," he leveled plainly. "I do."

"I know, I just want to make you proud."

"If I haven't let you know how proud I am of you, then I am the one at fault. You are an extraordinary woman! You'd have to be with my blood in your veins," he said playfully. Lyla hid her smile in the pillow. "Now, is that the end of it all? Are we straightened out?" he asked quickly. "I know I have been preoccupied, but I couldn't help it. You know that. Being at the top of the mountain may provide a mighty view, but comes with a mightier weight on your shoulders."

Martin couldn't imagine what unbelievable situations a top level vampire would deal with. A hell of a lot more than anything that ever crossed his desk at Beaumont's.

"No, yeah, I think we're good now," Lyla answered, looking more relaxed now that she could see she was no longer in hot water.

"What about Enzo?" Martin chimed in. "Are we going to be in trouble with anyone for that?"

"Who?" Owen asked, looking briefly puzzled. "Oh, that bothersome brat out front?" He snorted. "No. No one will give a hoot about him."

"Are they going to be happy you finally got him?" Martin asked excitedly.

From what he understood of how Enzo had avoided any punishment, it must have been embarrassing for the top vamps to not be able to catch him.

"What's he going on about?" he asked, turning to Lyla. "Why would they care?"

"He's been wreaking havoc all over town and getting away with it," Martin insisted. "Won't they be glad you finally caught him?"

"Finally caught him?" Owen scoffed. "I doubt anyone even had—excuse my language — that *cockwomble* on their radar, to be honest. We deal with problems on a much grander scale than that pipsqueak. Someone of his sort is easy to deal with. Poof, gone. Easy." His fingers snapped loudly, and he laughed.

Martin didn't join in on the joke, seeing as he was almost *poof, gone, easy.*

"I see." He looked at Lyla, who lifted a shoulder and frowned at the revelation.

It seemed even she believed Enzo to be a bigger deal than he was. It was easy to think that when he was in your face and threatening your life. An ant may fear an ant, but they meant nothing to a cat, he supposed.

"I don't mean to sound crass or cruel, but you must understand, just like when you were human, not everyone makes it to the top. When you do, life becomes more complicated in some ways, but most certainly easier in others. If everyone had the powers and abilities that I have honed over centuries, could you imagine the abuse? If someone like that Enzo character had access to all that I do? Mankind would be wiped out in days, and then where would we be? Hungry, for one."

However much he wanted to balk at the unbalance of power, he could see his point. The universe needed checks and balances to keep monsters like Enzo under control. Knowing that there were most likely some in positions of power who were just like that jerk, he could see how dealing with them would be more of a concern than a small town newbie. The world outside of his town always seemed large and far away. Now that there was an underworld within it, everything expanded by leaps and bounds.

"I should say thank you for sparing me," he finally said.

"I would never have gone against Lyla's wishes, so your gratitude belongs to her," he gazed at her with prideful love. "She always gets it right in the end. That's why I'm always here to provide whatever I can to help her build herself up. That part is easy." He again snapped his fingers.

Martin began to ask why he didn't set her up poshly like the vampires in the fictional stories, like the one he saw himself as in his daydreams before the wise man's words repeated.

Then where would we be?

If Lyla had been handed the world on a platter as the woman he first met, she would have been mentally frozen in that moment, never needing to grow or better herself. They were really taken back to the point of being babies in the world, with all new life lessons to coincide with their all new pulseless lives.

"That being said, I need to be on my way, so if there is anything you need?" Owen waited for Lyla's response.

"No, I'm good. Thanks for coming all this way and helping us out." Lyla stood from the couch.

"Of course, my sweet lamb. Anything for you," he gushed, rising to give air kisses to her cheek. Martin swallowed the humor of seeing Lyla return the gesture. "Keep me updated on your progress." He turned to Martin. "How rude of me! You're a member of the flock now, aren't you? Is there anything I can do for you?"

He knew better than to ask for the ocean side castle and he knew he couldn't give him back heart beat. "No, I don't think so," he finally lamented.

Owen frowned. "Nothing? Really? You have a virtual genie standing before you and you can think of nothing that's troubling you?"

He was safe, his family was safe. That was all he could ask for.

"Now that I don't feel like everyone is out to kill me, all I can think of is keeping my job."

Owen regarded him with a look of knowing. "You're struggling to find work now? That's a common problem when you've first been turned." He nodded solemnly.

"Well, I have a job. I was able to make it work for nights, but I'm worried the store will close and I'll have to find somewhere else." He ruefully shook his head that he was back to the same old problems. "I don't know how I could make that happen."

Owen reached up, tapping his own lip in thought. "What's the reason for the worry of the business?"

Martin nearly growled at the thought of Chance Beaumont's clueless face. "The guy that's running it is pretty well running it into the ground. He's the reason I stumbled into Enzo's orbit in the first place."

Owen bobbed his head to the door. "That one? That *Enzo* was being problematic with the owner of your shop?"

"Just as problematic as the owner, really," he answered bitterly.

"Right. So, I'll purchase the shop and eliminate the problem. Good?" he said with the ease of someone offering to bring ice to the party.

"What? No. Wait. You can do that?" Martin couldn't believe he would offer such a gesture.

"Of course I can!" he chuckled as if he'd never spoken to someone so naïve. "Like I said, for us at the top, there is a lot that is easy." Once again, he loudly snapped as he said the word. "I'm impressed enough with your *go get 'em* gumption to pull yourself up and find a way to make it work. Sounds a lot like my Lyla, except you're doing it the right way. You two are going to learn a lot from each other."

The ease with which he could solve his problems was shocking. More so, he considered his wording. "By eliminate, you don't mean you'll kill him, do you?" He hated the guy, but he didn't want his blood on his hands.

"Do you want me to?" Owen questioned, looking intrigued.

"No. I definitely don't."

"Then I won't," he concluded. "See? Easy!" Another snap of his fingers crack in the air.

Lyla gave Martin a congratulatory clap on the back and addressed her sire. "Thanks Owen. We'll make you proud."

"I'm sure you will." He put a hand on her shoulder. "Especially once to take a position at this shop of Martin's."

"What? No!" Her shoulders slumped as Owen laughed.

"You'll do great," he assured her. "I really do need to fly, though. Martin, would it be alright if I said goodbye to that daughter of yours? She is such a pip!"

His head spun at the speed with which things happened with Owen as he called out for the others to join them in the living room. No wonder Lainey was so keen for her to call him.

"Is everything alright?" Nadine asked nervously when she approach her husband.

"Yeah," he blustered with a dazed grin. "We're good."

Owen took a knee to speak to Harper. "It was very nice to meet you, young lady. I hope I get to visit you again in the near future."

"You can come over and watch *Veromika* if you want to," she offered with a friendly smile.

"I would like that very much. I need to get back to work now, though. Could you do me a favor and open that door for me?"

She did as he asked, skipping to the front door.

Martin wondered why he didn't open it himself. As he considered if it was a regal habit or another vampiric quirk, Owen gave her a wink, lifting his arm high in the air. Bringing it briskly down, his body erupted into dozens of tiny brown bats that swirled around her head and then out the door.

"Wow! He can do it! He can do it just like *Veromika!*" she cheered and watched them all disappear into the night sky.

Nadine snatched her back from the porch, where nothing of Enzo remained. "Good God, Martin! What was that?"

"It's another new one for me, too," he sighed. He had to admit it was a pretty cool trick. One he hoped he lived long enough to learn. "Did you know he could do that?" he asked Lyla.

"Yeah, that's one of his favorites. As you can tell by his suits, he's a wee bit of a showoff," she remarked, looking out the door to the moonlit sky.

That he may be, but to Martin, he was a lifesaver in more ways than one.

"What now, guys?" Lainey interrupted. "What's the plan?"

Martin looked at the clock on the wall. It was still a few hours until sunrise. "I really just want to go home."

"Done. You all ready to go?" Lainey asked, pulling out her van keys.

"I'm always ready to leave the beach," Harper murmured with her nose wrinkled.

They filed out of the beach house with Nadine voicing her concern about the van not having seat belts as she locked the door. Once they had settled in the back, it wasn't long before the hum of the road was beneath them and she and Harper were snoring away.

Lyla leaned against the van's wall, consumed with her own thoughts of the night and Martin left her be, choosing to enjoy the first peaceful moment he had had in days.

The ride home took longer than the speed Lainey had fled in; this time traveling within the traffic laws she had disregarded previously. Pulling into the driveway, he shook Nadine awake and bundled Harper into his arms.

"Thanks guys. That was a hell of a night, huh?" he called out to the pair.

Lyla crawled up into the passenger seat.

"One of many, I'm sure," Lainey joked. "Take care, alright?"

He wished them the same and headed inside.

"Martin, I am way too tired to get into any of this now. I just want to put on fresh jammies and crawl into bed with you, alright?" She yawned widely.

"Damn, Martin! What happened? I've been going nuts! Where did you guys go?" Dan swirled into view, nearly nose to nose with him. Martin took a step back, giving himself some distance.

"I just need to know that there aren't going to be anymore surprises for a while," Nadine half pleaded with a sleepy smile, taking Harper from his arms.

The small girl lifted her head to see Dan, looking them all over with concern. "Mr. Jack! I have so much to tell you! I just met someone you might know!"

Nadine stopped and turned to Martin, who was waving Dan away with his hands. "What does that mean, Martin? Is she saying that her imaginary friend is friends with *vampires?*"

He rubbed his fists along the sides of his head, staring at Dan, who was now satisfied they were alright. "Not exactly."

"Not exactly? Martin, for god's sake. What now?" Nadine stood at the bottom of the stairs, watching Martin decide what to say. He decided, like Lyla's new plan, that honesty was the best answer.

"He doesn't know any vampires other than me. Well, he kind of knows Lyla."

Dan waggled his eyebrows at the mention of her.

"What in the world are you talking about?" she blurted, officially out of patience.

"He's a ghost, Mommy!" Harper cheered, pointing at the space in the room where he stood.

"A ghost," she echoed.

"Yeah, she's telling the truth," Martin admitted, his face twisted when he waited for her response.

"You're telling me we live with a ghost?" Her face was flat and tired.

Dan let out a whoop at the revelation. "I didn't think you'd ever tell her. This is so—" His eyes drifted over Martin's shoulder to the open front door behind him. "Whoa! Who is that? Hello, gorgeous."

He didn't want to turn around. He wanted to walk straight upstairs, crawl into bed, and hold his exhausted and unbelievably forgiving wife, but he knew he had to turn around. "Shit."

With a coy smile on her face and a tiny wave, Agatha stood just inside his house.

"What?" Nadine sighed.

"Apparently we now have ghosts…plural."

"Oh, for god's sake!" Nadine cursed. "I'm going to bed." She stomped upstairs without another word, with Harper gleefully calling out to their new guest to come see her room.

Closing his eyes and rubbing at his forehead, he conceded that she had the right idea. They would live to see another day and deal with it then. Although, if they kept collecting stragglers, Martin knew they'd need a bigger house.

At least now he knew they could afford it, since he still had the night shift.

MARTIN'S PLAYLIST

About the author

Katherine Dempster is a Canadian writer of paranormal and horror thrillers. A life-long reader and fan of the macabre, she lives in the countryside beside a small lake, pretending every day is Halloween.

You can visit her online at:

Facebook @katherinedempsterauthor

Instagram @katt_dempster

X @para_norma1

Also by

Katherine Dempster

The Corpse Flower Colony

Into the Lake

In Sheltered Shadows and Other Short Stories

The B.I.T.N. Assignments

-Welcome to Aumbry Valley

-Welcome to Dunhope Manor